Emylia Hall was born in 19__ __ __n countryside. She is the author of *The Book of Summers*, which was a Richard & Judy Summer Book Club pick in 2012, *A Heart Bent Out of Shape*, *The Sea Between Us* and *The Thousand Lights Hotel*. She lives in Bristol with her husband, the writer Robin Etherington, and their young son.

Praise for Emylia Hall:

'[An] extraordinary story by an author who's fast becoming one of our firm faves' *Sun, Fabulous* Magazine

'Lush, romantic escapism' *Mirror*

'This atmospheric, slow burn of a read is perfect for the end of the summer' *Daily Mail*

'An utterly beautiful story, brimming with romance and tinged with loss . . . Hall's sensuous, vivid prose draws you in and holds you captive until the last page. This is a summer read to be devoured' Lucy Clarke, author of *The Sea Sisters*

'A perfect summer read' Tiffany Murray, author of *Diamond Star Halo* and *Sugar Hall*

'*The Sea Between Us* is that rare beast – a beautifully written, intricately observed love story that's both lyrical and enchanting . . . a novel that deserves to be savoured' Hannah Beckerman, author of *The Dead Wife's Handbook*

'A delicate, atmospheric, regretful tale, but full of redemption too. I absolutely loved it' Richard Madeley

'Highly evocative and a joy to read' *Sunday Express*

'Beautifully nuanced' *Spectator*

'Emylia Hall __ __ __ __ __ __picture . . . an addictive __

'A novel that glints with passion, loss and doubt' *Marie Claire*

'Fantastically evocative and sun-drenched with a twist' *Stylist*

'As tender and insightful as it is gripping. The novel speaks of life's value and potential – and of Hall's, as a writer' Susan Fletcher, author of *Eve Green*

'The prose is an art-form in itself . . . a story that grabs the reader and completely immerses them in a picturesque world from the first to the last page . . . beautifully written' The Book Bag

'We were utterly blown away by this novel. Vivid and heartbreaking in equal measure' Novelicious

'Haunting and full of vivid prose . . . a novel to be devoured in a couple of sittings' *Lady*

'[A] vivid coming-of-age story' *Woman & Home*

'A poignant story of first love, desire, friendship, tragedy, grief, and self-discovery, in a stunning location' We Love This Book

'A thriller, coming-of-age story and love letter to Switzerland, all in one' *Good Housekeeping*

'The writing is so pretty you'll fall in love with the setting . . . We guarantee you'll be saving up your pennies and catching a flight to Switzerland before you're halfway through' *Heat* magazine

'A touching coming-of-age story' *Image* Magazine

'Heartfelt and evocative' *Grazia*

'[An] emotive novel not to be missed' *Star* Magazine

'Hall confirms her talent for romantic but original prose' *Big Issue*

The THOUSAND LIGHTS Hotel

EMYLIA HALL

REVIEW

Copyright © 2017 Emylia Hall

The right of Emylia Hall to be identified as the Author of
the Work has been asserted by her in accordance with the
Copyright, Designs and Patents Act 1988.

First published in Great Britain in paperback in 2017 by Headline Review
An imprint of HEADLINE PUBLISHING GROUP

1

Apart from any use permitted under UK copyright law, this publication
may only be reproduced, stored, or transmitted, in any form, or by any
means, with prior permission in writing of the publishers or, in the case
of reprographic production, in accordance with the terms of licences
issued by the Copyright Licensing Agency.

All characters in this publication are fictitious and any resemblance to
real persons, living or dead, is purely coincidental.

Cataloguing in Publication Data is available from the British Library

B format ISBN 978 1 4722 1202 3

Typeset in Sabon by Avon DataSet Ltd, Bidford-on-Avon,
Warwickshire

Printed and bound in Great Britain by Clays Ltd, St Ives plc

Headline's policy is to use papers that are natural, renewable
and recyclable products and made from wood grown in well-managed
forests and other controlled sources. The logging and manufacturing
processes are expected to conform to the environmental regulations
of the country of origin.

HEADLINE PUBLISHING GROUP
An Hachette UK Company
Carmelite House
50 Victoria Embankment
London EC4Y 0DZ

www.headline.co.uk
www.hachette.co.uk

For my family, with love and gratitude

If I can stop one heart from breaking,
I shall not live in vain.

Emily Dickinson

Be not inhospitable to strangers,
lest they be angels in disguise.

Inscribed on the wall of Shakespeare
and Company, Paris

one

KIT RAN AS IF THERE WAS SOMEBODY CHASING HER. SHE pounded up and over the Downs, past the kite fliers and the dog walkers and the tiny children rattling along on scooters. She didn't stop until she reached the edge of the Avon Gorge. As she leant over the wall, the man in the ice cream van peered out, then ducked back inside. Far below her, the mudbanks glittered in the late-afternoon sun. Kit pressed her fingers to her eyes as stars crowded her vision, and waited for her breathing to settle. She checked her watch. Visiting hours began at six o'clock. There was just time to race back, change and compose herself. To practise what she was going to say one more time before going in.

One question, that was all she had. One question made of five words, and none of them as frightening as those she'd had to learn recently – words like *refractory*, *palliative*: the unwelcome vocabulary that had entered the lexicon of their little family. As she left the edge of the gorge and started back towards Clifton, her heart was beating in double time, but it had nothing to do with the speed that she ran at, or the miles she'd covered. The question charged along with her.

Kit didn't normally run in the afternoons. She preferred the very early mornings, when the toes of her trainers would turn dark with dew. She'd head for the open sky, the vast stretches of grassland where, in the fragile light, it was possible to believe in the safety of infinity. She felt brave then, armoured, so that when she returned to the still of the house, she could talk to her mum about the things she'd seen. The fox that was so dainty on its feet, eyeing her uncannily long, and not without accusation. The rose light over the river; the way the suspension bridge appeared to rise up, dream-like, mist billowing beneath it. The honeyed blur of a lone retriever as it chased a flock of gulls. It took away the taste of the night, such talk.

Maybe you could get a dog, her mum had said the other week, and Kit had tried to play along, said it'd be less trouble, a decent swap, in fact, when actually she was thinking that there might come a day when such a companion would be welcome. A chirpy little terrier, perhaps, or a soft-eared spaniel, with a coat you could bury your face in without explanation or apology.

When her mum had fallen ill, when nothing about it had looked good, Kit had moved back to be with her. A decade ago Bristol had been her university city, and after she'd left, heeding the call of London, her mum had chosen to make it her home – as if she wanted to continue to inhabit the same spaces as her daughter without quite intruding on her independence. So Rosa had moved there in Kit's footsteps, swapping the crooked rooms of their Somerset cottage for a rented flat high up in one of the wedding-cake white terraces, a once-grand house carved into pieces and left to time: fusty carpet, chipped-paint railings, but with windows big enough to let the sun dance in, and a shared garden to the front with a moat of rose beds. Until a few months ago Kit had been one of the transitory faces in the hall – the daughter who visited sometimes at the weekend, a bag over her shoulder, taking the stairs two at a time as she raced back to her own world.

She'd been in an airport when her mum had telephoned: Lisbon, waiting to fly to Oslo. Her laptop balanced on her knees, she was having trouble connecting to the terminal's Wi-Fi, a deadline getting away from her. Her phone rang, and as she answered, she hadn't been able to stop irritation seeping into her voice. *I got the results back*, her mum had said, her tone as formal as a schoolmistress's, her Italian accent barely there; but it was the pause that followed that told Kit what she couldn't bear to know. In that moment, she'd vowed to move home.

The motion of her afternoon run stayed in her, and she moved mechanically through a shower, a change, the dragging of a comb through her wet hair. Then she glanced around her, absorbing the contents of her mum's flat; the life it still had in it. The chalkboard shopping list with *bread, milk, tomatoes* smudged in pink. The wooden rocking chair and its purple cushion, a library book face down, pages splayed, as if its reader had just got up to make a cup of tea, or answer a ringing telephone.

The hospital was an ominous hulk of a building, its outward appearance promoting no certainty of bright futures. Kit wished for flower boxes at the windows, or a fluttering flag, some visual manifestation of optimism. On the way in she paused at the revolving door, waiting for a man and his little daughter to pass through it. The girl was curled into her father's neck, her face hidden, and was sobbing noisily. Kit hoped she was crying because she'd been denied the promise of pizza again for tea, or because she'd wanted a toy from the hospital gift shop, or any other small, but no less bitter, disappointment. Their eyes met, hers and the man's, and she gave him the closed-lip smile that visitors always swapped in the halls – the look that said, *This is hell, but here we all are, because where else can we be?*

Inside, the nurses greeted her. Anne, with the Kirby grips and the clumpy shoes, and Roksana, with purple-streaked hair and a smile so kind it could split you in two from across a room. Kit adopted the same falsely bright tones she always did, though for whose benefit she didn't know. They were doing the best they could, perhaps that was why. They all were. But the question that had chased her over the Downs gave her away. It felt desperate, grasping; slipping her facade. It had no place among the gentle fortification of cards and flowers and paperback novels. Nor did it sit with the sweet and sonorous music she shared, passing an earphone – *Here, Mum, you'll like this*. It had taken her by surprise, this sharp desire to suddenly know, and shocked her too. For to ask was to acknowledge, however implicitly, that her mum's time had all but run out. Kit hesitated in the corridor, feeling her conviction already fading.

As a small girl, maybe five or six, she had asked about her father. Because someone in the playground had stared at her as if she was crazy when she said she didn't have one. *That's impossible! That bird over there has a father. That dog.* So she'd asked her mum outright, as they sat across from one another at teatime, twirling spaghetti. *I hate to admit it*, her mum had said, in a tone that was uncomfortably distant, *but I never knew him very well. And he turned out to be . . . not very nice. Not very nice at all. And then he died before you were born, so . . .* She'd drifted then, and it had felt an act of cruelty – even so young, Kit had been sensible to that – to attempt to bring her back.

So she'd stayed kind. Until she was leaving for university, that last night at home, in the garden of their old cottage, Deer Leap; the place Kit had been brought to as a baby, Tuscan soil still in the tread of her mum's shoes. They were up late drinking sparkling wine, their bare feet aching with cold, as bats had swept overhead. *Everyone says that university is about figuring out who you are,* she'd said, *but . . . I'm never going to know, am I? Not really.*

She'd felt the heat of Rosa's look, and for once, instead of it quieting her, it stoked her flame.

'Is it because you're ashamed,' she'd said, 'that you didn't love him? Italy's Catholic, right? And back then I guess randomly sleeping with someone you didn't really know was considered . . .'

Rosa had been very still. In the gloom of the garden, Kit hadn't been able to observe her expression. She'd floundered on.

'Because, you know, that wouldn't matter to me, Mum, it wouldn't matter to anyone these days. People sleep with more or less total strangers all the time, and if you get pregnant that's just unlucky, and . . .'

Her voice had tailed off as she'd looked at the shape of her mum, and she had rubbed her nose, for it had started to prickle as if in warning.

'Or . . . was he married?' she'd edged.

'Not that you'd ever have known it. He certainly had me fooled.' Rosa's voice had been thick, choking in on itself.

An affair. She'd never have pictured her mum as the slighted other woman, somebody tempting but not sufficient. She seemed too uncompromising for such a role. Kit had wanted to say, *Did he know about me?* Even if she'd been just a bump beneath a dress, a love child, the strange fruit of a moment of madness, had he known, before he'd died, that there was a baby on the way?

'He already had a child,' Rosa had gone on, 'and . . .'

It had taken a moment for Kit to realise that her mum was crying. Rosa never cried. Not ever. She was as consistently featured as a portrait in a gallery. Twelve years on and Kit could still remember the precise feeling of regret, the guilt that had shot up and down her body in hot spears. From the woods behind she'd heard the sharp clap-clap of a pigeon's wings, and it was as though it was the sound of the topic being released, startled, flapping, making its break with noise and flight. Never to return.

'I'm sorry,' she'd said, in barely a whisper. Then, louder, 'I won't ask again. I promise.'

In the years that followed, whenever she needed to caution herself, to give pause and consider the consequences of an action, Kit would remember that feeling: the folly of pretending you had the faintest clue what it was like to be somebody else.

She pushed open the door. Rosa turned to her and lifted a hand, and Kit waved back, her eyes burning.

Her mum's face had always been sculpted, her cheekbones

high, her brow arched, but now she was only gaunt. A pea-green silk scarf, loosely arranged at her neck, offset the shocking paleness of her skin. Her lips, too, were defiantly bright. She'd always worn lipstick; *Rose for Rosa*, she used to say, not dusky pink but fierce red. She'd snap out a mirror and apply the colour in deft strokes, never needing to correct a smudge or start again. Lately, Kit had found it hard to look at her. Other times all she wanted to do was gaze, drinking up that very second, that minute, that certain graspable moment.

Rosa was the kind of woman who'd always turned heads, caused conversations to falter. In the untamed Somerset countryside she'd cut an unlikely figure, with her blue-black hair that was sleek as feathers, her bright lips and pristine wellington boots. Battle dress, she'd called it, as she swept on mascara and polished her shoes, even if she was just going out to gather blackberries, or pick daffodils at the end of the lane. Later, on the streets of Clifton, she'd been luminous. But it was never for men, the care she took. For all those who'd knocked at her door with lavish bouquets and murmured promises, she'd never let any of them in. It must have killed them, and how teenage Kit had laughed about it, lying back on her bedspread, bicycling her legs in the air, thinking of all the men in the West Country, hearts blown wide open by her untouchable mum. And how she'd once wanted to look like her! Kit had always felt herself a pale imitation: smaller, slighter, hair that curled in the rain, eyes a liquid blue. *You look*, her mum had told her one day, *exactly like my grandmother did as a girl*. But what relief she'd felt, to know that it wasn't *him* she took after. That her mum didn't have to look at her and be reminded of what she'd lost; what she'd never really had.

'The sun hurts my eyes but I refuse to have the blinds

7

drawn,' said Rosa now. 'Not on a day like this. Spring sunshine, it's the best kind.'

Her tone was light, bright and unnaturally giddy. Did the drugs do that? Kit made a mental note to ask the nurses. She went to her and hugged her as tightly as she dared.

'You could wear shades. Movie-star style.'

'Perhaps just lower them a little, would you, darling? Just a little.'

Kit went to the window, glad of the occupation. Outside there were trees in blossom, puff-headed with pink flowers, rude with health. It was the worst time to ask. It was the only time. How would it be to know?

She flicked the blind, and a ladder of light fell across the bedspread.

'Mum,' she said, not quite turning, 'what was his name?'

The revolving doors spat her out, and she stumbled. Swore. A cluster of smokers turned to look at her, then quickly away again. Kit stood rooted, unsure which direction to go in. People came and went. Cars passed. It seemed to her remarkable that, outside the hospital, the world was as she'd left it.

She stared down at her hand. The strange collection of letters, scratched in biro, rising like a sudden birthmark.

'Thank you,' she had said, moments ago, curling her fingers around her palm, impossibly grateful. 'Thank you.'

'All these years,' Rosa had said, her voice sounding as though it belonged to somebody else as the words bumped into one another, 'it was important to me to believe in what we had. The life . . . I'd made for us here.'

'What we *have*, Mum, not what we had.'

'Oh, don't cry, darling girl, never cry.'

But she was, and she couldn't stop. She'd just held her mum's hand, and silently willed her not to go anywhere. To stay, always. When Rosa spoke again, Kit almost didn't hear her. She had to ask her to repeat it.

Kit. He didn't die.

Then her mum had lain back against the pillow, her eyes closed, spent by what it took to say it twice. Spent by what it took to say it at all.

two

VALENTINO LIT HIS LIGHTS EVERY EVENING JUST BEFORE DUSK, like a boy who still believed in magic, like an old man who could remember when he used to. As his guests congregated on the terrace for *aperitivo*, they'd witness the illumination, a sight as sparkling as the drinks in their glasses. But it wasn't until later, when the sun dropped and the dark rolled in, that they were granted the full spectacle; then forks paused on the way to mouths, and toasts were made, as a ripple of appreciation spread across the dining room. Most of Valentino's lights were hung high in garlands and appeared at the flick of a switch, looping from the roof to the lawn, strung between trees, and twined amidst vines on the trellises. Others he lit by hand: a candelabrum at the terrace edge, Chinese lanterns swinging from the boughs of a cork oak. Sometimes the children who stayed tried to count them, charging about the gardens, calling, *One hundred and seventy-three! One hundred and seventy-four!* Occasionally he encountered a smart-arse, like the engineer from Cologne who blew out one flame then beckoned him over – *You missed one!* – with a snigger intended for his apologetic-looking girlfriend, but Valentino would simply shrug, and smile, and turn away.

He hadn't been born on the island of Elba, but for nearly thirty years it had been his home. He'd seen the seasons turn, admiring this trick of endless renewal. In spring the rains came, water pooling on balconies, cascading down the steps to the square. Oceans of pink flowers appeared overnight, flooding the clifftops with colour and scent. In summer the roads were lit by fireflies, and the undergrowth was studded with the sticky heads of wild strawberries – everywhere the unbelievable blue of sea and sky. Autumn was dry-roasted, and olives scattered the ground like green marbles. Stews bubbled on stovetops, spiked with berries and dark meats, and the sea brought new treasures, thick lengths of mullet and mussels as big as your fist. In winter the island was mistral-whipped, and the few who'd stayed went about with bent heads, their hats pulled down, occasionally rewarded with days of near-impossible lightness and brightness: a crisply cut horizon that invited thoughts of far-flung places, and the contentment that there was nowhere else you'd rather be. Living through the island's seasons was, Valentino thought, like inhabiting a beloved poem. Much as he knew it by heart, it still possessed the ability to strike him afresh, some new gem of meaning emerging from an old, familiar line.

Aperitivo was magic hour at the Hotel Mille Luci, and his favourite part of the day. Valentino welcomed his guests to the terrace as Abi offered Negroni and Aperol spritz – vivid drinks in misted bowl-shaped glasses, cut with curling orange peel and ice. Oliviero carried out an ever-changing banquet of antipasti – tonight vast platters of *pizzette*, tiny plump focaccia stuffed with provolone and salami, bowls of sweet figs wrapped in prosciutto, and bouquets of grissini, made with rosemary from the garden and glinting with decadent diamonds of salt. As a ritual, it was an unabashed but elegant form of pleasure. Everybody was united in a simple appreciation of the moment, and the anticipation of all that was to come. That was the way to live, Valentino thought, and not just in the hour before dinner.

With ten rooms in the hotel, the crowd usually numbered twenty or more. A good size. You could give something of yourself to everybody; you could remember all the names. Tonight he would be speaking four languages – German, French, English and Italian – moving between them as though they were all just different words in the same tongue.

'*Guten Abend*, Max, Steffi. Hey, Jurgen, Nikki, *buonasera*!'

The Berger family came from Bavaria: a pair of tall, athletic parents, Max a ski instructor, Steffi once one, and their boys, mad-happy six-year-old twins. Between the four of them they were white-blond and tanned brown. They were sitting at their usual circular table by the giant-flowered hibiscus, their conversation made up of whispered admonishments and yelps of unfettered enthusiasm. The Bergers preferred Prosecco to cocktails, and so Prosecco was what they drank. Valentino topped up their glasses, then moved to the boys, gesturing to their *limonata* as though to add the illicit fizz.

'Oh, you're driving? Next time, next time.'

It was the same joke every evening, and they always snorted with laughter.

Then there were Francesca and Veronika Alessi, the elderly sisters from the mainland city of Perugia, one with a tight grey bun, the other a ragged bob, dressed in matching cotton tunics and wide-legged trousers. Veronika had a lively laugh, eyes roving for mischief, while Francesca was more sober in spirit – though was rarely without a glass of something in one hand and a book in the other. They sat across from one another, popping olives and crunching breadsticks.

'Signora Alessi, and Signora Alessi, good evening, dear ladies. Was it a happy day? Did you make it to Villa dei Mulini?' he asked in Italian.

'We certainly did,' said Veronika. 'I never appreciated what a tiny man Napoleon was until I saw the bed he slept in.'

'But a grand ambition, no? He built our roads, you know, drained our marshes; he should never have left us for Waterloo.'

He stooped to pick up Francesca's dropped napkin, and laid it gently back across her knees. She thanked him with her eyes.

He went next to the three boys from the university in Turin, who were clustered near the antipasti tables, hungry as gannets. He'd seen them coming back from the beach late at night, girls on their arms, the lit ends of their cigarettes bobbing in the dark. They possessed all the ease of youth. One of them, Ricardo, was dressed more casually than usual, in the black and white striped shirt of Juventus.

'He wants them to buy Capello, he's wearing it for luck,' said his friend.

'Capello from Torino? And how will that sit at the next Derby della Mole?'

They laughed. 'Depends if he scores.'

'Damned if he does, damned if he doesn't,' said Valentino, and shook each of their hands before moving off.

'*Bonsoir, madame, mademoiselle*,' he greeted the pair from Paris, the preposterously glamorous Nina and her long-legged

13

stepdaughter Lucille. It was their second day and he was still yet to see them exchange more than a word or two with one another. Upon their arrival he'd made the mistake of referring to Nina as Lucille's mum, and the girl had cut in, correcting him with *belle-mère*. Nina had taken it in her stride, and passed the handle of her suitcase to him before walking off. Now she sat pinching the stem of her wine glass, while Lucille fiddled with the phone that she held in her lap.

'*Bien coordonné*,' he said, nodding at the colour of Nina's dress and the shade of Lucille's nail varnish.

'Not deliberate,' insisted Lucille.

'*Mais belle*, all the same. Shall I ask Oliviero to talk you through the menu tonight? He can tell you about the ricotta our friend Gino makes, and the aubergines from our gardens.'

The two women were bonded in the agreement that time with Oliviero was a fine idea, and Valentino felt sure he saw a look pass between them – for once a complicit smile.

He cut back into the kitchen, and when he came out again he saw Isabel. Dear Isabel, *bella* Isabella, all the way from England. She was their most loyal guest. Coming down just after seven o'clock, elegant in a navy linen dress, her only adornment the necklace she always wore, with its silver locket. The intervening year seemed to have passed in no time at all when Isabel returned. He kissed her lightly on each cheek, and handed her a Negroni.

'I've been thinking about this first *aperitivo* all year long,' she said, taking a sip, closing her eyes.

'As have we.'

'I try it at home, you know, a glass of something, a few nibbles, but it's not the same. It never is.' She waved her arm, seeming to encompass everything with the gesture: the rolling lawn, the bauble-decked lemon trees, the galaxy of tiny lights, even, perhaps, Valentino himself.

He offered her a bowl of olives, and she plucked one.

'And *vongole* tonight?' she asked.

'Of course,' he said. 'Everything as usual.'

'You've no idea how happy that makes me.'

'I hope I do,' said Valentino. 'How are you, Isabel? The summer, it's been kind so far?'

'Kind enough.'

'Your garden?'

'Oh yes. And my herbs have really taken off. The marjoram's quite stolen the lawn. I should have brought some for Oliviero, but then that'd be rather like taking coals to Newcastle,' she smiled at the wrinkle of his incomprehension, 'or like ice to the Eskimos. And you? You're well? You look well.'

An hotelier's job was to look after people. That was how Valentino had always seen it, and he had pledged to uphold his role with dedication and commitment, every hour of the day. It was down to him to ask how people were, if there was anything they needed, if he could assist with their bags, their itinerary, the angle of their sunlounger. Help choosing a wine? The fastest way to the beach? Did you have a good journey, a good day, a good stay? Few ever turned his enquiries back on him. Except for Isabel. Most people had some grievance in their life – however buried – and he had come to learn how to read the disappointments, the faraway looks and the hesitancies. Perhaps she too possessed this ability; hurt recognising hurt. *Are you all right?* she had asked the second year she'd come, nine summers ago now. What had he been doing? Nothing out of the ordinary; uncorking a bottle, perhaps, or straightening the table linen. *Are you all right?* The question had been extraordinary in itself, but more startling was his desire to answer with a truthfulness he rarely permitted, even when conversing with himself. That first time he'd waved it away: *Very well, very well*, he'd said, because he was, wasn't he? Essentially?

'Very well,' he said again, nine years later. '*Grazie. Grazie.*'

three

THE WOMAN FROM THE PARADISO DROVE A VINTAGE LANCIA, and she took the turns of the road with an abandon bordering on recklessness. The night breeze kicked up her hair, mussing it, messing it, hair that had been so smooth as they'd danced in the crush of hot and liquid bodies. The Paradiso was closed throughout the Elban winter, but as summer arrived and the tourists and seasonal staff along with it, the club – with its lasers that swept the sky, and beats that crossed the water – opened its doors. He'd met her a week ago at the bar as she castigated Giuseppe for serving her sparkling water without ice. They'd got talking, and seemed to like what one another had to say – certainly adequately enough to not dilute their physical attraction. They'd danced then, and their bodies had fitted together in a promising way. The music was too loud for talking so they'd kissed instead, and dancing and kissing had carried them through from late night until the white blaze of morning. Tonight, when they'd met again, after Oliviero had closed his kitchen and bid the guests *buona notte*, they'd simply picked up where they'd left off. It was barely after midnight, and they were already driving back to her place. The starlit water fell behind them as they swung into the hills behind Portoferraio, deep into the chestnut woods where the scent of wild garlic tanged the air.

He smiled at her sideways, and placed his hand on her knee.

'Where are you staying again?' he asked.

'Why, can't you wait?'

He laughed, and she clicked her indicator, spun them up a palm-lined driveway, tyres spitting gravel.

'It's all right,' she said. 'You don't need to.'

A white stone villa was illuminated, a clean, bright block, and palatial enough to draw a low murmur of appreciation from him.

'Nice place,' he said.

'What did you expect?'

There was a question. What did Oliviero expect? If you didn't have high expectations, you were never disappointed. His grandmother had said that to him once a long time ago, his dear nonna, with her darned stockings and flower-print housecoats, and he'd never forgotten it. Certainly she'd seemed to live her own life by that adage; reality didn't bite her, because she never got too close to it. Where the bread on the table had come from, what her son was out doing when he should have been with his family, these were questions she'd refrained from ever asking, because if she had, how could she have coped with the answers? That was no way to be, in Oliviero's mind. But he knew that if he ever tried to explain it, he'd sound high-minded, disrespectful to the sacred Italian institution of family. He might even come apart in the places he was patched.

'Dangerous question,' he said, climbing out of the car. As he rounded the bonnet, he threw an arm around her shoulders and they climbed the steps together. In her heels she was as tall as him, which made her an awe-inspiring prospect: Carlotta, a lawyer from Rome, a fast-talking woman who danced like she'd climbed all the way inside the music – frenetic and somehow untouchable. But it had been her suggestion to leave the club early, so perhaps this last was untrue.

He'd never had to try with women. Even as a schoolboy, as his friends were pestering and blundering their way into uncertain clinches, it seemed all black-eyed Oliviero had to do was smile, and he got what he wanted. Which was what, precisely? Another question he wasn't sure he had the answer to. He was thirty years old: young enough to feel like his life was still ahead of him, old enough to know that the past was irretrievable. While the ambitions of his personal life were indistinct, professionally he was perfectly happy. His *cucina* was everything, and it was the surety of cooking that Oliviero had always loved. It was like a code of honour: *Do right by me, and I'll do right by you*, the ingredients seemed to say, as meat browned, sauces thickened, and egg whites stiffened into snowy peaks – everything happening just as it was supposed to.

Carlotta turned her key in the lock. 'There's no such thing as dangerous,' she said. 'It's all a matter of perception.'

It was blithe talk, and he didn't mind it. Most people went about in their bubbles, never even realising it until they burst. He followed her inside.

A couple of hours later, after they'd undressed on the stairs, her dress a puddle, his jeans left on the landing, after they'd fallen into the first bedroom they came to, where they moved together with a rhythm that made their dance-floor efforts look pedestrian, Carlotta slipped into the shower. And just as

Oliviero was thinking of joining her, he saw the gilt-framed photograph. Carlotta in a fur hat, her face pushed close to a grey-haired but youthful man, the spike of the Eiffel Tower in the background. He took it into the bathroom, held it up, and she squinted at it through the steam.

'You and your brother don't look so alike,' he said.

'Ah.' Then, with a quick smile, 'Again . . . what did you expect? Not that I'd be single?'

He rubbed his chin, and his stubble crackled. 'I expected you at least to tell me,' he said, finding his nakedness to be, for the first time that night, an undermining factor.

'Whatever happened to blissful ignorance?' she said, laughing. 'And come on, honestly, would knowing really have made a difference?'

The night around him was still. Oliviero walked back down the hill towards the port, his shirt loosely buttoned, the cool air pleasant on his chest. The loss was not his, and it probably wasn't hers either, though as she'd chased him with wet footprints across the room, the shower still hissing behind her, you'd have been forgiven for thinking otherwise.

four

KIT'S JOURNEY BEGAN LONG BEFORE SHE CLOSED HER MUM'S door behind her and hurried to the waiting taxi. Before she checked her bag, to be sure that a mysterious force hadn't caught hold of her passport, spiriting it from the zip-locked pocket in which she'd tucked it – a nervous tic that had never before, in all of her travels, afflicted her. Before the small sigh – the relief to finally be on her way, knowing that whatever lay ahead, it was now too late; forward motion had taken over. For all the journeys that are made on the spur of the moment, with clothes yanked from the washing line, and no more of a route to follow than the heart's pull, there are those that are agonised and analysed, worried over day and night. For Kit, 'To go, or not to go?' had transcended the question she'd carried with her into the hospital.

She moved through two airports, and the train journey, in a state of semi-consciousness, mechanically doing just what she had to do. She was aware of people around her, holidaymakers at the periphery of her vision, children with miniature back-packs and bony knees, parents drinking coffee and sharing newspaper supplements, but stayed entirely within herself, plugged into a pair of earphones. She'd been a travel writer for years, a professional wanderer – but this? This was different.

It was two and a half months since everything had changed, twice over. Perhaps her mum had gripped her secret – not just Kit's father's name, but his continued existence – so tightly, and for so long, that letting go of it meant relinquishing much else too, for when Kit went to her the next day, determined to find a way to talk, she had the distinct impression that she was altered. Worsened, surely? she asked the nurses, and they were duty-bound to confirm it. In the days that followed, her mum's decline eclipsed all else, and it was only later that Kit taunted herself with wondering how things might have unfolded differently, if Rosa had unfurled her startling truth sooner, or been granted the time to colour it more completely. And if, when her mum had said 'He didn't die, Kit,' she'd found the courage, the equanimity, to try and draw out her story there and then. But Rosa had looked so pained, as if every word hurt her, and with the customary cautiousness she'd learnt since childhood, Kit had pulled back. Six days later, Rosa Costa had slipped away in the night, taking whatever else she might have wanted to say to her daughter with her. Kit had thanked the doctor and the nurses, then left the hospital for the last time, her mum's bag in her hand. The only other thing she could remember about that day was that the sky had been unforgivably blue.

Caring for her mum had been consuming, testing her as she'd never been tested, but loss, loss took up everything, and was an occupation unto itself. She had never thought of grief as a physical thing before. Some days she was left so heavy, so leaden-limbed, that she thought she'd never be able to move again. Other days she felt so very insubstantial that the slightest puff of wind might blow her away across the rooftops. She had stayed on in the Bristol flat. She still called out *I'm home* every time she walked through the door, but she'd begun to no longer expect an answer.

Then had come the day when she had, simply, nothing left to do. She'd completed the last of the abundant administration that death required. She'd sorted through all of her mum's belongings, objects that she'd never be able to see as ordinary; her dressmaking chest with its carefully folded fabric, the assorted boxes of cotton and pins and sketchbooks. She'd taken three bags of clothes to a charity shop on a street she knew she wouldn't walk down again.

What could she do now, except carry on with some semblance of a normal life? Knowing that it would always be lacking.

But there was *him*.

Valentino Colosimo.

Kit had gone over to the kitchen table, and flipped open her laptop, as though she was about to do any number of everyday things. Instead, she'd tapped her father's name into the search engine, her finger hovering, hesitating, before hitting Return. Results had filled the screen, but there was, astonishingly, only one exact match: a lone pin, in all of the Internet's vastness.

On the ferry from Piombino, Kit found herself looking up and out; never before had she felt so precise a sense of moving towards something. For all the illness that had dwelt in the Bristol flat with them, and for all the engulfing absence that had followed, she hadn't been able to imagine leaving. But now, as

23

she leant on the ship's railing, she wondered if she could ever, in fact, go back.

They glided away from the port and executed a wide, slow turn. As the ferry gathered speed, a gust of warm wind caught her hair, her skirt. She felt a faint flutter of anticipation. It was almost the same feeling she had whenever she embarked upon a new trip, but not quite. At some point in her childhood she'd asked her mum why they'd never gone to her homeland, or anywhere abroad, and Rosa had said they simply couldn't afford it. But one day her mum had come home with a giant globe in her arms, every country marked out in candy colours. Kit had spun it, her chin propped on her hand, her eyes flicking past the whir of Eritrea, the Hague, Port of Spain. She liked to think that this was how her wanderlust had begun. Maybe she was born with an itinerant spirit, the desire for flight running deep inside of her. Perhaps their world of two was too containing, so what a thrill it was to spread her wings, to wave her mum goodbye at the door and alight somewhere new. Then came the job at the travel magazine. Subediting. Correcting grammar. Sometimes taking liberties, rehashing whole paragraphs, to inject the kind of wonder that the globe-spinning girl wanted to believe in. An editor who saw something in her and offered her a break, watched how she took it with both hands and gave her another, and another, then a better writing job altogether. It was liberty, tethered by purpose. Freedom that came with responsibility: to try to capture the spirit of a place. But she'd never written about Italy.

An island romance, Kit had told her editor. She'd related the legend of Maria and Lorenzo, the star-crossed lovers whose sorry fates were celebrated every year at the Lovers' Festival on the Tuscan island of Elba. A thousand burning torches illuminating the cove of Innamorata, everybody turning out to celebrate true love and revel until dawn. 'That's the thing about this festival,' she'd said. 'It's the Italy us Brits want to believe in, isn't it? Passion, romance, commemoration, all on an island that looks too beautiful to be true. So that'd be the piece: forget Juliet's balcony – is there another place in Italy that epitomises what it means to truly love?'

Her editor had tipped her head, eyed her sideways. 'And you'd undercut it, I suppose, reveal it as nothing more than a show for tourists?'

Kit gave her a non-committal smile. 'And look, there's even a hotel on the island named for the legend – the Mille Luci – the Thousand Lights. That's where I'm going to stay.'

Later, she marvelled at her convincing tone, considering that, perhaps, this was part of her inheritance: the ability to slant the truth to suit her means.

Now she moved closer to the railing, and there it was, already in view, the island of Elba: its shape gently undulating, the discernible rise and fall of mountain and wooded hillside. It would be easy for her to sidle close, to watch him under the cover of her profession. There, he would be compelled to interact with her. *Hi, Kit Costa, love child. You screwed my mum, in every sense, and then she told me you were dead. Nice to meet you.*

She lifted her face and inhaled deeply, filling her body with all that the air had to give.

As they approached Portoferraio, its buildings became distinct. They were painted the colours of Neapolitan ice cream – strawberry and vanilla, with chocolate-brown shutters. There was a fort high on the hill, rimmed by trees with foliage as neat as parasols, and a harbour full of bright white yachts. The ferry swung on past and docked beyond, at the considerably less frivolous-looking port. There Kit streamed from the boat with the other passengers, picking their way through the cars as they crossed the burning tarmac. She wandered past an uninspiring strip of shops, each filled with gaudy fashions, and discount perfume. A hair salon. A down-at-heel café with a dark interior, just one man sitting hunched behind an espresso machine. Scooters bearing catalogue-worthy couples blasted past, engines sounding like a wasp caught in a glass. Families strolled together, children skittering ahead, wearing T-shirts ironed by someone that morning, carrying beach inflatables that had earlier sat propped in the porches of their homes. Everyone she passed seemed to know exactly what they were doing and where they were going.

When Kit was somewhere different, she always felt she could become somebody different too; try on other lives, or take her own and slot it in somewhere else. There was an exquisite pleasure in laying new prints: the wanderer stealing in. But as she ventured from the ferry, she felt for the first time like an uneasy outsider, and was certain that nowhere she had ever travelled had felt as strange to her as that sunny port town on a weekend afternoon.

She saw a sign for the bus station, and before she could lose what was left of her nerve she went in and bought a ticket. Just as she was stowing her wallet back in her rucksack, she saw the little tin nestled in there. She'd meant to take it out on the top deck of the ferry, surrounded by nothing but sea and sky. She zipped the pocket carefully and told herself that another moment would present itself. That it was better to wait until something, until anything, felt right.

five

KIT STEPPED OFF THE BUS AND INTO THE SLAMMING HEAT OF mid-afternoon. It was supposed to be under a mile to the hotel, but ahead the road twisted and turned with hairpins and switchbacks, the surface liquid with mirage. The bus rumbled off, and she sank down on the verge, her arm wrapped round her rucksack.

I want to go, she thought, her throat contracting. Reverse it all. Back on the bus, the boat, the train, the plane, a taxi hurtling through Hotwells and into Clifton from the bottom. Round the gardens, up the stairs, three flights, push open the yellow door, calling out, *I didn't go through with it!* Then they'd open wine, and the two of them would find a way to laugh about it: the whole foray nothing but a foolish aberration.

She heard the approaching roar of a motorbike and drew up her legs, aware, suddenly, of her perilous position at the side of the narrow road. Instead the bike slowed down and stopped beside her. *Here we go*, she thought. She set her features to unbothered, disinterested, her default travelling look when passing men fancied their chances, but when he removed his helmet, said *Ciao, signorina*, she struggled to keep it that way. The remarkable thing was not so much that she'd noted his beauty – the kind of male beauty that, in another time and place, might have proved difficult to look at, because she'd have found her eyes sparkling all too obviously – but the fact that she saw something for herself in it. Rather like somebody looking at an idyllic picture in a holiday brochure and for a transporting moment seriously imagining themselves within that landscape, before the barriers of reality came crashing down.

He said something that she didn't understand.

'Sorry, but my Italian is . . .'

'Ah! I said if you're waiting for a bus, you're on the wrong side of the road. And there isn't one for an hour, I think.'

His English was smooth, easy, and with the dance of his accent his words were nowhere near ordinary.

'I just got off the bus.'

'So you're waiting for a lift? Come on. Where are you going?'

He held out his helmet. She hesitated. It didn't feel like a proposition, just a straightforward offer.

'The Hotel Mille Luci. I'm going to Hotel Mille Luci.'

'It's just down the hill,' he said. 'It's safe. Freewheeling all the way, okay?'

'I'm not worried about the bike,' she said.

'Just the rider?'

'Not even that.'

'It's a nice walk,' he said. 'Good views. But after a long journey? *No, grazie.* You're on holiday: take it easy.'

She looked worn, and felt it too. He couldn't know that her day had begun in the pale light of dawn, with a gruff but talkative taxi driver speeding her through the streets of a still-sleeping Bristol. Then a plane, a shuttle bus to Pisa, a train that skirted the Tuscan coastline, a ferry into the way-off blue, that last jolting bus ride up into the hills, swinging round sheer drops, briars scraping the windows. Now, after all of that, her dress was creased and sticking to the small of her back. Her hair was wild and there were grey smudges beneath her eyes: the mirror in the bus station toilet had told her that. This last could be seen as the mark of her early start, rather than the indelible print of endlessly interrupted nights. Someone who grafted too hard, perhaps, wound tight as a bowstring with workaday pressures. She could pretend to be that person. That person was easy.

'I'm actually here for work,' she said. 'I'm working.'

'Yeah? Nice job.'

He smiled, a spark of curiosity in his eyes, but it didn't flare into a question.

'It's been a long journey, though,' she said, 'you're right there. Elba's not all that easy to get to.'

'It's a world away,' he said, with a boyish sort of relish. He held out the helmet again, and this time she took it. She hoisted her rucksack onto her back and climbed on. He spoke to her over his shoulder.

'You have to hold on to me. Is that bag okay, not too heavy?'

'Not too heavy,' she said.

So close to him, she saw the way his buzz cut tapered to a point, and she had a sudden desire to place her thumb against it, feel the bristle of his hair. He wore a thin silver chain, and the creases of his neck were tanned darker. He smelt not of engine oil, or sweat, or any of the things she might have imagined of a motorcyclist on a hot day – instead a cool, crisp scent of lemon and rosemary. It was a long time since she'd noticed the details of other people. She placed her hands on his waist, and felt the hardness of his body, the warmth and solidity of him. She immediately lightened her grip.

'Hold tight,' he said. 'It's steep. Okay, *andiamo*!'

It sent her dizzy, the intensity of the sun and the spinning road. The sea, appearing around every bend, tilted before them. He rode slowly, as if he wanted her to enjoy the sights. There were densely forested hillsides and towering cacti, and the ground was scattered with the bloated fruit of the prickly pear. Verdant as it was, the scrub at the side of the road was dry as tinder; one strike of a match and flames would lick up towards the sky, swallow the island right up. He turned his head, mouthed 'Okay?' She nodded, shifted her hands on his waist, and felt a flicker of desire that was so sudden, so entirely involuntary, that she shut her eyes. Willed it to happen again. His body between her hands, the heat of the bike beneath them; couldn't they just ride on? Sweep down the hill and along the coast, her holding on to this dark stranger, him opening something in her that was out of her control and, for once, welcome – not the dumb weight of grief or the fuzz of bewilderment, but a wilful abandonment to who knew what. Lust? Lust had no place in this trip of hers. It had had no place these last months. But here it was, gusting in, shocking her body into a realisation of its own existence, and all its strange currents. She felt a flood of relief. Of gratitude, even, for the presence of spontaneous feeling that wasn't sad or bad.

He swung off the road. The engine died.

'Your hotel, *bella signorina*.'

'That was fast,' she said.

'You want to go round again?'

She removed the helmet and climbed from his bike. As she stood looking up at the sea-blue gates, he waited beside her. She took in the sprays of giant palms that canopied the approach, the profusion of oleander in all shades of pink, the dazzle of water beyond. She'd seen it all a hundred times before, peering close, enlarging the image on her screen until it had fragmented beyond recognition, yet still the sight startled her. The letters of *Hotel Mille Luci* were set in stone, glinting with turquoise and jade. Kit's toes curled in her sandals, and the gravel crunched in reply. She felt a trickle of perspiration at her brow and wiped it away. She'd rehearsed her first words, and was ready with them. While she had a smattering of Italian, she didn't want to try and use it. Nothing to make her stand out, or appear ingratiating. Nothing to make her look as if she was trying to belong.

'You don't want to go in?' he said.

The madcap desire to flee with him had been replaced by an equally absurd wish for him to accompany her inside the gates.

'Do you know this place?' she asked.

His hand went to his head and he rubbed his hair. It was so short it bristled. He laughed. 'I know it a little.' Then, as if she was easier to read than she'd thought possible, 'Come, I'll show you. Can I take your bag?'

She shook her head. 'It's okay, I don't need . . .'

'It's my pleasure.'

He spoke with such simple conviction that she believed him.

As they entered the grounds together, Kit snuck a sideways glance. The inches between them felt at once nothing, and too much. If she'd ever imagined turning up at her father's doorstep, it hadn't gone like this.

* * *

For all of the hotel's surface familiarity – there were the orderly white lines of the main building, the terracotta tiles of the terrace, the flickering light of the pool – the sensation of actually being there was one made of sensory details that she hadn't permitted herself to imagine. A cloying sweetness from the oleanders; poisonous plants, she'd always thought, but here they dripped their honeyed scent with wild abandon and she found herself breathing it in, unconsciously licking her lips. Everywhere was the ceaseless music of cicadas, an invisible orchestra. Racketing birdsong, far from the polite choruses of English garden birds – she half expected to catch a flash of a parrot's wing, the rainbow stripe of a toucan. What were Italian birds? And were island birds something else? She didn't know.

'You like it?' he asked.

Kit nodded. 'It's different . . .' she began. She stiffened, then, as a man came into view. He could have been anybody as he walked across the terrace – a guest, a passing visitor – but she knew he wasn't. It had to be him. She stood transfixed, her breath held. Her heart thrummed unevenly. If he looked up now, she thought, it would all come undone; he'd see through everything, without her saying a word. And wouldn't that be a relief, of sorts? If he looked at her starkly, revealing to her what her mum had always known and attempted to protect her from. Then they could each walk away, unencumbered.

She shook herself, and held onto the straps of her rucksack, her thumbnail pressing hard into the fabric. She watched as he moved with a quiet sense of ownership, breaking his step to straighten a chair, bending to pick up something small from the ground – a cigarette butt, maybe, or a popped button. Perhaps, somewhere amidst the birdsong, there was a whistle at his lips.

32

She tried to note the details, telling herself that she was a journalist and this was her job: his black trousers and open-collared white shirt, making him appear rather like an off-duty waiter; the glint of his shined shoes. It was easy to picture him spinning on his heel, uncorking wine and setting down menus. An hotelier. The host. Her host. That was all, nothing more.

'That's the owner.'

Kit took a breath. 'Valentino Colosimo, right?'

He was so solid, so real. Squarely built, broad in the chest, not the tallest, but not short either. His hair, once dark all over maybe, still so in places, but silvered too now, cut longer on the top and short at the sides. Neat. A neat man. That was a nice unemotional word. The kind of man to have perfectly trimmed nails, stubble making its brief appearance only after five o'clock. Cologne, maybe. Everything in its place, here in this hotel too, chairs at right angles, lawn trimmed, the abiding sea with its die-line horizon. An ordered life, fixed. She thought of the fact of herself. How she wished she could go on watching him, cloaked in invisibility. *He hasn't seen me*, she thought. Then, *He's never seen me*.

'Excuse me one moment,' the man beside her said, kicking out his bike stand, then, 'Hey, Papà!'

He broke away from her and caught up to Valentino, draping his arm easily around his shoulders. She saw how their smiles matched, how as he said something fast in Italian their laughter overlapped. Her heart sank. *Papà*. Together they walked towards her, her father and her half-brother, going about their day as if everything was fine and ordinary. Same blue sea. Another sweet sky. And on their lawn just another crumpled traveller, wilting from the length of her journey and the unrelenting heat of the sun.

* * *

'You must be Kit. Welcome!'

Valentino had his arms thrown wide, expansively. She was tongue-tied, and her cheeks burnt. She managed a nod.

How did he know it was her? Of the many thoughts that assaulted her, that was the first. Then logic intervened, and she thought of her email and booking, her apparent professional purpose. She'd hesitated using her real name for the reservation, but on tapping 'Costa' into the search engine she'd seen the thousands and thousands of results it yielded, in stark contrast to Valentino Colosimo's solitary entry. Costa was ordinary in Italy – all over Spain and Portugal too. She would be ordinary. But still, it had been mostly a relief to receive his straightforward reply over email. No curiosity. *Dear Miss Costa, I'm pleased to confirm your stay . . .* He was close now; close enough for her to see his eyes. Sky, she noted. They were the colour of the sky. Which meant they were the colour of her eyes too. He held out his hand, and she shook it.

He looked like a father, she thought then. Not hers, not necessarily – forget those eyes for an instant – but he had a solidity to him, a capableness. A surface impression, of course, that must mask his true character. *Not very nice.* Even though she'd been tiny, Kit had comprehended her mum's understatement. *Not very nice at all.* But he looked, to all appearances, like a pusher of swings and a kicker-back of balls. Keys and a wallet. A fixer of things. Was that how fathers were? She almost laughed, then, at the unlikeliness of it; a shrill, short, bird-like cry it would have been, almost certain to draw a strange look. She'd got better at checking herself, these last weeks. At first grief had made her drop in and out of the present and its rationality without warning. Drifting off mid-sentence. Leaving

34

a party before she'd found a drink. Flares of impatience at too-slow walkers in the street, and screaming at the wind as it blew her umbrella inside out.

'Let me take your bag, *signorina*,' he said. 'You didn't tell us the time of your arrival. I'm sorry, I would have arranged a taxi.'

His voice was warm, unhurried, his heavy accent belying his fluency. When he smiled, more creases appeared, crinkles by his eyes and at the corners of his mouth. But, she thought, he didn't look boundlessly happy. There was no laughter chasing his smile. Rather it was one of professionalism. His enquiries were polite, mere patter, his manner deceptively intimate.

'Really,' she said, 'it's fine.'

'Our guests don't usually arrive on the back of Oliviero's motorbike.'

There was no undercurrent to his tone. No teasing little suggestion that she'd perhaps enjoyed it too much.

'But you're here now. And for that we're very happy. Please, *signorina*, let me formally introduce you. Meet your chef, Oliviero.'

Oliviero stepped forward. He dipped an exaggerated bow, and grinned at her.

'Sorry, *signorina*,' he said. 'It was fun not to say.'

Again she felt the twist of something inside. It was, she told herself, embarrassment, not desire. Nerves, not anticipation. She'd confused these things before, that was all. As she smiled stiffly, she looked for some trace of herself in him, some small signifier – the position of a beauty spot, or the shape of his nose – and was relieved not to find it. It excused her mistake, the lack of resemblance. She'd anticipated there perhaps being a glamorous, long-limbed wife – Valentino's second, or third,

35

probably, after a lifetime of indiscretions of which her mum was just one – but not offspring, still living under the same roof, part of the business. Not someone else to be navigated.

'And this,' said Valentino, lightly taking her elbow and steering her down the path, 'is Mille Luci. In English, the Thousand Lights Hotel.' With a sweep of his arm he gestured to the emerald lawn, the clusters of strawberry bushes, the grove of silver olive trees tumbling down the hillside, the row of striped sun umbrellas, the vine-laden trellises. 'Your home, Kit,' he said, smiling, this time his eyes joining in too, 'for the week.'

Kit found herself smiling back then, and it was a strange thing, really, because it had come from nowhere and stayed longer than any had in months. She'd forgotten how it was, to smile like that, and she'd forgotten the feeling that went with it too, the warmth blooming somewhere in her chest, opening like a flower. Then she stopped, because she didn't know how she was supposed to feel, but she was certain that it shouldn't be this.

'*Grazie*,' she said, a creak in her voice. She felt him looking at her, and squinted instead at the sea, her hand held to her eyes. A small boat with a red sail was moving languidly. A light aircraft purred somewhere overhead. 'It's beautiful,' she said, because it was.

six

VALENTINO COULDN'T MEET ALL HIS GUESTS AS THEY ARRIVED, but he was happy when fortune and circumstance permitted it. The look on their faces as they rounded the driveway and took in the full spread of the place for the first time never failed to fill him with pride and satisfaction. The young British woman had seemed struck, certainly, by what she saw – though whether it was with pleasure he couldn't rightly say. He'd worried at first that she was somehow disappointed – perhaps she'd expected something grander, or imagined they were right on the beach – but he realised as he shook her hand, and relieved her of her bag, that it was tiredness that had her in its grip. Tiredness had a lot to answer for. People often arrived with that dazed look about them; a long trip, an early start, a near-miss on a hairpin bend with another crazy driver. A ride on the back of Oliviero's motorcycle? That was less usual.

His new guest's hesitation had reminded him of another British woman, Isabel, and the first time she had come through his gates. A coincidence, then, that Isabel should have arrived just the day before. This year – her tenth stay with them, always the same week – she had walked in as if she were coming home. The first time, she had seemed a very different person. He could remember everything about it. Her standing there in her bare feet, a pair of leather sandals dangling from her hand. How as he'd showed her to her room a gem-green lizard had darted across their path and she'd jumped at the sight of it. How she'd slowly taken in the blue bedspread, the white cane chair, the red-tiled terrace with its view of the garden, and the extra-ordinary weight she'd put on the word *grazie* as he'd pressed the key into her hand. Later that evening he'd served her Oliviero's clam linguine, and a slice of *torta della nonna*, accompanied by his own favourite wine, refilling her glass as he passed, with a small stooped bow. Isabel hadn't told him much about herself, not that first year, but he'd wondered. She'd walked as if physically burdened; her head bent, shoulders rounded and caving. But he'd seen a small change in her as the days passed. She'd found her own rhythms, as everyone at the Mille Luci did, and perhaps it was the precision of them that had brought some balance to other parts of her too.

It was another of the things he liked about his work, seeing how his guests fell into their rituals, how established they became, after only a handful of days. If he shut his eyes, a hundred images came to him, snapshots from all around the hotel, summer after summer: the doctor from Munich in a chair by the fig tree, reading a crime thriller, her bare feet resting on the flattened backs of her espadrilles; the red-headed Belgian boy breakfasting on his own each day, dropping croissant crumbs to Fortuna the cat; the couple from Napoli, the impossibly glamorous Serie B footballer and his wife, who played cards together on their balcony each night after dinner.

After ten stays at the Mille Luci, Isabel's habits were well grooved, and it pleased him to see how quickly she resumed them each year. She began each day with an early breakfast beneath the shade of the giant palm, as Abi was carrying out the first platters of cheese and ham and oven-warm *cornetti*. A little later, as soon as the covers were drawn back on the pool, she was waiting. He'd been surprised, that first year, by her body; out of the water she chose clothes that seemed designed to hide the gentle curves of her calves, the elegant shape of her waist. She'd turn twenty lengths or more, spinning backstroke to front crawl with expert precision. She almost always took lunch, unless she'd planned a day trip, to Marciana Marina or the dizzying Monte Capanne. Afterwards she liked to sit on the bench beneath the shade of the eucalyptus tree, crossing her ankles, peering out at all that blue. He'd told her once, on perhaps her second or third visit, that it was one of his favourite spots too. One afternoon, the first year she'd come, he'd been picking strawberries – thinking that all his guests had gone to the beach or were taking *riposo* – when she'd almost trodden on him. He was kneeling in the grass, and at first she must have wondered what he was doing. He was aware, suddenly, of the perspiration dampening his white shirt, his black leather shoes looking odd in the middle of the garden.

'Oh,' she said. '*Scusi.*'

He turned and smiled, opened his hand. 'A berry?'

She'd looked at him with a whisker of amusement, motherly, almost, as though eyeing a small boy with his hand caught in the biscuit barrel.

'No thank you,' then, 'Are they very sweet?'

'The sweetest.'

'Everything is so delicious here.'

They'd smiled at one another then. He'd tipped three berries into her palm. She'd cupped them as if treasure, and walked on up the garden.

It was nothing, an exchange like that. A good deal less effusive than many of the conversations he had on the terrace at *aperitivo*, or in the bar and by the pool. And yet. Hearts were opened by degrees, and the slightest shifting felt seismic to some. Oliviero had once said to him that in this job, you fell in love fifty times a summer. But he wasn't sure if Oliviero had ever truly been in love. He, Valentino, had loved enough for a lifetime.

As Valentino had left the young woman, Kit, in her room, closing the door gently behind him, he found himself wondering what her rituals might come to be, what rhythms she'd find at Mille Luci. She'd said she was here for work, and it had seemed important to her to stress that, so perhaps her time would not fully be her own. But she had to eat, so they'd make sure she had the best food. Oliviero, he could already tell, would be particularly eager to please in that department. She had to sleep; her room, the corner room, caught the sea breeze like no other, and it had a circular window in its roof through which, a guest had once told him, they'd seen a star burst across the sky as they settled into bed. That night he'd wish for her a shooting star. And a second slice of *torta della nonna*.

seven

OLIVIERO TOOK OUT HIS KNIVES. THEY WEREN'T JUST THE TOOLS of his trade but a gift, so he looked after them meticulously, folding them away in their leather pouch every night once service had ended. How innocuous they looked when sleeping, yet they could cut through gristle and sinew with the lightest nick.

There was a callousness to the preparation of some food, and it had bothered him in the beginning. Or, more precisely, his comprehension of the fact had bothered him: his self-awareness, as he'd brandished a studded metal club and pounded veal steaks, of the calculated violence required to prepare the meat. As he'd held a chicken in his hands, he'd felt discomfort at the shift of its ribcage beneath his fingers, winced at the nipples on a strip of belly pork. Fish had proved easier, particularly if he avoided the all-seeing eyes, for the scales and gills were reassuringly foreign, and crustaceans better still, spiked urchins, octopus, sunset-shell scallops looking more like something from a children's storybook than the living world. Valentino had caught him once as he'd been washing his hands at the sink. There was blood beneath his fingernails and he couldn't shift it. He'd scrubbed his hands until his skin was scalded red and steam was rising. *Hey, hey*, Valentino had said, and Oliviero had felt his hand on his shoulder while the other turned the tap off. *You're clean.*

How long ago that time felt, when every inch of him had jumped with unwanted associations. Back then, even his natural skill with a knife had been worry-making, when it should have been a source of pride. Slice open Oliviero, with one deft strike, and what would be revealed? Certainly his reluctance to accept the fact that this could be something he could be good at, that could be his, and his alone. That had taken time, and it was Valentino who'd given it to him, along with just about everything else. When Valentino said to him, *mio bambino, mio figlio*, his eyes shone with pride, and that did something to Oliviero – to know that you could make someone else happy just by doing your best.

They drank wine together, the two of them, long nights on the back terrace when the guests had gone for the season – finding a new balance in their relationship, and forging a way forward through their shared endeavour. Valentino had smoked in the old days, and now Oliviero's chef's whites were black, but much else remained unaltered. The sea, for all its surface changes, was a fixed presence, and he valued the constancy of the setting sun, the symphony of colour that was an Elban sunset. What was it about stretches of water that made people wait and watch and hope? He saw it in the guests, their eyes filled with longing as they gazed out beyond the carnival of palms, the sprays of oleander, the muss-headed olive trees. He saw it in Abi, who two years ago had been cleaning at a hotel in Napoli and now worked the front desk and helped wait tables. She offered painting tuition to guests sometimes too, her own work adorning the walls of the dining room. She'd left her family behind in Gambia, and when she watched the sea, Oliviero was certain she was seeing all the way to where her home had once been, sightlines bending round continents. She'd found happiness with Benito Ferrante, the sculptor who lived up in Alta, but just because you were content in one place it didn't mean you gave no thought to the others.

And Valentino. Papà Colosimo. Of all the watchers, he was surely king. In the long off season they'd sit together with their feet kicked up on the railing, the view just about swallowing them up. Or sometimes they'd go down to the rocks, settling a few steps from the water, biting the tips off cigars and splitting pistachio nuts into their palms. It felt as though they could talk about anything on those nights, and that feeling was enough, so mostly they just listened to the rising shrieks of gulls, and watched for the turn of a fish beneath a wave. He hoped other island dwellers knew a peace like this. The sea showing them what they wanted to see, and washing away the things they needed to be gone.

Oliviero set to work. His dark head was shaved, but he wore a red bandanna anyway, the donning of which was the signifier that his duties were about to commence, like a surgeon pushing down his mask. He was chopping onions, and he felt his eyes begin to burn. It was the only time he ever cried, since he was a boy anyway. He'd gone to a mirror once, seen the onion tears streaming down his cheeks, and stared at his reflection with intense curiosity. Then he'd wiped his eyes and gone back to the chopping.

They were a full house that night, as they were most nights, and before the main event came the electrifying support act: *aperitivo*. Usually he returned to the kitchen as the guests fell upon the food – there were the last preparations to be made for dinner, and a successful *aperitivo*, with its bitter, moreish drinks and abundant antipasti, made everyone hungrier than ever. It was Valentino who played the ebullient host, passing between his guests, looking upon them as fondly as if they were family. Tonight, though? Tonight Oliviero would stay awhile.

She was a journalist, Valentino had said, here to write about the island and the Lovers' Festival. She'd been friendly enough as she'd jumped on his motorbike, though unless it was his imagination, the air had cooled once they were inside the hotel gates. Perhaps he hadn't given her enough. Some female tourists seemed to expect him to lay on the *ciao bella!* and if he didn't, he was somehow disappointing them. It had been an easy enough facade to adopt as he went from teenager to man, that of relentless charm. It seemed, in obvious ways, to be made for him. But truthfully? He'd grown tired of it. He'd only realised quite how tired as he'd walked out of Carlotta's villa the night before, prickling with something like offence at his unwitting part in her game of casual infidelity. The fault was all his own. Superficiality responded to superficiality, didn't it?

She'd worn sunglasses, and while it was hard to get the full measure of a person without seeing their eyes she'd nonetheless radiated a kind of intensity, an enviable self-containment. What would she make of their little island? They didn't get too many British visitors to Elba, but still Valentino had had him learn the language, said if he was serious about being a part of the business then it had to be done. As an adult he paid attention in a way he never did in school. Hours spent poring over textbooks in the off season. Thumbing dictionaries. Valentino reading his tattered Agatha Christie novels while Oliviero listened to Neil Young and wrote down the lyrics. He was glad, now, of all that time spent.

She must have done this hundreds of times, new places, new people, but as she arrived at the terrace Oliviero thought Kit looked rather like a rare bird hovering at the edge of a lawn, fearful that a cat might emerge at any moment. It was endearing, the hesitancy. He excused himself from the boys from Torino and went over to greet her. He saw her glance towards Valentino, but he was engaged in conversation with the German family, the Bergers. Abi got there just before him, offering her a fizzing orange Aperol. He saw her take it, and proceed to drink it quickly. She wore a black dress, and her hair fell in loose waves.

'Hey, good evening,' he said, and now he could see her eyes. They were cloudy with tiredness, but still held the possibility of brightness; like the island skies in early spring.

'*Arancini?*' He held out a platter of the golden rice balls, oozing with mozzarella and sun-dried tomatoes. People wrote about his *arancini* in the guestbook. A doctor from Lyon once asked if he could send him some by same-day delivery, said he'd pay anything for it. He watched Kit take one. She held it between her finger and thumb, as if uncertain what to do.

'You *eat* it,' he said, but instead of smiling back, she regarded him with . . . what? Normally the looks he received were less complicated. 'Forgive me,' he said, one hand on his chest. 'Maybe you have a personal code? Don't ride on the bikes of chefs? I made you break that. I'm sorry. Really.'

'Well, I have to have some rules when I'm travelling,' she

replied, so steadily that he almost took her seriously. He laughed.

'Where were you before this trip? Somewhere cool?'

'Just in England. Doing England stuff.'

'Oh.' He felt irrationally disappointed, for he'd pictured her globetrotting, filing copy from café tables in Panama, Berlin, Nairobi. 'But you're a writer? You write about foreign places, vacation places?'

'A travel writer, yes. I . . . was on a sort of sabbatical.'

'Okay,' he said, 'best food you've ever had?'

'Bangkok.'

She bit into the *arancini* at last, and he watched, making no attempt to hide the anticipation on his face.

'Or maybe Goa,' she said, mid-chew, and almost with a smile.

He groaned, in mock – mostly mock – disappointment. He realised then how much he wanted to see it, that smile of hers. He tried to think of something else to say. Usually he didn't have to. He felt a touch at his shoulder then; it was the French woman, Nina, glittering with jewellery, and wearing an equally shimmering dress. '*Bonsoir, mon cheri*,' she said, leaning in to kiss him on both cheeks. Her perfume was an invisible cloud, and he resisted the urge to cough.

'I need another of those delicacies, *adesso*,' she said breathily. 'And you *must* tell me again how you make them.' She peered past him, noticed Kit, then looked pointedly back at Oliviero. 'Ah, *excusez-moi*. I'm interrupting.'

'You're not,' said Kit. 'Not at all.'

Nina raised an eyebrow, nudged Oliviero in the chest in pantomime fashion.

'Then you need to work harder,' she said to him.

46

Oliviero gave the laugh that he knew he was supposed to, but a quick glance at Kit told him that she took no pleasure in Nina's insinuation. She looked, Oliviero thought, entirely uncomfortable.

'I need to go back to the kitchen,' he said, but she wouldn't let him catch her eye, so there was no way of telling if she understood that he wasn't running away; it was his way of rescuing her.

eight

'*CHE BEL VESTITO!*'

The French woman had left to refill her plate shortly after Oliviero had made his exit, and Kit had been relieved to find herself alone. She started, now, as she felt a tweaking at the skirt of her dress. She turned to find a woman smoothing the fabric with her thumb. Her hair was pulled into a tight bun, and badger striped. She must have been well into her eighties but her lipstick was as red as the Negroni she held in her other hand, and the look in her eyes just as intense.

'*Ah, seta! Molto fine.* What beautiful silk it is.'

It was a gesture of her mum's, that quick, tactile investigation and appraisal of cloth. Oh the things you lost of people. The innocuous details that you didn't know you missed until you glimpsed them again. She resisted the urge to say, *Please do it again, please.*

'*Grazie,*' she said instead. Then, 'It's Italian silk, in fact. Vintage, I think.'

She practically purred, the woman, and looked at her with sharpened interest.

48

'And you, you are Italian too. Fresh, not vintage. Me, I'm vintage. But, *sì*, you are a *bella donna italiana*?'

Kit gave a small smile. '*Mia madre*,' she said, and somehow it felt like the surrendering of a secret. She exhaled, had another drink, the bittersweet Aperol fizzing on her tongue.

'*Tua madre!* Please, tell me more . . .'

She thought of telling her of the hours she'd spent as a child watching her mum sketch and snip and pin, first as Rosa made piecemeal alterations to their own clothes then, eventually, her bespoke designs, dresses that had adorned the windows of boutiques in Bristol, Cheltenham and Oxford. How she, Kit, had grown up whispering her secrets to a dressmaking dummy called Bella, and how the equable Bella continued to occupy her mum's room in Bristol, as headless as ever, and wearing an unfinished frock.

She thought of telling her that it was her mum who'd made the dress she was wearing now, and how it had arrived in the mail one day, rolled inside a padded envelope: an astounding informality for something so fine. But that was Rosa all over. She'd come across the fabric by chance, she'd said, finished the dress that same day, and therefore it had to be mailed – what good was there in waiting? Ideas were to be acted upon instantly. *Adesso!*

How would it be, to share some small portion of her mum with this eager older lady? If her interest was too scant, she'd regret it instantly, and if it was too probing then she'd regret that too. Cocktail conversation required an equanimity Kit didn't yet possess – not here and now, not in this place. Since she'd arrived she'd tried to stay conscious of Valentino's movements across the terrace, always at the periphery of her vision, but thoughts of Rosa must have distracted her, for he was upon them, this Gatsby-like figure, with his set smile and dark suit.

'*Buonasera*, Signora Alessi, Signorina Costa.'

Kit replied in a voice that lacked all conviction, and was grateful for the eclipsing response of Signora Alessi. She watched as the woman switched her hand from her dress to Valentino's arm, greeting him effusively. He dipped a small bow, and glanced at Kit, just suppressing a smile.

'This young girl, in her very beautiful dress, was talking to me of her Italian mother,' said Signora Alessi, in English. 'Wonderful, wonderful.'

'Ah, yes?' he said, with what seemed like genuine interest.

Kit's drink slopped in her glass.

'Yes,' she said. 'Look, I'm sorry, this is so rude, but while I remember, is it all right . . .' She lost her thread; his eyes were too intent. She took a breath. 'Dinner in my room, would that be okay? Room service? Just tonight. I've got this deadline, for another piece, and . . .'

'Of course,' he said, '*non c'è problema*. Abi will bring your meal to you.' He smiled, simply. 'I hope you complete your work. And join us the next night, yes?'

Freedom glimpsed, she rushed towards it. She excused herself from Signora Alessi, told her she'd enjoyed talking with her. She thanked Valentino, glancing ruefully at her watch as she did so, as if even now an editor was somewhere waiting, growing in impatience. Then she hurried from the terrace, not realising she was still gripping her glass until she was halfway across the lawn.

Earlier, when Kit had first closed the door to her room, she'd wanted to lie down and shut her eyes, to process her arrival, the fact of Valentino, the presence of Oliviero, but instead the room had insisted that she engage with it and take in its details. There was nothing overblown about it, you'd never call it luxurious, but it was, simply – and she'd felt traitorous to even think it – homely. The bed was made of white wood, and had a cornflower-blue cover. The floor was terracotta. White linen curtains lifted in the breeze that blew in from the sea. The view from the balcony was of olive groves and jungle palms, sprays of pink flowers and wide, wide water. Kit had lain briefly back on the bed and looked up at the circle of perfect sky above her head. *For God's sake*, she'd said.

Now, she closed the door sharply and leant back against it, unspeakably glad to have escaped the terrace. For all the indisputable charms of the hotel's cocktail hour – the vine-laden pergola, the lights glowing against the dusk, the profuse hospitality – it was an occasion that demanded more of her than she felt able to give. Perhaps, she thought dimly, that went for the whole trip. Her stomach pitched as she thought about Oliviero. Her reaction to him had been acutely physical – and it continued to be so, even if attraction had been replaced by utter mortification. She was sure she didn't need to worry about him feeling the same way, but that was scant comfort – her own embarrassment, however private, however contained, was more than enough. And Valentino. *Him*. It was his job to be pleasant, and maybe he was good at playing the role, but all the guests turning smiles his way, basking in his attention, was difficult to watch.

She looked over at the blue-painted desk, where earlier she'd set out her laptop, her pens, her notebook, a couple of copies of the magazine she wrote for. It was a workstation, but the paint of its scenery was still wet, and unconvincing. She needed to feel centred, so she went to the bottom of her rucksack and drew out her diary. Tucked inside its pages were two photographs of her mum, and she held them now. Everything else fell away, as she knew it would.

The first was the oldest picture that she had. Rosa's face was defiant with youth, her cheekbones sharp as blades, as she balanced the infant Kit on her knee. This was Rosa the year after she'd left Italy, before she'd had to tell anybody her lie, except perhaps herself. It was taken in the garden of Deer Leap, the place Kit had grown up, an old labourer's cottage on the fringes of a Somerset estate. Her mum had kept house for the man who lived at the manor, grateful that her introverted employer hadn't objected to her tucking the basket with the baby in a corner of the kitchen, that he hadn't minded when Kit the toddler had thrashed pots and pans with wooden spoons, or raced up and down the halls on a hobby horse made from a broomstick. These were the sorts of stories her mum had told her. This was the family folklore she knew.

The other picture had been taken just last winter, the day before Rosa had been set to begin a new course of treatment. It was Kit who'd insisted on the photograph. She'd held the camera at arm's length and they'd pushed their faces together as though making the two halves of a heart. Her mum had protested, said, *God, no, I look like death*, and they'd laughed, because what else could they do, but their eyes had the sheen of just-kept tears as they'd looked at the camera. They were out walking, determined to take whatever the day had given them – the rare winter sun, this time together. They'd begun at the harbour and trundled along past the children floundering in kayaks and the impervious-looking paddleboarders. They'd walked through the boatyard, stopping to watch a man paint stripes on a ferryboat. If they'd had the legs for it, they'd planned to make it to the riverside path by the Portway. They'd cycled it together several summers ago, out past the city, where the hills sprang patches of rock shining white in the sun, and dusted tracks winding who knew where. 'We could be in Andalucía,' Kit had said then, 'or Italy?'

'No,' Rosa had said, 'not Italy.'

They'd tired, in the end, and turned back. But Kit had slipped her arm through her mum's and talked of the two of them taking a trip the next summer, somewhere warm, somewhere beautiful. Rosa had hesitated, and something unspoken had passed between them. *Now there's an idea*, she had said eventually.

Kit held the photographs on her knee.

So, she said. *I'm here. Elba. But maybe you already knew that was where he was. Maybe you've always known. This hotel. The son.*

Signorina Costa. He'd greeted her just as if she was anyone; no memories – however old, however insignificant – stirred by uttering the name that had been her mum's too. That said everything, didn't it?

Kit looked down. There was a whole life between the two pictures. One before them too, that, however briefly, Valentino Colosimo had been part of. She bundled them back inside her diary, avoiding her mum's eye, unable to think of anything else to say.

Down the years, Kit had kept things from her mum, of course she had. She'd had no deep guilt from never declaring her week of lunchtime detentions for answering back to an ill-tempered science teacher when she was twelve. Nor the piece she'd felt compelled to tear from her dress when she was fifteen, for it had been better to pretend it had snagged on a fence than been burnt by the smouldering end of her own cigarette. Nor the boys. All the boys. Rosa had been tough on the male species; she didn't believe in the possibility that any of them might be good. *You're too smart for them, too* bellissima. So Kit's first time had stayed her secret. Sixteen years old, a party in the woods, the fingers of a black-haired boy weaving through hers, his tongue darting into her mouth. Him hopping, one foot caught in his jeans, her laughing, just for something to say, to do, then everything over so quickly. Then the wilting buttercups left in her tent the next morning; she'd have liked to have told her mum about them. Instead she'd cycled home, freewheeling, legs kicked wide, the wind streaming her hair like ribbons, and put on the yellow dress her mum had made her the summer before. Rosa had pursed her lips approvingly, said it looked better on her this year, that she'd grown into it, and Kit had wondered then if perhaps somehow she knew after all.

She searched for more. Things she'd never told because she'd thought they'd alter the way her mum looked at her, even by just a degree. The old man who'd fallen on the other side of the street and she'd cycled on past, because if she'd stopped she'd have been late for her first day at work, and at the time that had felt like an important thing, the punctuality. The pill she'd taken once, holding it on the tip of her finger, her eyes widening, heart pumping, no clue what it was or where it came from, then, regardless, letting it dance her all the way to dawn. How she'd lied to a friend, claimed flu and missed her birthday party, but really she was trying to stifle a crush on that same friend's boyfriend. Inglorious moments. Ill-advised. Dubious. Sure to provoke disappointment in a mum who seemed unimpeachable, but . . . None of it was in the same league. None of it was life itself.

A whole father. She'd stood next to him. Swapped words. He'd touched a finger to her elbow, taken his hand in her own and shaken it. He had a fading bruise on his thumbnail, and the tiniest of scuffs on the toe of his shoe. Was it only just now sinking in, the certainty of his existence? And how strange it had felt, as he'd walked across the lawn, to realise that he looked like just the kind of man she could imagine her mum once having loved; however misguidedly, no matter how fleetingly, and despite Rosa never admitting it.

The knock startled her, even though she was expecting it. And although she'd been told it was Abi who'd bring the tray, she was still surprised to see her standing there with her uncomplicated smile, her mass of tiny curls like a halo round her head. As she set down the tray Kit said *grazie* several times, and as Abi left she fell upon it, inspecting the contents. The *aperitivo*, however aborted, had done its work; she was hungry.

When Kit was small, her mum had often brought home leftovers from the meals she cooked at the manor; making their own separate food, therefore, had been a treat. Italian food was a treat. Kit had asked for green spaghetti for supper on Saturday nights long before everyone was buying jars of supermarket pesto. She remembered watching Rosa pinch ears of dough, *orchiette*, with a practised twist and a flick. She'd simmer a pan of tomato sauce for hours on end, bending to taste it reverently from the spoon, garlic casings scattered about her feet like old confetti. In later years she frequented a deli in Clifton, run by a smiling young Sicilian couple. She'd leave hugging a jar of marinated artichokes to her chest, and carrying a rustling bag full of pistachio-cream pastries. *Food makes life worth living*, she'd always told Kit. Now Kit looked down at the tray, and thought that whatever Rosa would have made of her trip, she'd have approved of this.

There was a roundel of charred and oil-brushed bruschetta, heaped with speckled borlotti beans and glistening tomato. She whisked off one cover to reveal spaghetti with well-rounded scallops and chopped nuts, and beneath another a piece of bright white grilled fish, adorned with sprigs of rosemary and fine-sliced garlic. Tiny roasted potatoes, cubed like dice and full of crunch. A plate with purple leaves of radicchio and the yellowish tips of endive and delicate curls of frisée. A wide slice of *torta della nonna* – she recognised it straight away – sugar-dusted, scattered with pine nuts. And there was a note, propped against a half-bottle of island *vino bianco*. Kit opened it, thinking it the bill for room service, but then she saw the name *Valentino*, signed in fountain pen at the bottom; a bold sweep.

I hope your first meal with us is restorative and pleasurable, it said. *All Oliviero's work! We wish you buon appetito! Anything you need, just ask. It would be our pleasure.*

She picked up the plate with the tart first, and wandered out onto the balcony. The air was warm and still; the hotel and its garden glowed. It was as if she was in the middle of an enchanted wood, and she stared into its depths; the lights against the night were spellbinding. Her vision blurred. The best person in the world had died and Valentino Colosimo had no idea. She took a forkful of tart, and felt her chest heave. She'd forgotten the flavour of the sweet custard, the toasted pine nuts. *Torta della nonna*, she said out loud. Granny's tart, it meant, but as a child she'd always called it *torta della mamma*, because it was her mum who'd made it for her, just as she had done everything else.

nine

DINNER WAS A DANCE. IT WAS SOMETHING TO BE CHOREOGRAPHED, the music provided by the clink of wine glasses, Abi's shoes tap-tapping across the tiles, and the murmur of conversation that changed as the evening went on, *animato, animato*, then rising, sometimes *forte*, always *grazioso*. Through five courses Valentino spun on his heel, waltzed between tables, tending to his guests even before they realised they were in need of something. As the meal wound to a close, people drifted to the terrace, beguiled by the illuminations. There they might drink a *digestivo*, and listen to the island's night music – the distant wash of surf, the chatter of cicadas. Young couples might slip away hand in hand, old ones too, smiling secret smiles. Others tucked themselves inside the bar, leaning back on cushions, balancing tiny cups of *espresso corretto* on their knees. That night the Germans, Steffi and Max, argued in hushed voices, as their boys, full of too much pasta and too much sunshine – or just enough of each – sleepwalked along in their wake. The elderly sisters took their customary turn round the edge of the garden, arm in arm, before returning to their rooms. Nina drank an amaretto liqueur, occupying a sofa on her own, her eyes closed. Lucille skulked by the covered pool, talking on her phone in an urgent whisper. The boys from Torino played cards and drank bottled beer. Only Isabel remained at her seat in the emptied dining room.

'Everything was all right?' Valentino asked, with a light touch to her shoulder.

'Wonderful. It's always wonderful,' she replied.

'Can I offer you something? A limoncello?' Then he grinned, saying it with relish, already knowing she'd accept. 'Or a grappa?'

'Oh, a grappa. Yes please. Why not.'

He brought over a bottle and two glasses.

'You might hear another English voice here this week,' he said. He sat down just across from her, his chair angled sideways. 'We have a writer staying.'

'A writer? How interesting. Will I know her books?'

'She's a journalist, I think. Covers travel for magazines, newspapers. She's here to write about the festival at Innamorata.'

'Oh, lovely! Romeo and Juliet, the island version. Well, it is a spectacle. But why isn't she staying at Capoliveri, then? It'd be much more convenient.' She sipped her drink and eyed him over the glass; there was something teasing in her look, and he liked it. 'Perhaps it's all an elaborate ruse and really she's here to review your hotel, Valentino. Was she at dinner? I didn't see anyone who looked terribly English . . .'

'She's part Italian. Her name. Her looks. And she dined in her room.'

'Then she's certain to be writing wonderful words tonight. How is Oliviero?'

'Running all over the island, when he isn't in the kitchen.'

'Girls?' Isabel smiled. 'Our modern-day Romeo. So there's nobody particular?'

'Never anybody particular.'

'He's young. Perhaps that's the way to be.'

'*Sì, sì*,' said Valentino, taking her words. 'When you're young, it's the way to be.'

He saw her eyes flick down, her hands holding on to one another. He'd always guessed her to be in her early fifties, Isabel, a decade younger than himself, though he couldn't be sure of it. There were times when she appeared so young, so girlish; on occasion he'd even seen her blush – he didn't think he'd ever seen an Italian woman blush like that – though it could always be wine, he supposed, the flare of wine and the after-burn of the sun. Regardless, the effect it had on him was that he lost his years too. Became the awkward youth, the ill-shapen teenage boy, that in fact he'd never really been.

'Do you think,' he said, fingers drumming the table, 'that she might be here to review us? The writer from England?'

Isabel laughed. 'If she is, then . . . well, I'll have to dispose of her. We can't have the secret getting out; they'll all flock here. Goodness, no, keep the Brits on the Tuscan mainland, that's what I say.'

'I like the British,' he said.

'And we like you Italians.'

They raised their glasses to one another, and Isabel stifled a yawn.

'I must leave you . . .' he said, getting to his feet.

'Of course you must. You've things to do. I, on the other hand, am going to go outside and watch the stars. See if they're all in order.'

'You're not tired?'

'I am, dreadfully, but I never like these evenings to be over.'
She stood up, smoothed her skirt. 'Good night, Valentino.'

He bowed, and wished her *buona notte*.

Oliviero came out of the kitchen. His chef's overalls were gone,
as was his red bandanna, and he wore a black shirt that he
buttoned as he walked. He clapped Valentino on the shoulder.

'I'll see you later,' he said.

Valentino nodded. 'Have a good night.'

He'd likely be headed for one of the bars down in Portoferraio
or Marino di Campo, with open-air dance floors and music you
had to shout over, if you cared to try at all. A million miles
from their tranquil corner of the island, though perhaps that
was why he was drawn there. There was something hectic in
Oliviero's soul; maybe that was how it was with all young
people. Valentino's own cautiousness had certainly never
rubbed off on him.

Valentino couldn't remember the last time he'd danced.
He'd never been one for it, even in his youth. He'd saved his
fancy footwork for the ring. It felt like a lifetime ago now, his
boxing. Never more than an enthusiastic amateur, but on the
right night he was quick on his feet, mule-strong, dogged.
Colosimo versus Di Angelo, June 1976 in Firenze, the feeling of
surety as he delivered the knockout punch after nine rounds.
For all his victories, he'd taken plenty of beatings too, often
going home with one eye puffed and swollen like a squashed
plum, his lip split. What he'd liked was the fight, and even if
he'd lost, the ringing of his head and the aching of his body had
felt like a good thing; his best efforts expended. His girlfriend
at the time had made him stop. She'd never understood it, what
could drive a man to lift his fists, and dance on his feet. His

wife, though, had been different. Sometimes he'd caught sight of her at the edge of the ring, her face raised, eyes blazing, and in bed later her nails tracked his back, the ferocity of her kisses imprinted in all the places he wasn't bruised. However physically spent he'd felt, she'd always stoked the fire that was left in him.

He rubbed the side of his face, his light stubble crackling. Fire and fight. It had been a long time since he'd thought of anything quite like that. He shook his head and picked up a tablecloth, folding it from end to end. Then he went to the next table, and the next. Like this he moved from small job to small job, ending up in his tiny office behind the reception, sinking into an old leather armchair. He would read a few pages of a book, perhaps. The newspaper. Sometimes the good-for-nothing cat would sneak in and curl up in his lap. He used to enjoy cigars but the doctor had told him to stop all that. There he'd stay until precisely midnight, when he'd go outside and do the rounds of the lights; flicking switches, extinguishing candles, robbing paper lanterns of their delicate glow. This too was his dance, and he knew the steps by heart.

ten

EARLY MORNINGS IN THE MILLE LUCI KITCHEN WERE EASY, breezy, and Oliviero had them to himself until the boy Bernardo, the *plongeur*, came down from the village. He always made sure he had a cup of hot chocolate waiting for him, a sweetener to start the day. Valentino had taught him a lot, but he also remembered how it was to do that job – that it was the small things that made a difference.

As a teenager, with an urge to stretch his wings, Oliviero had worked in a different kitchen, as the pot washer. Before every evening's service he'd join the staff, the working family, in a meal. The job itself was awful, his fingers scalded, skin cracked, his back aching from standing on one spot all night, and the pay was lousy, but that meal, oh, that one meal. The salty shock of ground anchovies. Roasted tomatoes that exploded in his mouth. Unctuous lengths of tagliatelle carbonara. That was why he stayed, working so late that at school the next day he'd fall asleep propped on his elbows, waking with a start because the teacher had thrown a stub of chalk at him, pinging off his ear with stunning, stinging accuracy.

He imagined, sometimes, going back to that first restaurant, disguised in his bandanna and blacks. Peering from the sanctuary of the kitchen to see the band of locals seated at their corner tables, legs kicked out and scheming. What would he cook? A showboating dish, like stuffed courgette flowers, a batter as light as air, the flesh of the vegetable sweet and spry and tasting of the garden it came from. Or maybe an escalope of veal, beaten until as thin as paper, smacked with a blunt object until his fingers ached. Or perhaps the answer was something simple: nothing but a bowl of pasta. Ah, but penne all'arrabbiata, of course. Angry pasta, that was what it meant in Italian, *angry*, and his version bursting with enough chillis to leave the diner in no doubt of the cook's intentions. So many options, so many interpretations. *See, I am accomplished, impressive, even. See, I don't care what you think. See, I'm angry, I'm angry still.* But then, after all these years, perhaps what was required was serenity. Tranquillity. A dish that tasted like a half-embrace, or the squeeze of a shoulder. Something generous, and familiar maybe. Carbonara; a rich and creamy sauce, smoky cubes of pancetta, thick ribbons of belly-filling tagliatelle; a scattering of optimistic young parsley. Or lasagne. Toasted cheese and smooth white sauce, the sun-bright taste of tomatoes and the homely flavour of good minced beef.

It was a fantasy that Oliviero rarely indulged in, because the thought just left him sad and angry, and not knowing which of the two emotions was the more just.

He had music, he had coffee, and there was flour on his hands: the day had begun. He rolled and buttered pastry for *cornetti*, to be served warm from the oven when they were plump and just flaking, best eaten with a spoonful of home-made jam. The

63

bread he'd made too: crusty ciabatta rolls, a gleaming lattice loaf, and a little-bit-sweet dark rye. During breakfast hours he'd cook eggs to order, pancakes too, and fry sliver-thin pancetta and herb-filled sausages he got from the butcher, Carlo, in Marciana Marina. For the first time this morning there would be strawberry focaccia on the table too. Instead of going out, he'd spent the night before in his room, going through his recipe notes, and decided that this would be perfect. Now he studded the plumped pillow of dough with the shining berries, drizzled the juices, and set it in the oven.

This done, he stood back, allowing himself a moment's pause – a sip of coffee. His eyes travelled to the window. The view wasn't panoramic. The kitchen was to the side of the hotel, in the shadow of a slope of pines, with a cluster of burly palm trees pressed close to its outside walls, but it felt, to Oliviero, sensationally exotic. Waving fronds, a swatch of sky; it was as though he were in the depths of the jungle. He often had the side door open, and if he took a break to smoke a cigarette, he'd crouch on his haunches out of view of the guests, and breathe in the coolness that came down from the trees. Valentino had talked once of opening up the kitchen, removing the wall that separated it from the dining room, saying the guests would enjoy watching him at work, the hiss and flame and slice of it all. Oliviero knew he'd rise to it, but to him the kitchen was sacred; a place of privacy, but also somewhere that the diners should never know too much about. What magician pulls a rabbit from a transparent hat?

He didn't hear her knock, not through the music, but he saw the kitchen door swing open. She was standing at the threshold, her hands full of her dinner tray.

'I'm just returning this,' she said, with a flicker of what

looked like embarrassment. 'To Abi,' she added, with unnecessary emphasis.

He bounded over to take it, as though the sooner it was in his hands the sooner they could forget the fact that she'd had to carry it all the way from her room.

'Sorry, sorry,' he said. 'Someone would have come to take it. We didn't want to disturb you last night, but this morning . . .' He slowed down, stopped. Smiled. '*Buongiorno, bella signorina.*'

'Good morning,' she said.

'You're awake very early. But you did sleep okay?'

'Yes. Surprisingly.'

'Surprisingly?'

She shook her head dismissively. 'Just . . . first nights in places,' she said.

'We're not like other places, I think.' He noted the empty plates with approval. 'You ate everything.'

She nodded. He saw a slight flare of her nostrils, a just-perceptible movement of her head.

'That's focaccia in the oven,' he said. 'Made with strawberries.'

'With strawberries?'

'I've never served it at breakfast before. Maybe you want to test it?' He glanced at the timer. 'It'll be ready in . . . one coffee's time.'

She narrowed her eyes. It wasn't lost on him that they were brighter than before.

'That's a unit of time?'

He nodded, held up his coffee pot.

'I'm going for a swim,' she said, indicating her shoulder bag in return, as if it too were proof of her intentions.

'So you need some energy. And now I've said the word "coffee", you have to have one, right? And you don't realise it yet, but you need strawberry focaccia too.'

'But . . . breakfast is from seven o'clock,' she said. 'I'm disturbing you. You can't have guests tramping all over your kitchen.'

Tramping. He didn't know the word, but he got the gist of it.

'I like tramping,' he said. 'How do you take it? A lot of milk, *si*?'

She hesitated. Then she said, 'Black, please.'

After Kit left, Oliviero felt strangely occupation-less. She hadn't stayed for his focaccia in the end. It needed another ten minutes, and she'd drunk her coffee like an Italian: fast, upright, refusing the seat he'd offered her. When the kitchen doors swung open again, he grinned. She hadn't been able to resist after all. But instead it was stout little Bernardo, instantly halting, filling his nostrils, asking what it was, that amazing smell. Oliviero had to laugh.

'And I suppose you want some with your *cioccolata*?' he said, awash with benevolence, because she'd woken up and come first to his kitchen. And that never happened.

eleven

THE DAY WAS BRAZENLY BEAUTIFUL. THE BREEZE IN THE PALM trees sounded like the rustling of dresses. The bougainvillea beamed. Kit took the path to the beach, hurrying now, not so much making up for lost time – it was early still, and she had no schedule – but desperate for the edifying effects of water.

The path zigzagged down the terraced slopes, past strawberry bushes and twisted olive trees and neat rows of courgette plants bursting with yellow flowers. She stepped from one paving stone to the next, narrowly avoiding the garden's minute population: a lime green lizard darting past her, an army of intrepid ants hefting a berry between them. For all the manicuring of the grounds around the main building, this stretch of the Mille Luci had a wild quality. The air was full of the hum of insects. The sweet scent of ripe fruit was everywhere; bound for focaccias, perhaps, if Oliviero's was a success, and she was sure it would be.

That morning she'd set out to prove to herself that there was nothing strange about anything, not beyond the conventional strangeness of encountering a hitherto unknown sibling. His kitchen was a different sort of space to anything she'd expected. Ceramic bowls full of lemons and their leaves, twisted plaits of garlic, a shelf creaking with jars of home-made jam and pickled vegetables. It was congenial, when she'd expected something stark, industrial. He'd held up his espresso pot like she was a friend dropping by, but as they'd waited for it to whistle and hiss, she'd shifted on her feet, feeling like anything but.

She paused in the shade of a juniper tree, laid her hand on its trunk. She was lower now, the sea a slim band of blue. The strong coffee, so hastily drunk, had sent her buzzing. She breathed levelly. Emptied her head of new concerns, brought the old ones to the fore. Had her mum known this place? Not the hotel, surely, for the website had said it had opened twenty-eight years ago, but the island? Elba? Kit felt sure that she hadn't. Because surely, no matter how piercing the hurt, if you'd been a part of something this beautiful, wouldn't you carry it with you? How could you stand hand in hand with your tiny daughter on the pier at Clevedon, faces stung by the wind coming off the water, wellingtons sluiced by rain, and not say *Let me tell you how the sea can be.* Or butterflies; watching the cabbage whites that chased through the garden at Deer Leap, how could you stop yourself from talking of the painted wings you'd seen?

The beach itself was a slender band of sand, decked with sunloungers, their parasols yet to be unfurled. To the sides there were slabs of rock, as smooth and grey as elephant hide. Later there would be towels patchworking every available space, a nut-brown attendant keeping a languid eye on the loungers, but for now Kit had it to herself. She kicked off her flip-flops and stepped out of her dress, and walked towards the water. The heat of the sand was rising, the sea already as warm as a bath. She waded, then dipped below the surface, swam away from the beach with fast strokes. Further out, cool currents wrapped themselves around her, and she flipped onto her back, felt the pleasant shock as the colder water prickled her scalp. She floated like a lily pad, her arms and legs starfished, as she stared up at the sky. It could devour you, all that blue, and she was ready to let it. If there were waves at all she barely noticed them. She'd swum in plenty of seas, but none had ever seemed to combine stimulation and relaxation quite so perfectly. She felt more present than she had in months and months. Kit breathed deeply. Left to drift, her mind rolled this way and that, following inlets, lapping into sea caves, flooding into places where it had no right to be. Abruptly she turned onto her front again, and began to stroke a fast crawl back to the beach. It was supposed to be a quick dip, to restore clarity. Because her first thought upon waking that morning hadn't been of her mum, and here, of all places, that felt disloyal.

Kit's hair was wet from the shower as she went in for breakfast. She took a table on the terrace, beneath the shade of a vast umbrella-like palm, and was brought coffee by Abi.

'You slept well, miss?'

'So well, thank you.'

'And dinner, it was good?'

'Very, very good.'

'You help yourself from the buffet for breakfast.'

Kit had seen it as she passed through the breakfast room, the extravagant spread of fruits and jams and cheeses and meats and pastries. She'd also noticed the way the windows were open to the garden, inviting the day in; the sprays of bright flowers set on every table, the languid turning of the ceiling fans. The paintings on the walls, splashed canvases, beach scenes in rainbow colours, spiked heads of palms and dazzling sea. If she were anybody else writing a piece on the hotel, she would have wanted to talk about that space.

'Could I perhaps just have some eggs?' she asked.

Abi smiled and nodded, disappearing without asking her what kind. Perhaps they only served their eggs in one way: Mille Luci style.

Her mum had made the best scrambled eggs, and when Kit was small, if she was ever ill, eggs were what she gave her. In a small and heavy-bottomed pan she cooked them as slow as they would go, stirring in butter and salt only at the last. Those scrambled eggs had always been the most comforting thing Kit could imagine, far more than the sum of their parts.

She sat back in her chair, hidden behind her sunglasses. She knew Oliviero would be confined to his kitchen, but Valentino was nowhere to be seen either, and that was an unspeakable relief. From her place of safety on the far corner of the terrace, she surveyed the scene. Perhaps Valentino didn't work in the mornings. Maybe he'd stayed out late the night before, silver-tongued and silver-haired, carousing his way along the coast. He could have scatterings of illegitimate children, popping up like mushrooms in the forest, for all she knew.

'*Buongiorno*,' said Oliviero. 'Again.'

Sauntering across the terrace, he looked like the arrival of an extravagant kind of midnight: black eyes, black stubble, black chef's garb.

'How was your swim?'

'There was no one there,' said Kit. 'It was lovely.'

'Best time to go. Yesterday,' he said, 'I swam before work.'

'Wow, that would have been really early.'

'Or very late.'

'Dark or light?'

'Both. The sun came up as I got out of the water.'

She thought he'd be the kind to enjoy the theatre of a packed beach, strutting down the runway to the shoreline.

'I went out,' he said, 'in Portoferraio. Couldn't sleep afterwards. The water, it's good for thinking, isn't it?'

She wondered what he'd been thinking about. What possible complications could visit the life of this man who freewheeled on his motorbike and measured time in coffee?

'The focaccia,' he said, 'it's gone already.'

'So it was popular, then?'

'I should have kept a piece for you. I'm sorry.'

'I had my chance,' she said.

'You should have taken it.'

His smile tipped, his eyes crinkled. She tried hard to look away, but found she couldn't.

'I'll make it again tomorrow,' he said. 'Eggs. Abi said you wanted eggs. How do you like them?'

'Um . . . I don't really mind.'

'Okay. I make my best eggs. And tomorrow morning, when you swim, you should follow the rocks to the next cove. It's tiny, but very beautiful. My favourite. One of them, that is to say. The beaches on this island, they're *bellissima*, there are some the tourists never find, and . . .'

He faltered, and she wondered then what her face had been doing, if it was marred with something that made him feel that his conversation wasn't wanted.

'*Allora* . . . eggs.'

71

To her relief, he left her, and she watched him go. She saw him wave at the two little blond boys who were pelting up and down the lawn, chasing an orange sun of a ball. She saw him stop to greet the French woman and her daughter – *Bonjour, madame, mademoiselle* – then carry on his way.

Half-brother. It was so unlikely a thought that she wanted to laugh.

The eggs, when they came, seemingly just three or four sips of coffee later, were scrambled. Served on a sea-blue plate with a sprinkle of parsley, a crunch of black pepper, and glinting with butter. One forkful, and Kit had to admit they were about as perfect as anyone else's scrambled eggs could ever be.

As Kit left the terrace, she was aware of the day stretching out before her, and having no clear sense of what to do with it. It was a rudderless, flattening feeling. She passed a young family carting their beach bags and inflatables. Identical twin boys, the two from the lawn, darted ahead in their jelly shoes, while their parents followed behind them with a purposeful stride.

'*Morgen*,' said the woman. She wore shorts and a bikini top. Kit glanced at her flat stomach and muscular build, the scar that ran the length of her knee.

'*Buongiorno*,' she said back.

They carried on past, a vision of blond hair and tanned skin. 'Jurgen!' she heard the father call. 'Nikki!' His hand went to his wife's shoulder as they descended the steep garden.

They were so complete a unit. Father. Mother. Boys, times two. At home, they would each have their places at a dining table, their favoured chairs. A shoe rack in the hall, full of big and little pairs. They wouldn't need anybody else but each other, a family like that. But there would be doting grandparents anyway, elders who read the boys fairy tales, stories that were no more magical than their own ordinary lives.

Suddenly Kit felt acutely lonely.

If she had ever hankered after a male figure at home, it had only been to even the balance: a ramshackle, absent-minded man, perhaps, with frayed elbows and biscuit crumbs on his jumper, someone to offset her relentlessly immaculate, ruthlessly correct mum. Someone who might occasionally slouch. Or sleep in. Or wipe away a tear as the credits rolled on a soppy film. *You're far softer than me*, Rosa had said to her once, and Kit had imagined herself spongy and insubstantial, more porous than she'd have liked. *No, gentler, I mean gentler*, which was a better word, but Kit could never tell if her mum considered it to be a good thing, gentleness. When Rosa fell ill, when the self-reliance that had been her defining feature was forced to falter, so too did Kit's. Oh how she'd wanted to feel that there was somebody else there with her. Somebody to whom she could say, *She seems a little better today, don't you think?* Or, through a wash of tears, *This is so fucking unfair*, and know not only that they understood the utter pointlessness of such a feeling but also that they were experiencing it every bit as powerfully as you. Someone whose job it was to look after you, even if, in the muddled aftermath of heartbreak, you might find it was your job to look after them. But this father she'd imagined in such moments was never actually hers: his long-ago death was the least of the reasons for his ineligibility. Despite him now having a name, and a life after all, a good-for-nothing man like Valentino Colosimo would remain, forever, good for nothing. The very obliqueness of her desire – this vague notion of a decent father – had stopped her feeling too treacherous, even if Rosa's lines continued to ring in her ears: *All men are useless*, amore, *we're much better off without them.*

'Kit, *buongiorno.*'

The way he said her name made her heart jump. *Kiiit*. Hers was a name that had always sounded a little brusque, far too stubby, yet here it was as drawn out as a caress, the kind of sound you might make to soothe a restless child. She turned, and he stood looking just as he had the day before: white shirt, black trousers and an easy smile. The beauty of his hotel was everywhere around him, with its perfect eggs, immaculate ocean and beds that meant you woke up forgetting, even for just a second or two, what really mattered.

'Everything is all right?' he asked.

He was unapologetically, implausibly living. And among all the many complicated emotions that this fact elicited, unjustness was, in that moment, the one that struck her most.

twelve

'*SIGNORINA?*'

'Sorry, I'm fine, just . . . too much coffee at breakfast.'

'It is strong stuff, it's true,' he said. 'Would you like some iced water?'

'Thank you, no.'

He didn't wish to detain her. Intruding upon any guest's privacy was a grave mistake for an hotelier. But to be sure that she knew he was there for her? That much was important.

'You're happy with your room? You have everything you need?'

'Yes. Thank you. It's great.'

'And your work,' he said, 'it went well last night? You finished it?'

He saw her hesitate. 'Well, not finished, but . . . progress. Some progress.' Her hand went to her hair self-consciously.

'Well, have a good day. And if you want anything, if there's anything we can do to make your stay more pleasurable . . .'

'Thank you,' she said, cutting in. 'It's all fine.'

He was holding her up now, he could see it, so he stepped

aside, and gestured with his arm to the day that lay beyond them both. She turned to go.

'Oh, and *signorina*, will you be joining us for dinner tonight?'

'Okay,' she said, 'sure.'

Her answer fortified him. 'Don't work every hour,' he said. 'See something beautiful. Enjoy our sunshine.'

She gave a small wave, then cut it short abruptly, as though she'd thought better of it. He raised his own hand, picking up where she'd left off.

When Abi had danced about the terrace with her broom, when the tables were laid afresh for lunch with immaculate white cloths and glasses that held the sunlight, Valentino and Oliviero would sit beneath the majesty of the giant palm and talk of the dinner to come. Which, invariably, led to talk of their guests.

When Valentino had first opened the doors of the Mille Luci, he'd wanted to make a place where people could retreat from their worlds for a while, then go back to them with brighter eyes and happier hearts. Wasn't that what all holidays were, at their best? You carried them with you long after you'd shaken the beach sand from your shoes. He believed that a few well-spent days of leisure could provide a simple and beautiful thing: an appreciation of the present moment, something that could be too easily lost amidst life back home. Dozing on a cushioned lounger in a patch of sunlight, the wind rustling the eucalyptus above. An iced *limonata* to hand, or a perfect crescent of watermelon. The prospect of a fine meal. A crystal sea. A chestnut-lined trail to hike the length of. Soft almond biscuits, served on a sunshine-yellow plate, with a coffee that took your head off then set it back down more smartly than

76

before. These were things that could be found at any number of places up and down the Elban coast, but Valentino had made it his mission to show people the way to them. To offer them the *amaretti morbidi* when they were just-baked, to bring a second cushion to the lounger, to sketch out the map that led to the copse of strawberry trees and the view that made even the most world-weary of travellers stop, an involuntary smile spreading clean across their face. Some guests, some weeks, just needed more coaxing than others.

'The Alessi sisters are taking a painting lesson with Abi. That's good to see. And Steffi Berger is interested too, though she's never held a paintbrush in her life, she says.'

Abi's pictures were throughout the hotel, seascapes and beach scenes, as much inspired by her memories of Bakau and Cape Point as her home on Elba. Sometimes he'd catch a guest just staring into one, caught by its magic.

'On the subject of the Bergers, the little boys,' said Valentino, 'Jurgen and Nikki, they struggle to stay up late for dinner, don't they? They were asleep in their spaghetti one minute, then throwing green beans at each other the next. Overtired. Not a restful meal for them, or their parents.'

'Maybe they should teach them to be better behaved,' said Oliviero. 'I wouldn't have been allowed to get away with that.'

Valentino held up his finger. '*Certamente, no*. Or maybe we serve pasta and ice cream for them in their room? Donna could watch them, while Steffi and Max have a meal on their own.'

'Every night?'

'If they want.'

They offered the services of a babysitter, Abi's friend Donna driving over from Marciana Marina, but often families preferred to dine together at the Mille Luci. The Bergers, however, had struck Valentino as the kind of parents who did what they felt they should do, rather than what they really wanted. Doubtless they considered their holiday as a time for the family to be together, patching their frayed relationship with boy-shaped sticking plasters. He'd seen the dark scoops beneath Steffi's eyes, heard the rapid spit of her tongue, and seen the hangdog look on Max's face; one was tired of admonishing, the other tired of being admonished. There was something else there too, he was sure of it. It was as palpable as the scar that streaked Steffi's knee.

'And we should change their table for the evening. Let them have one in the window.'

'Move Nina and Lucille?'

'No, just nudge them along slightly. They won't notice. And if they do, we'll offer them more Prosecco. In fact, we'll bring them Prosecco anyway. Prosecco for everyone.'

'They don't look very happy to be on holiday together,' said Oliviero. 'They hardly talk to each other.'

'Nina's husband, Lucille's father, was supposed to be here too. They changed the booking at the last minute. He had to work, apparently.' Then, 'I don't think they've been married very long.'

He'd noticed the way Nina's fingers went to her ring, turning and twisting it. Tipping it, every so often, so as to admire the glint of diamond.

'It's the last thing I'd have wanted at that age,' said Oliviero, with feeling.

'I know that,' said Valentino, a hesitancy in his voice, 'but . . .'

'Or maybe it's just what they need, to be forced upon one another. To get to know each other without anyone mediating.'

78

Whenever Valentino's faith in what they were doing was shaken, Oliviero always found a way to restore it. Perhaps that was the job of the younger generation: to bring the hope. And when Oliviero wasn't around, he went to his visitors' books. He had a shelf full of them, where *grazie*, no matter the language it was written in, always meant something different. There were cards, and letters too, saying the things his guests felt they couldn't write in the book that lay on the reception counter, maybe because behind them there was a husband jangling his car keys, or a wife checking their passports, or their children standing on their tiptoes, craning to see what was going on.

I think this holiday saved our marriage.

Your hotel has made me believe in beauty again.

No one has ever been this kind to me before.

Instead of only thinking of what could have been, or what is – and despairing of the fact of both – this week I've been able to see what could perhaps still be, and whether that day arrives or not, I'll be forever grateful for the hope of it.

This last was from Isabel, the card she'd sent after her first stay. She'd only written once, but her return visits were, he thought, continued testimony to her appreciation of Mille Luci. He didn't keep this card of hers inside the drawer with all the others; instead, nine years ago, he'd slipped it inside a leather-bound notebook, and there it stayed. He rarely took it out, for he knew her words by heart. The thing was, he understood exactly what she meant. If he had considered himself capable of such articulation, he might have written those words down himself. For while his hotel would never bring him total happiness, it had, nonetheless, lent a colour and light to his days that he'd once imagined was gone forever.

'I'm a little worried about the young British woman,' he

said. 'Or British-Italian, I should say. Signorina Costa.'

'Kit,' said Oliviero.

'Yes, Kit. Isabel thought she might be here to review us, you know.'

'Then there's no way you can be worried.'

'I don't think she wants to be here. Not really.'

'She travels for a living; I suppose we're nothing she hasn't seen before.'

'I don't know if it's that . . .'

It was so small a thing, so insignificant that he might almost have missed it. As she'd stared out over the view of the grounds, he'd seen her take a quick breath, a tiny gasp from just-parted lips. It was, he'd thought, as if the sight was filling her right up, blowing her heart wide. For all her guarded looks later, in this she hadn't been able to help herself. It was disarming, seeing that in someone. You wanted to make it happen again, and again.

'I'm going to ask her out for a drink,' said Oliviero. 'She can't work all the time. And being on your own, that's not much fun in the evenings.'

Valentino's hand went to his head, smoothed his silvered hair. He didn't like the idea, but he couldn't say why.

'Maybe she enjoys being on her own,' he said. 'Besides, she's a guest. Even if you didn't know it when you picked her up on your motorbike.'

'*Basta* . . . I gave her a lift, that's all.'

Oliviero hadn't minded a little gentle jibing in the past, but this time he seemed to resent it. He looked boyish in that moment, his brow furrowed. Valentino could see the youth he'd been, someone who could be as introverted as he was garrulous, who'd dwelt in the easy spaces of girls and parties because there was simplicity to it, a closeness without intimacy. He wanted more for him, he always had, but who was he, really, to talk about happiness?

'Anyway, it's only ever been an unwritten rule, and . . . You wouldn't mind?'

Valentino shrugged. 'I think . . . she values her privacy, that's all.'

He was ignoring the fact, of course, that Oliviero was the kind of man that a lot of women would undoubtedly enjoy the attentions of.

'Maybe,' said Oliviero, 'we finally throw out the rulebook, written or unwritten. Isabel?'

'There is no Isabel,' Valentino said. 'Not like that.'

Oliviero leant over, laid a hand on his shoulder.

'You deserve to be happy, Papà,' he said.

'Deserve?' Valentino shook his head, not simply to disagree, but as if to rid himself of the notion entirely.

They'd talked like this before, and it never ended well. On between-season days, when mistrals tore at the junipers and sent waves leaping high above the rocks. As more wine came out, talk of God joined them at the table too, and Oliviero seemed to welcome it, with his staunch belief in right and wrong and the consequences of all actions. *Justice is divine*, he had said once, a long time ago now. *Whatever wrong turns we make on earth, and however we think we've righted them, we're always answerable before Him*. This was no piety, but a boy putting his faith in a higher power to settle the account of our lives. Valentino had chewed on his cigar and let him talk on, because he could see that he wanted to, that it made him feel better, and God (or whoever) knew, he didn't want to deny him that. When it came to Oliviero, he had a lot of making up to do. The boy had said to him once, *I know you've lost your faith*, but that was to suggest it hadn't happened wilfully, that it was simply temporarily mislaid and he might, eventually, find it again. He'd replied, simply, *I don't think I ever had it*, which wasn't exactly true, but when it came to God and justice and any of those things, Valentino didn't feel he had any other answer.

Oliviero gave a one-shouldered shrug, and stood up.

'Okay,' said Valentino. 'Ask her. Just remember she's a journalist. You don't want to end up in her story.'

thirteen

IN THE WHITE HEAT OF THE AFTERNOON, OLIVIERO KNELT IN his herb garden. He picked basil, smelling the musky sweetness on his fingers in a manner that bordered on superstition. He couldn't walk past rosemary without trailing his hand through its soft spikes either. Sometimes when a warm breeze was blowing he'd catch the scent of all the island's herbs, wild fennel, oregano, calamint: it was the best perfume he could imagine, the essence of Elba. A place where there was always something good cooking.

He crossed from the garden to his kitchen, a bunch of basil in his fist. He saw the Italian sisters coming towards him, and threw up a hand to wave. Francesca and Veronika greeted him in their own separate ways – one with a knowing smile and a pinch of his cheek, the other with a curt little nod. After spending the morning sightseeing at Marciana Alta, they told him, they were headed back to their rooms for a late *riposo*. They wore matching floppy hats and clumpy sandals and their walking sticks tip-tapped across the terrace in perfect time.

'So did you brave the Capanne?' he asked.

'Idiot boy,' muttered Francesca. 'What do you think we are, mountain goats?'

'We wanted to,' said Veronika, 'well, I wanted to, but the contraption that takes you up there, I don't know, I couldn't put my trust in such a thing.'

A chairlift ran up the mountain, the most basic kind, looking like a string of birdcages. Oliviero went up more often than most. He visited the top of Capanne at least once a summer, sometimes twice. It was dizzying, the view, but somehow clarifying too. Things were put into perspective at such a great height. Mundane worries could be left far below. Was it also that he felt closer to God, up amidst the clouds? As if His very face was close enough to touch. From the summit you could see the entirety of Elba, and all the way to the remotest islands of the archipelago, Pianosa, Capraia, Montecristo, and Gorgona, the prison island, where inmates harvested grapes for wine and tended cows and gathered hens' eggs. Valentino had suggested that they added the fine Gorgona wine to their list, but Oliviero hadn't seen the point, not when perfectly good vineyards on Elba could do with their custom, but some part of him still wondered how that wine tasted. What it would be like to drink a glass, knowing who'd made it.

'It's been running for more than fifty years,' he told the sisters. 'It's solid. It's safe.'

'Or,' said Francesca, 'on its last legs. And here I speak with some experience. I can die without seeing that view, I can tell you.'

Oliviero smiled at Veronika, who sighed, her narrow shoulders rising and dropping. 'I wonder if it wouldn't have been incredibly beautiful. Worth swallowing any fear for. I'll suppose I'll never know.'

He looked at her. She might faint on the way up, sent dizzy by the heat and the height and the sensation of the ground falling away beneath her feet. Or she might experience a sensation of perfect weightlessness, and infinite possibility. He knew what it meant to him – the ascent, the arrival – and perhaps it would mean something to her too.

'I was thinking of going up there myself this week,' he said. 'If you wanted to come with me . . .'

'Oh no, *caro*, you don't want that.'

'You're mad,' said Francesca. 'She'd drop dead on you halfway up.'

'What about tomorrow? Sunshine all day, clear skies. We'll see all the way to Corsica.'

'Oh,' said Veronika, her cheeks colouring, her head dipped. 'You don't want to go up there with an old woman like me. *No, no*.'

He'd never taken anyone to Capanne. It hadn't felt right. But this was different. 'Yes I do,' he said. 'And if you're scared, I'll hold your hand. But you won't be. You'll love it. It's a date. Okay?'

He saw her then, Kit, crossing the top terrace. And Veronika noticed too.

'Go on, go on, don't let us stop you,' she said, and when Oliviero looked at her he saw the twinkle in her eye, the mischievous smile at her lips.

'*Ciao*,' he said. '*Ciao, bella*.' He held out the basil to her, as if it was a bouquet. 'Go on, smell it. You don't have basil like this in your British supermarkets.'

'I grow it in a pot on my windowsill, actually,' she said, dipping her head to sniff. 'And it smells just as sweet.'

To his surprise she took a leaf, popped it in her mouth.

'But, okay, it doesn't taste quite like that,' she said.

She'd caught the sun on the tops of her shoulders, and where the strap of her top had shifted he could see a paler line of skin. Her cheeks, too, had colour, and she looked altogether more relaxed. He realised he was just smiling dumbly at her.

'Your work's going well?' he asked.

'Yeah, okay, thanks. I went to Marciana Marina today, actually.'

'But you're writing about the Lovers' Festival?'

'Change of scene. I worked from a café there, ended up staying for lunch.'

'Which one?'

He felt territorial, suddenly. Luca did a decent spaghetti con frutti di mare at his place, jumping with garlic and chilli and whatever the sea had yielded that morning, and the peach tarts at the café on the piazza were, he had to admit, a slice of sweet delight. His own pear tart, made with the lightest almond pastry, was inspired by the creations of old Signora Rinaldi, and he'd told her as much. He'd earned a cuff about the head for that, then a kiss on both cheeks after she'd tasted a slice.

'I can't remember the name,' she said. 'It was overlooking the sea. Then I went up into the old town, the fishermen's quarter. Just wandering about.'

'The Cotone,' said Oliviero.

Once, years ago now, Oliviero had spent a night sleeping on a bench in Marciana Marina, and nobody in the world had known he was there. He'd stayed on the beach until the dusk had rolled in, then followed the path into the Cotone, up narrow cobbled streets where the contents of people's homes spilt out into the alleyways: bicycles and buckets and spades

86

and washing lines flapping with beach towels and grannies' knickers. Flowers everywhere. Windows pushed open to the evening, with the sounds of television grumbling away in the background, or the spit of a sauce on a stovetop. He had wandered these pathways and let the burble of other people's homes comfort him. The elderly bench-dwellers had greeted him with *buonasera*; they had the same swollen ankles and well-worn clogs and crêpe-paper skin of old-timers everywhere, but had seemed to him to be possessed of a contentment that was particular to Elba. It wasn't the worst place in which to end your days. He'd wondered if they'd have greeted him so cordially if they'd known why he was there. He'd gone on to sleep rough that night, in a park a few steps back from the water. He'd laid himself down on a bench, listened to the fluttering of moths beneath the halo of a street light, while just along the coast an oblivious Valentino had turned out his thousand lights, and whispered *buona notte*.

'Do you like what you do?' asked Oliviero suddenly. 'You're happy, with your job?'

'I love it,' she said. Then, 'Not always. Not every place. But . . . it's an adventure.'

'So this,' he waved his arm, 'we're an adventure?'

She looked as if she was about to say something, then changed her mind. She nodded.

'I like that,' he said. 'Valentino thinks staying at the Mille Luci should be about discovery. Discovering what makes you happy, you know, what makes you relax, or feel excited. Or . . . inspiration. You know? I guess it's the same thing, discovery, adventure.'

He lost her eye contact then; she was looking down the terrace past him, shifting on her feet.

'And you, you like it here?' she said. 'You like your job?'

'I love it. It's everything.'

They were looking at one another now. He wanted to keep her there, was searching his mind for something more to say.

'Costa . . . So, I want to ask, you're Italian?'

'I was born in England.'

He tapped his heart. 'Here, though? *Italiano*.'

She smiled at that, and made to walk on, but he caught her arm. Just lightly, two fingers gently pressing, but he felt her flinch. He stepped back, as though he'd gone too far and was trying quickly to remedy it, but at the same time blurted out what he'd wanted to ask her since she'd arrived.

'Would you like to go for a drink later?'

She hesitated, seeming to appraise the intentions of his question.

When Valentino talked to him of love he had to look away, because he'd seen what it could do and he didn't like it. It was far simpler to live a life ungoverned by the heart. As far as he knew, he'd never hurt anybody in this way. He'd never made a promise that he didn't feel he could keep. Occasionally, though, he met someone who gave him pause, and made him reappraise things. Carlotta from two nights ago was one such woman; the assumptions she'd made about him were ill-founded but, at the same time, comprehensible, and he hadn't liked it at all. Kit, in a different way, was another.

'I have to work,' she said.

For someone else, it might have been because she didn't seem remotely interested, the challenge holding all appeal. But he'd never been needy in that way. The things he had to prove, they weren't to do with sex. They weren't to do with love, either, he told himself.

'Just after dinner, you know. We take my bike, go a little further this time, a little faster. There are good bars not so far from here, not exactly Roma or Milano or . . . I don't know what you like. New York? Tokyo? But nice, you know. Marciana Marina, where you were today, it's cool at night. Tranquil, but . . . a good place. And . . .' He was watching her face, and even though he'd never done it before, back-pedalled so fast; he saw that there was nothing else for it. '. . . and that's all great if you're on holiday, but you're here to work, so . . . you have to work. *Allora*.'

'But . . . thank you,' she said.

He waved his hand dismissively. 'Sorry, okay?'

'Sorry?'

'For asking. I would never usually ask a guest.'

She let out a laugh. 'I can't believe that.'

And, perversely, it gave him hope, that laugh of hers. A hope he still believed in even as he watched her walk away across the terrace and disappear around the corner. Even as he continued to stand in the space she'd so abruptly left, until he heard the approaching tap-tap of a stick, the shuffle of sensible shoes. It was Veronika, giving him a consolatory pat on the shoulder, and a look that said, *You can't win 'em all, my boy.*

fourteen

FOR HER FIRST RUN ON ITALIAN SOIL KIT CHOSE A DIRT TRACK
that wound through the chestnut forests up behind the hotel. It
was an inland climb, with the sea falling away behind her; if
anybody was out there swimming, before stoves were fired or
dough was kneaded, she wouldn't see them this way.

It was chilly in the woods, the just-rising sun yet to burn
through the canopies, and she moved quickly, her elbows
pumping, driving the sense back into her. She tried to think of
nothing but the movement of her body, the music coming from
her iPhone – rapid electro beats, a buried vocal – inviting no
particular reverie. But she wasn't let off that easily.

The day before, she'd made two mistakes, and the lingering
taste of them had woken her early.

The first was not her rebuttal of Oliviero, but the reason she
hadn't given him for it – and the realisation that had swept in
afterwards. When she'd left London to be with her mum, her
job had come with her, but the man she'd been dating for a
handful of months hadn't: an ellipsis at the end of their not-
quite relationship, for they'd each known it was over, without

it needing to be said. Since then she hadn't felt like having so much as a drink with anyone. What date wanted to hear about the Christmas stocking her mum had once sewn her, and how she'd turned her flat upside down looking for it, as though the disappearance of that childhood relic was like losing her mum all over again. Or the fact that every day a different memory fell into her head; like how Rosa had walked her to school on her first day and slipped a chocolate coin in her coat pocket for her to find later as she stood on her own in the playground; or the jugs of cloudy lemonade she'd make every summer, that always left their lips tingling and citrus-kissed. And how the remembrance of such things made her lose whatever thread of conversation she was tenuously hanging onto, how she didn't trust herself not to say *I'm sorry, this just feels . . . completely pointless . . .* and get up and walk out, without having the strength to adequately explain why.

But Oliviero? She'd refused his offer not because of the loss of her mum, but because of the fact of their shared father.

Her second mistake was agreeing to talk with Valentino.

He'd been at dinner the night before, moving between the tables, working his crowd with easy smiles and effortless small talk, jumping from one language to another.

'*Buonasera, bella signorina,*' he'd said to her.

'*Buonasera,*' she'd replied.

He'd poured her wine, stepped back as he waited for her to taste it, his face professionally expectant.

'*Grazie,*' she'd said, with a nod.

'Tonight for you we have . . .' and he'd reeled off the menu, as he did to every guest. But he'd seemed to take longer over it with her, adding embellishments.

'. . . and the pasta, which is named for "ears" in Italian, for the shape is like . . .' his hand went to the side of his face, tweaked his ear, 'something like this. And it's a very traditional pasta. Dense, you know? Needs a robust sauce. Delicious. It's my favourite.'

Had he always worked in hotels? Had he ever been in the heat of the kitchen, or was he a perpetual front man? Was that how her mum had met him, as he came to her table, poured a little wine in her glass, and made her feel special? Then left her twisting in the wind.

'You had a good day today?' he'd asked. 'The writing, it's going well?'

Kit had sensed the eyes of the woman at the next table on her. She'd been the only other person dining alone, and Kit had felt sure that she was British. It wasn't so much the fairness of her skin or the modesty of her linen dress that had given her away, but the powers of perception that so many foreign travellers seemed to possess: the ability to recognise their own, even from a distance, without a word being spoken. She'd looked immeasurably comfortable, this woman, as she'd spiked radicchio leaves with her fork, and lifted her wine glass with slender fingers. She'd smiled at Kit.

Kit had replied with something affirmative but uninformative. Valentino had nodded with enthusiasm, as though she'd treated him to some rare insight.

'Excuse my interrupting,' the woman had said, 'but Valentino is a rich source of information about the island. There honestly isn't anything he doesn't know. It's worth you taking advantage of him.'

Her voice had been soft and pleasant and full of warmth, but Kit had felt her mouth tighten. She'd wanted to say, *There's something he doesn't know*. She'd glanced at Valentino and seen how his chest had puffed a little.

'You're writing about Innamorata, yes? The Lovers' Festival? I can talk to you about the legend, if that helps.'

'It's a wonderful story,' the woman had said, 'and he tells it really very well.'

'I know the story,' Kit had said. 'But . . .' She'd hesitated, scratched her arm. 'I guess it'd be useful . . .'

They'd looked at one another, Kit and Valentino.

'If you want,' he'd said. 'Tomorrow afternoon?'

Kit ran on, trying to empty her head. She had to admit that the landscape seemed to be doing its best to distract her. It sent her a cloud of tiny peppermint-green butterflies. Her steps stuttered as a polecat, or a stoat, or some other long-bodied creature, cut across her path. A sudden break in the treeline, a slice of sea and sky so wide, so true, so blue, that she just had to stop and submit to it for a moment. And then a blackbird, a common garden blackbird, chirruping as though its life depended on it. She felt the accustomed burn at the back of her eyes, a tightening in her throat. 'Blackbird'. Her mum used to sing that song to her. *It's yours*, she'd always said, *it's your song*. She had told the same story over again, as though Kit had never heard it. How one night, when her daughter was a tiny baby, she'd been feeding her, propped up in bed, the cottage window open to the sky, and as Kit had sucked on and on, and night had turned to dawn, a blackbird had come and perched on the window ledge – a female one, tawny-feathered – and burst into song. They'd looked at one another, the blackbird and Rosa, as if they understood one another perfectly; what it was to mother, these gaping mouths and their hungry young. From then on Rosa had always sung 'Blackbird' to her daughter as she rocked her to sleep. And every time Kit heard the story, she'd always said the same thing back. *I thought it was because my hair was dark. Aren't I the blackbird?* No, Rosa would laugh, *the blackbird's the blackbird. But it's still your song.*

After the run, after a cool shower, it felt easier, somehow, to walk through the breakfast room, to help herself to a plateful of fruit, to order pancakes from a smiling Abi, to drink a second coffee. Valentino passed her table, his voice full of a smile as he said, *I'll see you this afternoon, an espresso on the terrace, perhaps?* Oliviero brought her pancakes to the table, dusted with icing sugar and bursting with berries, and gave a small bow as he set them down. *Buon appetito*, he said, just as if she was any other guest. She tripped back, *Grazie*, just as such a guest might.

Maybe, she thought, this was how to do it. Forget everything. Have an ordinary stay. Write an article. Go home, back to normal life. But the life she knew had ceased.

'You didn't swim this morning?' he asked, then. 'I was out early. The light was very beautiful.'

After he'd gone, she got up too. She left her pancakes untouched, and went to her room.

At three o'clock, Kit took a seat overlooking the garden. She held her notepad in her lap, pinched her pen between her fingers. Her sunglasses hid her eyes.

Valentino set down a small tray, two tiny wells of espresso, a small jug of frothed milk, a bowl of biscotti, every piece studded with almonds and dark chunks of chocolate.

'Oliviero makes the best biscotti,' he said, offering them to her. 'I can't resist them when they're warm.' He bit into one with a crunch that struck her as faintly obscene. He grinned, 'I can't resist them when they're cold, either.'

He didn't look like a man who gorged on biscuits – he had a hard, muscled look to him, a frame built for labour. If he'd been crumpled, or porky, he might have been somehow easier to accept; he looked as though he'd live forever.

'So how much do you know?' he said.

Kit felt a heat run through her body. She hoped, prayed, that it hadn't burst through her cheeks. She picked up her coffee cup, and set it down again without drinking.

'About Maria and Lorenzo? Some. Just . . . what I've read. Oh, wait . . .' She fumbled in her bag and took out a Dictaphone. 'Do you mind?'

He shook his head. 'Of course.'

She placed it between them, and pressed a button. Nodded. 'Okay.'

'Okay, so the story changes a little as different people tell it,' said Valentino. 'As all stories do, you know. But this is what is . . . understood. It's 1534, and Maria is the daughter of a merchant, from a very wealthy family. Lorenzo, he's got no money at all. So poor. They first meet on the beach – it's called Innamorata now, you know *innamorata*? It means "in love", named for them, of course, but before, it was called something else: Cala de lo ferro, Iron Cove. It becomes their place, a special place for Maria and Lorenzo to meet, to spend time with one another, and, eventually, to marry. In secret.'

He wasn't telling her anything she didn't know, but she found herself hanging on his every word. She searched for double meanings, with the paranoia that he knew exactly who she was and was doing a very good job of hiding it; just as he was hiding his own malevolence, the dark forces of his character, beneath a veil of bonhomie. She was struck, as she listened to him, watching the movement of his mouth as he said *love*, the way his hands followed his talk, punctuating it with precise, deft gestures, that when it came to Valentino, for the first time since her mum had died, she had been able to choose how to feel. Grief permitted no such liberty. She had decided to look his name up on the Internet. She had decided to come to Elba. She had decided, now, to sit across from him at this terrace table, hearing him tell a story that she already knew. And she could decide whether to look at him as her father, and hate him with all of her mum's passion – a passion Rosa had hidden from Kit, but that had been, after all, powerful enough for her to kill him dead. Or . . . she could let him glide on before her, simply the committed host of a charming hotel.

Next he spoke of pirates, their capturing of Lorenzo, Maria's desperate bid to save her beloved, the loss of him, and the loss of her, leading to a watery grave.

'Then, after a hundred years, a Spanish nobleman is . . . banished . . . is that the word? Sent away, forever. He comes here, to Isola d'Elba. He had great shame. His family want nothing to do with him. And he chooses Maria and Lorenzo's beach as his home, builds a house. One night, he sees a young woman on the rocks, looking for someone, calling out a name with . . . desperation. Later, when he talks of it to the villagers, they tell him it is the ghost of Maria. He is a . . . romantic man, I suppose, a spiritual man, or whatever, and he feels very strongly that this is the truth. So, the next night, he lights a thousand lights . . . how you say . . . torches? Like candles. All the way along the beach, to help Maria find Lorenzo – if she comes back again, that is to say. He lights them every night until his death many years later. It is this gesture that has become the symbol of the festival. Now every year at Innamorata there is a procession, people carry these lights, these torches, and they dress in traditional costumes. A young woman, she plays the part of Maria. There's a boat race to find the shawl she lost in her efforts. It's become . . . a fantastic spectacle . . . something the locals enjoy, dancing until dawn, on the beach with the lights. Tourists, too. Everybody comes to Italy looking for romance – that's what we do, isn't it, *passione*! And they find it at Innamorata.'

'Not everybody comes to Italy looking for love.'

'Not love. *Romanza*. People want seduction, and it's here in our landscape, our architecture, food, language. There's much beauty here. Even the small things. Take this *biscotti*, one small taste and you would see,' he lifted his eyes theatrically, 'true romance.'

'Romance,' said Kit, with a puff of disdain. 'It's all just show, though, isn't it?'

'Watch a sunset from our rocks and I don't think you will see anything wrong in a little bit of show. The sky on fire, the water too. Truly *bellissima*. And then you take a drink on the terrace, and you look down and see the same colour in your glass. Maybe it's small things, but . . .'

'And you called the hotel Mille Luci because of the myth of Maria and Lorenzo?'

'The legend, yes.'

'So you believe it?'

'It's a good story.'

'But you believe in . . . its message. Everlasting love.'

'I don't think that's the only message.'

'When people dress up in costumes, and dance all night, and

light their lights, that's what they're celebrating, though, right? The idea that love can last forever.'

'I think Italians like a good party,' he smiled.

'Right.'

'But . . .' he rubbed his chin with the flat of his hand, 'I think some people believe that, yes. Most people, probably. You need to tell yourself something, don't you? Perhaps love is the story that people tell themselves.'

'The way you keep saying "people" . . . so you're speaking for everyone, then?'

'No, not everyone. Not at all.'

'But you think you understand people,' said Kit. 'What they want.'

'I'm sixty-three years old,' he said quietly. 'I hope a little, by now.'

'And you include yourself in this . . . explanation.'

'Explanation?' There was a flicker at his jaw. 'For why people go to Innamorata to celebrate on a summer's night?' He picked up his coffee, drank it in one. 'I don't go to the festival.'

'How come?'

She asked it too sharply, and he looked momentarily taken aback. Then he reset himself.

'I don't like crowds so much. Oliviero goes. The guests often go. We organise transport, of course. So on Saturday, if you wanted to travel with us . . .'

Kit cut in, unable to stop herself. 'I guess I'm just trying to understand how people here really feel about this story. The festival. If it's all for fun, for show, or if . . . if it goes deeper than that.'

'Well, *francamente*, do the British believe in Romeo and Juliet?'

98

Kit had seen a production when she was at school, when a troupe of actors had performed it in the sports hall. She'd felt the spittle of Romeo rain down on her bare legs as he'd bemoaned his fate in a language that was supposed to be English. Kit hadn't cried once, and she'd laughed out loud when the girl sitting next to her had pointed out how tight Mercutio's breeches were, and how you could see just about everything if you looked hard enough. Then, three years ago, she'd gone to see the ballet rather than the play, and without a word being spoken she'd understood all that she'd missed when she was thirteen.

'And it must be a coincidence, of course,' said Valentino, 'that Shakespeare set it in Italy.' He smiled at her again.

'My mum,' said Kit, and felt her voice crack. She glanced down at the Dictaphone, steadying herself, swallowing the lump in her throat. 'She always said to me that the truest love was between a mother and her child. That the other kind, the supposedly romantic kind, was . . .'

The only person you can ever rely on is yourself. Love just isn't worth the pain, bella. Such sentiments might as well have been stitched letter by letter and hung above their fireplace. 'That's Amore', Dean Martin had sung. How many times had that song racketed about their old kitchen, bouncing off the Formica, as Rosa had taken it apart note by note, turning up the volume to abhor it all the more? *This is love*, she'd said, pulling her daughter close, *the only kind*, and Kit, maybe seven, maybe eight, had buried her face in her mum's apron, smelt the washing powder, and a lingering scent of fried onions.

'You said, "she always said" . . . excuse me, but, she's . . . no longer with you?'

Strangely, she hadn't thought of it, acknowledging the loss

99

of her mum to anyone. The mother of the journalist Kit Costa, that is, not the woman Valentino had once known. Her hand went to her sunglasses, her hair.

'I'm sorry,' he said, gently. 'Please. Continue.'

Kit stared at the Dictaphone. The cassette continued to turn, emitting a low whirring. She would replay the section later and have to fast-forward, the empty crackle too excruciating to hear. Her impatience, her snippiness hardly any better.

'What about people who've been hurt by love?' she said, in a softer voice. 'Who give it their all and still come away with nothing? What's left to believe in then?'

He rubbed his chin. 'We're never left with nothing,' he said eventually.

She leant forward, her finger hovering over the Stop button. It was a pointless conversation to begin with.

'I think,' said Valentino, not quite done, 'your mother's right. There should be different words for different kinds of love. Because *amore* on its own just . . .' he waved his hand, 'it's nothing. It can't do it. It can't hold all there is to hold. Somehow we think it should be a simple thing, this love, this *amore*. But it's not simple, it will never be simple . . .'

She hit Stop.

'. . . not as long as we live,' he finished.

Kit lifted her gaze to him, and for the first time in their conversation, she found him not looking back. His eyes had gone to the water, and it seemed to fill them.

If he had been any other person, she might have said, *I understand that, I think you're right – especially when it comes to family*. And it would have shocked her, to find herself thinking like that. To acknowledge that, amidst her love for her mum, there was also the hard, gleaming, undeniable fact of a lie, and that this changed things. Not enough to make her feel differently about her, but enough to make her think of how it could, if she permitted it. She reached across and picked up the Dictaphone. Valentino was looking at her again now, his eyes returned to normal, his face set in a smile.

'And how many people attend the festival each year?' she asked, turning over the page in her notebook.

fifteen

VALENTINO COULDN'T DECIDE WHETHER TO WEAR A TIE FOR dinner; sometimes he did, sometimes he didn't. He held one up to his collar and looked in the mirror. His shirt was white, and the tie was deep blue, and although they were only halfway through July, his skin had already reached the dark tan it had by summer's end. His hair had once been the colour of chestnuts, but now there was a lot more grey than anything else. *Not grey, silver*, Oliviero liked to say to him, pronouncing it with relish.

Had they ever really talked about love, he and Oliviero, in the way he had, however briefly, with Kit Costa? He knew the answer was no. The boy had never wanted to, but she, Kit, had taken just as fierce a pleasure in dismantling it as Oliviero might have; maybe they'd get on well after all, the two of them.

Costa. That was another unsatisfactory thing about the afternoon's conversation. He hadn't asked after her ancestry. Did she look completely Italian? Not necessarily. Her eyes were as blue as his, and they were hardly typical. His mother had always pinched his cheek, laughing that she had no idea where he'd got them from, for where were the blue eyes in the Colosimo line, or the Locatellis?

Unsatisfactory. Was that the right word? After all, what had he really hoped their conversation would achieve? That she'd lavish praise upon his hotel? Say that she was no longer writing about the festival, but about the proof of love that she found all around her at the Mille Luci? *Mah!* He took his tie and knotted it tightly. Stared himself down. So much for growing wiser the older he got.

He bent closer to the mirror, checking his nose. Hairs sprouted there now, and had for a long time, but he was quick with the clippers. Ears too, they had to be watched. He often wondered what it might have been like to age with a woman alongside him. Whether he would have noticed the changes in her body as sharply as he noted them in his own. He'd always kept active, but there was a softening to aspects of his frame these days – although, he thought, as he turned in the mirror, this was probably only obvious if you were to touch him, which meant that, apart from an excessively tactile Oliviero – always with the back-claps and the sudden embraces – this particular secret was safe. It was vanity, and he smiled at the foolishness of it. But vanity had never been his problem, therefore he allowed himself a little of it from time to time. If it meant taking a moment to pick the right tie to go with the right shirt, and feeling some sort of satisfaction that his gut didn't hang over his trousers like old Tomasso's in La Zanca, then vanity was all right by Valentino. He thought then of Isabel. The sun spots on the backs of her hands. The creases at her neck. The softness of her upper arms. He'd seen her every summer for ten years, and for him she hadn't changed at all, but he supposed if she was standing in front of a mirror now, she would find small ways in which she'd think perhaps she had.

Valentino felt quite certain that had he grown old with a woman alongside him, he'd have loved every change in her body. It was a map of life, wasn't it, your skin. He'd have traced every line with the tip of his finger, and known they'd walked each of them together. He'd have cupped handfuls of fat – if it were there to be cupped – kissing it, praising it; and if it wasn't – if she had grown to be stringy and bent in the style of Signora Marco – then he'd have adored that too.

But he had earned the right to no such reverie.

Kit had been disdainful of his talk of the complexities of love, doubting the words that were coming from his mouth, and well she might. She was young. She probably hadn't made any mistakes yet, nor felt the blow of anybody else's. She hadn't wanted a sermon, just a few details about the love story that people on this island liked to believe in. She'd been more cynical than he'd imagined, that much was certain, her manner punchier than he'd thought it could be. And then there had been the mention of her mother, the past tense. *Unsatisfactory*. He felt, again, that he hadn't conducted himself in quite the way that he'd wanted to. Perhaps he'd been too much hoping she'd tip her head to one side, appraise him with those true blue eyes, and say, *But why did you really call your hotel the Mille Luci?* And would she have turned that look of wonder on him then, the one he'd glimpsed so briefly the day she arrived? Hardly. She'd probably have thought it was the most pathetic thing she'd ever heard.

Isabel was down early for *aperitivo*, and their paths crossed in the dining room. She wore a navy dress and an enquiring smile.

'How did it go?'

'Oh, you know,' said Valentino, 'I talked a lot. All of it useless, probably.'

Inside, the stage was set for another Mille Luci dinner. Baskets of golden focaccia, salt crystals glinting, sprigs of rosemary like carefully placed bouquets. The salad table appeared like an exotic garden. Oliviero had scattered walnuts and sliced oranges and blanched green beans, mixed dressings of oil and vinegar, and there were mustard seeds glinting like pearls. Just a handful of times a summer they served a salad made from the petals of sunflowers, and it looked like a cloud of yellow butterflies had alighted on the plate. It was on the table that night, and he smiled to see it; how could you not?

'My mother,' said Isabel, following his gaze, 'used to make fairy cakes with marigold petals. But marigolds, of course, are ten a penny. Sunflowers! What have we done to deserve such beauty?'

'Don't we always serve it this week in July?'

'Oh, so you do,' she said, 'in honour of Maria and Lorenzo, perhaps.'

'Perhaps,' said Valentino.

Isabel's hand went to her necklace. An unconscious gesture, and one that was as much a part of her as her arch smile and low laugh. He could still remember the one and only time that she'd shown him the picture she carried inside her locket. He'd asked, carefully, tentatively, *What was he like?* and after giving him the most extraordinary look, she'd told him. Then she'd reached inside her blouse and drawn out her locket and showed him the picture. He'd carried on smoothing tablecloths and straightening chairs and eventually found a way to say, *Thank you, thank you for showing me.*

He offered her his arm, and she took it, and they walked out to the terrace.

The other guests drifted down, called by the lights and the sparkling drinks and the cumulative hum of conviviality. Max and Steffi together, their boys back in their room, where they were curled on the sofa, their spaghetti-stained faces resting in the crooks of their arms. Nina and Lucille, not quite talking, but not arguing either. The sisters, Veronika and Francesca, chuckling like hens.

'Oh my,' said Veronika, catching Valentino's hand, 'that boy of yours. He took us both, you know, all the way up to heaven itself.'

'You liked it, Monte Capanne?'

'Liked it? *Mamma mia*. We loved it. We loved it, you dear man.'

'So you went too, in the end, Signora Francesca?'

'I didn't trust her not to die on him, going all the way up there. I went to supervise.'

'He packed a picnic. Prosciutto. Oranges. *Schiaccia*,' said Veronika. '*Santo cielo*, the taste of that *Schiaccia*!'

Oliviero's version of the traditional Elban cake was loaded with dried fruits and nuts, generous daubs of island honey and lavish splashes of sweet Aleatico wine.

'So much alcohol in it, no wonder we were giddy,' said Francesca, waggling her finger at him.

'I will never forget that view,' said Veronika. 'I will never forget this day.'

The honorary grandson. That was another role that Oliviero slipped into with ease, when among a certain type of older guest. He was dedicated to doing good, that boy, and he always had been. Not something hereditary, then; more of a reaction to circumstance, perhaps. In that way they were similar, at least. There had never been a guest who hadn't loved Oliviero. In fact Valentino was certain that a few had loved him too much. But he'd always been staunch before, never so much as a drink with any of them, not outside of *aperitivo*. He couldn't have asked Kit out yet, for he hadn't mentioned it again. Perhaps he'd changed his mind. Thinking of Kit, Valentino looked for her on the terrace.

'I saw the writer getting in a taxi,' said Isabel, as if reading his mind.

'She left?'

'Well, surely only for the evening?'

'Of course,' said Valentino, hurriedly. 'That was what I meant.'

Later, in his office, as the guests lingered on the terrace beneath the garlands of lights, he poured two fingers of grappa and drank it back, savouring the burn. Fortuna, the no-good cat wound his way around his legs and gave a small growl of pleasure. Valentino bent down and tickled him behind the ear. Fortuna had pitched up on the lawn one day, years ago now, training his wide-set yellow eyes on Valentino as if it was he who was the imposter. *Well excuse me*, Valentino had muttered, and it had made him smile, talking to a cat like that, and so he'd let him stay. Oliviero had accepted his presence grudgingly – *You'll have to improve your manners if you want to live here with us*, Valentino had overheard him saying, *and mind you keep away from the guests*. It had been Oliviero who'd named him Fortuna.

Dinner had been the success it always was. The roasted

peaches served with scoops of mascarpone had been particularly fine that night, caramelised to perfection. And he was sorry that Kit hadn't been there for the sunflower salad. She'd ordered her taxi from the front desk, but when he'd spoken to Abi later, she hadn't been certain of her destination.

'Did she say she would be missing dinner?' he had asked, as if it had mattered.

'Yes,' said Abi. 'Yes, she did.'

Valentino wasn't sure that he could remember another guest who'd seemed able to take or leave them quite so easily. One and a half breakfasts, only one dinner in the dining room. It was unprecedented. He wasn't concerned that she would write an unfavourable review of the hotel. That wasn't what kept him awake that night, after he'd flicked the switches and extinguished his candles and sent his lights to sleep. It was the disquieting thought that he might be missing something. He, who prided himself on reading people, and giving them what they needed; small things of course, for what was a second cup of coffee, or a perfectly turned slice of tart in the grand scheme, but he had a stack of letters and a shelf full of visitors' books to reassure him that such things did, in fact, matter. He wanted his guests to be happy. And Kit Costa didn't seem happy. It was that simple. Wasn't it?

The next morning, as he passed through reception, he heard the telephone ringing and ringing. Through the window he saw Abi watering the hibiscus flowers. He picked it up.

'Hotel Mille Luci, *buongiorno*.'

The voice on the other end of the line hesitated, then said in a rush, creaking with the threat of tears, 'I didn't know who else to phone.'

'*Signorina* . . . it's Kit?'

'I thought . . . perhaps Abi . . .'

'What is wrong? Where are you?'

'I went out running and . . . I fell. I've hurt my ankle and I can't walk on it. I can't even stand on it. I . . . I'm sorry. I didn't know what to do.'

'Where are you?'

'I don't know. Somewhere in the woods. I took the path up behind the hotel, the one that's signposted, and then forked off to the right. Maybe three or four kilometres? I don't want you to have to . . .'

'It's nothing. I'm coming,' said Valentino. 'I'll find you. Twenty minutes, maximum. You'll be okay? Until then?'

'Okay,' said Kit.

He took Oliviero's motorbike, a powerful, jumpy scrambler that crashed through briars and brush with seeming relish. It had been years since he'd been on a bike, and he might have enjoyed the ride, the way he stood high on the pedals, feeling it twist and jerk beneath him, but all he could think was how important it was to get to her, to find her before those tears that had threatened on the phone spilt. Before she fainted, for even though it was early, the sun was already throwing its heat, eating through the forest's ceiling as if it were tinder. Before she doubted his ability to do as he'd said.

Oliviero had wanted to go instead, but he had eggs to crack and *cornetti* to watch and a fruit salad to finish composing. *You'll be able to get her back safely?* he had asked, and Valentino had made a dismissive noise as he'd turned the key in the bike and felt the engine roar beneath him. He'd ridden scooters in his youth, they all had. Bare-headed. Bare-chested, too. Sometimes he'd had a girl on the back, her hair unspooling, her dress fluttering. They'd spent whole summers tearing up and down the old neighbourhood, engines whining – all sound and fury, really – as they flicked their cigarette butts and affected nonchalance.

In the woods, he tried for a short cut and the bike bucked him, its front tyre hitting a rock. He didn't go down as hard as he could have, a dense rosemary bush softening his fall, but he struck his elbow, right where the pain was all too acute. He clutched it with his hand as he swore beneath his breath. Getting slowly back to his feet he felt like a knight whose mask had been knocked askew. An old man trying to pretend that he wasn't. He gunned the engine, and kept his eyes on his path.

He found her sitting on a log, her head bent to her knees. One leg was stuck out, stiff as a rod, her ankle puffed up like a balloon.

'*Bella signorina*,' he said, kicking the bike to a stop, wiping the sweat from his forehead. He ignored the trickle of blood that came from his elbow. '*Stai bene? Stai bene?*'

When she lifted her face to him, it was clear she'd been crying.

'You're here,' she said.

They took it slowly. He wanted to carry her, but she insisted on hopping. He tried to take as much of her weight as she'd give him. She winced, her face pale, and he saw, and felt, her relent a little then. He helped her onto the bike, explaining apologetically that she'd have to put her arms around his waist. He tried to make a joke, something about him being a little broader than Oliviero. Her fingers held the loose fabric of his shirt, but as soon as they got going, she tightened her grip. It was so unfamiliar a sensation, and he felt, then, how very precious this cargo was. He had to get her home. Before he'd helped her onto the bike, he'd placed Oliviero's helmet on her head, and he'd noticed how she looked down at the ground as he fastened the clip at her chin, and how young she'd seemed as she did so, no more than a child.

He rode carefully back through the woods with her, his own head bare. The bike's engine was loud, but he had the impression that he could hear the crunch of the path beneath the tyres, the whispering of leaves in the trees above, the in and out and in and out of her breath, as if every sensation was heightened. As the ground steepened, her hands tightened again around his waist and he felt a pain in his side that he hadn't noticed before. He must have caught himself in the fall, or pulled one of those old muscles of his at the jolt. He winced, but to anybody else it might have looked like a smile.

sixteen

OLIVIERO TURNED UP HIS MUSIC AND WIPED DOWN THE KITCHEN surfaces in deft figures of eight. The palm fronds splayed the shadows behind him. Earlier, Valentino had come in and said in a buoyant voice that the doctor had been and gone and it was nothing but a nasty sprain – rest and ice, ice and rest. It seemed to Oliviero that Kit's acceptance of Valentino's assistance had restored his purpose.

Outside, the temperature was climbing with the sun. The day was already piping, the sea bluer than blue. He felt bad for her, stuck in her room, but Valentino would suggest a lounger in the shade, on her terrace or beside the pool or on the lawn. Hell, he'd probably equip her with a bell to ring, so they could be easily summoned. *Limonata.* Fruit salad. A scoop or two of ice cream with a splash of chocolate sauce, as though she were a child who needed cheering. He thought of granita then, a whole bowl of it. Crystals glinting with lemon juice. The iced crunch as you took a spoonful, the explosion of tart sweetness. If he made it now, it'd be ready by mid-afternoon, when the sun beamed so heavily it looked as if it would fall from the sky. That was when he'd take it to her.

When he was a tiny boy, his nonna used to make him granita on the hottest days, and every effort of his own – there in his chef's overalls, with his gleaming kitchen, and a freezer the size of her front room – was a studied attempt to match what she'd done with ease in the cupboard-like kitchen of her high-rise apartment. He thought of the rayon dress stretched over her boxy bosom, her legs as thin as matches, a woman who looked as though she'd topple at any moment, and perhaps that was why her forehead was always so creased, living under the constant threat of gravity asserting itself. What a cook, though, what a cook. And her granita, no more than an assembly job, some might say, nothing to it, was the best of all. Oh, the searing headaches that accompanied that first bite! How he'd chew on through them, spoonful following spoonful, the ear-splitting cold of crunching ice, juice of peaches and pears and strawberries running down his chin. He'd sit on her balcony, the chair kicked back on its hind legs, his feet propped up on the railing, eyeing the smoking towers of the steel mill, the water swilling at the seaweed-strewn beach. Another scoop of Nonna's ice, and sweeter thoughts would come.

'*Salut.*'

Lucille's tone was nonchalant, as if she had a cigarette dangling from her lips, and was speaking out of the corner of her mouth. He stifled a smile.

'*Salut, Lucille. Comment ça va?*'

She stood with a hand on her hip, posturing in her swimsuit, her eyes hidden by enormous sunglasses. She smelt of freshly sprayed perfume. He rubbed his nose, wanted to sneeze.

'What is that you're taking?' she demanded in English.

'Room service.'

'For the British woman?'

He nodded, without wondering how she'd guessed.

'Can I have some?' She said it like a challenge, her voice hardened in case of rejection.

'Sure, I'll bring you some. Where are you sitting?'

She fluttered her fingers in the direction of the pool.

'Where's your . . . where's Nina?'

'*Pff.*' She made a small sound of dismissal. 'We don't go everywhere together, you know.'

She was probably sixteen or seventeen, but pushing for older, furious that time was holding her back from what she considered to be all the good things. She seemed a nice kid, with a nice life, and if Oliviero had been like her, he wouldn't have wanted to blow past these days.

'Nice to come on holiday,' he said, 'just you women.'

She liked that. She might not have agreed, but she liked his perception of the dynamic, her own status.

'*Oui, mais* . . . I was supposed to go to the Côte d'Azur with my friends.'

'The Côte d'Azur? I'd rather be here, I think.'

'*Non, mais* . . . Even with your mother? Your *step*mother?'

He gave her a smile. 'If she was as cool as yours . . . definitely.'

She rubbed her nose. She looked younger, suddenly.

'I'll bring you both some granita. Give me twenty minutes, okay?'

'How old is she, the *anglaise*?'

He shrugged. 'Very old. Like me.'

* * *

'Hello?' he said as he knocked. Tentatively at first, then with more force. He heard the scrape of a chair. 'Kit? It's Oliviero from the kitchen. I have something cool for you.'

A pause. Then she said, 'Come in.'

She was on her terrace, arranged on one of the loungers from the pool. Her leg was propped on a yellow cushion, an ice pack across her ankle.

'I have a new pack for your foot,' he said. 'And . . . some ice for *you*. You know granita?'

She shook her head. Her sunglasses were pushed up on her head, and she was still in her running gear; a vest, short shorts. He took in the physical toughness of her, the jut of her collarbone, the ledge of her calf. She didn't look like someone who often had to ask for help.

'What's granita?' she said.

'The best thing. How's your foot?'

'The swelling's gone down,' she said. 'Thanks.' Then, 'It's . . . embarrassing, more than anything. Phoning up like that.'

'He's been wanting an excuse to take my bike out,' said Oliviero, waving his hand. 'And luckily you're an experienced passenger.' He wanted to add that he wished it had been him who'd picked up the telephone, and been the one to find her. But instead he said, 'Hey, you want me to change it, the pack?'

Kit leant forward, stretched. She dropped back. 'Do you mind?'

Her foot was pale, and shaped like a cartoon foot, slender, high-arched, the kind a prince might slip a missing shoe onto and find it fitted perfectly. Her nail varnish was the colour of tangerines and chipped at the edges. A bruise bloomed at her ankle.

'Doctor's verdict?' he said, as he reset the ice pack carefully.

'Up and about tomorrow, maybe even tonight. Just taking it slow.'

'Good news.' He passed her the bowl. 'Now, for you, granita *al limone*.'

She hesitated. 'I don't know if . . .'

'Please. Just taste it.'

She took a small spoonful. Then another. Closed her eyes.

'You like it?'

'Thank you.'

'When it's hot, you need granita.'

'Is it really just . . . ice? With lemons?'

'Sure. Too good for feet, though. There's some sugar in there too.'

She looked down at her hands, pushed her nails together.

'Everyone's being . . . really kind.'

'We look after our guests. It's what makes us happy. They're family, you know?'

She set down her spoon, the bowl balanced in her lap. He followed her eyes, to the run of sea and sky.

'So your work, you can take a day off?' he said.

Maybe she thought he was angling to invite her out again, because she ignored the question, and asked instead, 'How long have you had the hotel?'

'We opened in '88,' said Oliviero.

'And you grew up here?'

'On Elba? No. But Toscana, yes.'

'So you didn't always live here, at the hotel?'

'No. Not always.'

She looked as though she was calculating something, her brow furrowed. He considered taking a seat on the corner of the chair beside her, but he didn't, in case the movement changed anything. She hadn't asked him any personal questions before.

'How old are you?' she said.

'Thirty.'

She nodded, as if he'd confirmed something she already knew.

'Me too,' she said. Then, 'But this place, someone else was running it before Valentino took it over?'

'It was a private house, an old villa, but it was falling apart. He changed everything. He did it himself, mostly. Brick by brick. How do you say . . . a labour of love.'

She stared at him. It felt to Oliviero like Kit could put more in a look than any woman he'd met, but it didn't mean he was able to read what it meant. She must have shifted, for the pack had all but slid from her foot. He reached to adjust it, and she watched him. He saw her start as he set it back across her ankle, as carefully as he could. He took a risk then, planting himself on the chair beside her. Nothing to give the impression that he was settling in, just . . . taking a seat. In her lap the bowl of granita was starting to melt, just glistening. He wished she'd take another mouthful.

He saw then that her eyes burnt in the way that his had once. Perhaps this was what kept drawing him to her: the fact that Kit felt somehow familiar to him. There was something in her, and she wasn't giving it up, and he respected that, the strength it took. But he'd also learnt that, perhaps, it took an even greater strength to let it go. To unclench just that bit, to meet another's eye and say, *What it is, is* . . . His thoughts began to turn down a particular track, the road less travelled. That was one of the poems in Valentino's books that he pored

117

over on winter nights, one that he'd given to Oliviero to help with his English. It was okay, the poem, but Neil Young did it better.

Kit shifted position, sat a little straighter. The ice pack held. She leant her head back against the rest, and closed her eyes briefly. He saw a tear slip from beneath her lashes. She said, 'I lost my mother not very long ago. She had cancer. I don't know what that is in Italian.'

'*Cancro*.' Then, 'It's the same.'

'I'm not normally this . . . pathetic.'

'Not pathetic, not at all.' He lowered his eyes, then glanced back up at her. 'I lost mine too. I'm sorry.'

A mother for a mother. He didn't tell her he'd lost a brother, too, years before. Danilo, with his massive pupils and sweating palms and a drug-induced sense of anything being possible, anything at all, until he'd stepped into the sky from five floors up.

She looked at him intently. 'I'm sorry,' she said eventually.

'No, it was a long time ago.' Tentatively, 'But you? It was . . . more recent?'

'May.'

'This May? Shit. I'm sorry.'

They sat for a moment, in the new quiet.

'Your father . . .' he began, but she just shook her head. He knew that look. He understood it.

'Have some more granita,' he said instead, 'before it melts.'

seventeen

KIT'S PAIN WAS SUBSIDING. THE DOCTOR HAD BEEN A DELICATE woman, with strong hands and thick glasses and no English whatsoever. Valentino had translated. Valentino had done everything that day, it seemed, and she'd had to let him. He couldn't have known how it felt, the submission, and she hoped she'd betrayed no sense of it. If pain showed in her face then her ankle was a convenient scapegoat. After she'd hung up the phone, she'd briefly, and violently, sobbed. By the time he'd burst into the clearing, looking half-beaten up himself, she'd composed herself, so it had seemed unfair when again her eyes had burnt, her throat clenching at the sight of him. But somehow she'd managed to hold herself together, until they'd descended by motorbike, and, having no choice but to hold on to him, her tears had spilt again. How grateful she'd been for the engine and the birds, the spitting of gravel and the cracking of sticks. The helmet she wore too, with its visor pushed all the way down.

At the Mille Luci, Valentino had carried a lounger to her terrace, and returned to her, his arms full of cushions. He'd given her a couple of glossy Italian magazines, belonging to a guest who'd departed that morning.

I'm so sorry, he'd said, *for your pain. If there is anything I can do, you will say, yes? Nothing is a problem.*

Then he'd left her and she'd stretched out, her aching foot hoisted high, the sun blasting, all the colours of the garden popping, and she'd pushed her sunglasses up onto her head because she didn't want to dampen a thing. Then she'd hit a wall, felt the full slam of it. Whatever motivation had brought her here, by plane and train and boat and bus, it was changing, but into what, she didn't know. She wasn't certain she even knew its original shape. Although wasn't that how it had always been? For as long as she could remember, ambivalence and contradiction had permeated everything. She'd always disliked her father, although she hadn't known him. He might have been dead, but his patent absence had given him eternal life. He had never deserved her mum, but her mum had given something of herself to him, regardless. Kit was a mistake: the worst thing to happen to an affair. And yet here she was, and she wasn't a total disaster, was she? Lines crossing lines, everything and nothing making sense.

She wondered briefly if the painkillers the doctor had administered were something else, because as she lay looking out over the gardens, she'd felt a strange sort of peace descend. A feeling that perhaps it was all right to exist in a suspended state like this, somewhere between a lie and the truth. Then Oliviero had brought the granita, and she'd learnt that Valentino had suffered tragedy too.

He was sitting forward, his elbows resting on his knees, his hands steepled at his chin. She noticed for the first time the nicks and scars across his fingers. Chef's hands. They were into a new space, it felt now; while she hadn't planned to say a thing about her mum, not one word, in the end it had felt okay. As if it was one less deception. Something, somehow, had lifted.

'This place is nicer than you thought, isn't it?'

'Why do you say that?' said Kit.

Oliviero opened his hands in a gesture of unknowing. 'A guess.'

She shifted on the lounger. It was hard to assert oneself when prone.

'My professional opinion,' she said, 'would be that you don't charge enough. You could charge a lot more.'

'We want anybody to be able to come.'

Of the other guests she'd seen, it was only the French woman and her daughter who had the obvious sheen of wealth about them.

'But people will just think there's a catch. They'll look at your website and reckon that the hotel can't possibly be as good as it looks, because it doesn't cost enough to stay here.'

She was talking nonsense, and she knew it. What traveller didn't love to unearth a hidden gem, for their expectations to be surpassed? Oliviero looked bemused, and if he was laying it on, playing the charming innocent, it was deftly done.

'But it *is* as good,' he said, 'isn't it?'

There were five-star hotels that couldn't match the food. Exclusive resorts where the views were no better. And the Mille Luci had another quality, one you couldn't design or install or ever really teach. It could only ever come from the people who worked there.

'My professional opinion,' she said again, 'is that it's kind of misleading.'

'I just work out what the food costs, and . . . Valentino does the rest. He makes the prices.'

'What, out of the goodness of his heart?'

It came out more combative than she'd intended, but Oliviero didn't take it that way. He nodded with enthusiasm.

'It's true,' he said, 'he has a heart of gold.' Then, running his hand across his head, 'Do you like Neil Young?'

It seemed to Kit an abrupt change of subject, but she went with it. 'I don't really know Neil Young.'

'How is that possible?' he laughed.

She saw how his eyes changed shape then. He looked different, not like anyone. She could feel herself smiling back, and it seemed more effort to stop it, although later she knew she'd berate herself for it, oscillate between sweating and denying the meaning he might take.

'It's possible,' she said, wanting to add that of the many things she didn't know, Neil Young was the least of it.

'There's a guy who plays his songs. He's only about twenty, this skinny kid from Milano. Calls himself Neil Younger, which is kind of funny, I guess. He's playing in the square at Marciana Marina on Thursday night. He's pretty good. Was here last summer too.'

She took a spoonful of his granita. It had lost its icy bite, but it was so sweet, so cool. She held it on her tongue, swallowed. She knew where this was going. How could she stop it? Plenty of ways. She could ask what had happened to his mother, for she'd taken Valentino for divorced, not widowed, with no more to go on than her own prejudices, the scant but certain knowledge of his roving eye. She could ask why he considered his father's heart to be quite so golden, when it couldn't be, not at all, because Kit's mum didn't get things wrong; she'd always done what was best. Sometimes, just sometimes, the young Kit had worried that because she didn't know who her father had been, it made her one half less substantial. As though one side of her body was liable to disintegrate at any moment: her left foot, her left arm turn to dust. But then all she had to do was look at her mum, and know that one person could be everything. She rubbed her face with both hands.

'If your foot's better, do you want to go?'

She felt a pull inside.

'"Old Man". "Only Love Can Break Your Heart". "Harvest Moon".'

It took her a moment to realise that these were the names of songs.

'I can't,' she said, and right up until the words left her mouth she didn't know whether she'd say yes, or no, or something else altogether.

Valentino had left her a walking stick. *Just in case*, he'd said. It was made of honey-coloured wood, and was smooth to touch. She wondered whom it had belonged to. She tried her weight on it, feeling foolish, but it made all the difference, and she tapped her way across the room. She was wondering whether to attempt to make it down for dinner when a knock came.

'*Buonasera, signorina*,' said Abi. 'How are you?'

Kit said that she was okay, she was fine, doing much better.

'Would you like dinner in your room again this evening?'

'Actually, that would be great. Thank you.'

The door closed and she sat down on the edge of the bed, resting her hand on the stick. She felt a small hole of disappointment open up inside of her, though quite who or what it was for, she wasn't sure. When the knock came again, it was Abi with the tray. She set it down, Kit thanking her.

I guess this is easier, she said to herself, as she lifted the domed lid to reveal wafer-thin breaded veal, topped with a wedge of lemon, tomato spaghetti, a salad of cured ham and daubs of mozzarella and golden crescents of nectarine. A nut-encrusted chocolate tart. There was a note, telling her the names of the dishes. Then it said, *If you wish for a digestivo, ring down to reception. On us, of course.* It was signed *Valentino*, the sweep of the V looking like a sail full of wind.

Her mum used to make escalope Milanese. They hadn't had the money for veal in the Deer Leap days, but when her dresses were selling, Rosa spent her earnings on the best kind of food. *What else is there?* she'd say to Kit, as she hammered their steaks, the contents of the kitchen rattling around her. A neighbour had come over once, poked her face around the door, saying, *We heard the most terrible noise, is everything all right?* and Rosa had pointed down at her tomato-sauce-spattered apron and said, *The game is up*, laughing shrilly. *The crazy Italian, she'll probably call me now*, said with something approaching glee. But this was not typical behaviour. It was a memory that stood out, for usually Rosa took pride in her self-containment, her ability to live a life that didn't rely on others, the caprices of their opinions or affections or loyalties. When Kit left for London, she worried her mum would be lonely. Rosa had a friend or two, women she went for occasional coffees or glasses of wine with, but not the kind she'd call on the telephone on a Sunday night, when there was nothing much to say except this and that, the kind of minutiae true friends granted each other with grace. Was there anybody who'd ever known the truth? Who'd seen the swell of her stomach, the shattered pieces of her heart, and heard the words *He's dead to me, so he might as well be dead to my daughter too.*

Kit cut into the veal, twisted spaghetti on her fork.

Maria and Lorenzo's lights were shining, all one thousand of them. Kit paused on the terrace, leaning on her cane. The sound of the sea was just discernible, and a breeze rustled the palms. She caught the faintest scent of something. Menthol cigarettes.

'Good evening,' she heard.

Isabel was sitting by herself. She held her cigarette as though she was an unaccustomed smoker, a little aloft, as if she wasn't entirely sure it wouldn't burst into flames at any moment.

'I heard about your fall. What rotten luck. Are you all right, my dear?'

'It's already much better,' said Kit. 'I feel a bit stupid, really. I called here in such a flap.'

'I would say they were very happy to help. Is it stopping your work?'

'Not really,' said Kit. 'Not at all.'

'So long as you can still get to the festival at the weekend.'

'Quite,' said Kit, although it was a word she rarely used in that manner. *Quite.* As if she was exaggerating her Englishness for Isabel's benefit. It was her fourth day on the island, nothing, really, compared to all her past travels, but the sound of Isabel's voice was, that night, a comfort. She didn't want it to stop. Isabel gestured to the chair beside her, and Kit lowered herself into it.

'Where do you live, in England?' she asked, stretching out her leg.

'Just outside Oxford,' said Isabel. 'Where are you?'

Between places. Between everything.

'London for a while, but Bristol now. I was at university there.'

'Oh, so was I,' said Isabel. 'I do like Bristol, ever such a lot.'

Kit was ready to exchange the usual noises whenever Bristol was mentioned, agree on the fact that it was neither too big nor too small, how it was laid-back but dynamic, all of those things, but instead Isabel spoke again.

'I've often thought about moving back there myself. I teach English to foreign students, that's a transferable enough occupation, I know, I've just always felt rather stuck in Oxford. Unless . . . there's Italy, of course. Perhaps one day, Italy.'

'You'd live here?'

'Oh, I already do, in a manner of speaking. In mind, if not in body. One week every summer I'm here, but it lasts me a long time, the anticipation before, the memory of it afterwards. I have one of Abi's paintings on the wall in my kitchen, and it helps on the grey days.' She lifted her cigarette to her lips, took the smallest puff. 'I suspect I'm on Elba much of the time, in one way or another. Would you like to join me?'

She proffered a bottle of wine, and Kit saw the spare glass. She wondered whom she'd been waiting for. Somewhere inside the hotel there was Valentino, and Kit had intended to take him up on the offer of a *digestivo*. A hard, cool glass of grappa, perhaps, and she could have thanked him then, with a drink like that in her hand, because she'd realised that she hadn't actually said those words to him, and for today, they were due. A brief thank you, then a drink on her own, that had been her plan. But Isabel was one of those people in whose company she felt immediately and inexplicably comfortable. She had a pervading softness about her. Not weakness: tenderness. Despite her slight frame, hers was an enveloping, cushioning presence.

How unlike Rosa she was in that regard. Strangers had been drawn to her mum for plenty of reasons – the women who came for dress fittings glowed from her charm, and left wearing a new self-possession, a confidence that Rosa seemed to have stitched into her creations for them alone to find – but few, if any, broke through the surface acquaintance. Her mum had always seemed as if she didn't need anyone, not really, and close up, people found that discouraging. Except Kit. Her need of Kit had never been in doubt. Sometimes Kit had wished she could have removed the urgency from Rosa's love, but now? Now she'd do anything for a purposeless phone call at seven o'clock in the morning. To stand in line at the perpetually crowded post office to reclaim yet another missed parcel – a swatch of fabric or a batch of almond biscuits or a cutting from a magazine about a place that Kit had already been to, already written about. To hear another impassioned speech about never letting anybody hurt her, about being accountable only to herself.

'Are you sure?' said Kit. 'I'm not disturbing you?'

'Not in the least.'

Kit swirled the wine in her glass, took a sip. 'Wow, that's nice.'

'Isn't it? Made here, of course. *In vino veritas*. This is one truth I'm very happy to hear.'

'So do you always stay here? At the Mille Luci?'

'I do. I couldn't go anywhere else. How did you find it? There aren't too many British here.'

'I was reading up on the Innamorata legend. For my article. The name came up in a search.'

'On the Internet? I suppose that's how people find everything these days,' said Isabel. She stubbed the last of her cigarette in the ashtray, fastidiously, as if the threat of fire was still not quite over. Kit suddenly had the urge to smoke herself. She took another sip of wine.

'How did *you* find it?' she asked.

'Oh, quite by chance.'

Kit waited for her to say more. Isabel topped up their glasses, although they didn't really need it.

'It was all rather spontaneous. I got off the ferry, then I got on a bus, then I walked for a bit and . . . I smelt the most wonderful smell. I realised how enormously hungry I was. For the first time in weeks, months, years really.' She glanced at Kit, gave a small smile. 'I was terribly sad when I first came here. And, quite against all odds, I had what can only be described as . . . a lovely time. So I came back. And back again. And again. It's an extraordinarily beautiful part of the world, the island of Elba, and this corner of it, this hotel, is . . . the best of it.'

Kit stared hard at her glass. She could feel Isabel looking at her, and didn't trust herself not to say, or do, something stupid. Isabel's voice was so soft and measured, weighted with sincerity.

'It's become something of a ritual, I suppose. I've come back every year, the same week, for a decade now, and counting.'

'For the festival?'

'Oh no, the festival is insignificant, really. It's a lot of pageantry, very pretty, but I don't come for that. I come . . . I come because . . . I believe in the magic of the place, I suppose. I felt good here once, when I never expected to feel good again. Sorry, I'm rambling . . .'

'No, please, go on.'

Isabel looked at her, gratefully almost, as though she thought she was being indulged. But Kit hung on her words.

'Only that . . . perhaps we're all creatures of habit in some respects. We fill our days with small, repeated patterns. Our years, too, tend to roll on in much the same way. Then something happens that changes everything. And suddenly all those ordinary things that we took so much for granted from one day to the next appear exceptionally luxurious, and no longer for us at all. A cup of tea while sitting on a step in the garden in the sunshine, entirely unencumbered, thinking of nothing but what to make for supper? What a rare kind of bliss that is. I struggle to find it at home, even now I struggle, but I find it here, after a fashion. Only Oliviero is in the kitchen, which is a great improvement, and instead of tea we have the very best coffee.'

'And Valentino . . .' edged Kit.

'Ah,' she said. 'Yes. Valentino. I'm inordinately grateful for Valentino.'

'Why?' The question popped out too quickly, startling, like a cork from a bottle, in inexpert hands. 'Sorry, it's just . . . I mean, why?'

'What is your article about?' asked Isabel, as if she needed the answer before she could give her own. 'The hotel?'

'No,' said Kit, 'no, it's not.'

'You're not a reviewer, then?'

'Not on this occasion.' She hesitated. 'I'm here to write about Innamorata,' she said, but after Isabel's sincerity, it felt like a line. She mustered a grin. 'Everlasting love in La Bella Italia. You know the sort of thing.'

'He's kind,' Isabel said. 'That's what it is. He's very, very kind.'

'Right.'

'Which makes him an excellent hotelier. Incredible, really, I can't imagine there are many like him. He's kind to everybody.

But, I suppose in the way that true kindness works, it always feels as if it's especially for you. It's as though,' she said, 'somebody's seen all the way inside of you, and given you the very thing you wanted, before you'd even, perhaps, realised it yourself.'

Kit cradled her glass. I've got this wrong, she thought. There must be another Valentino Colosimo somewhere else, the real one, the bad one. The one that someone might make dead because they couldn't bear the thought of them being alive. She looked across the table at Isabel, and saw the emotion in her face, her shining eyes. She was, Kit thought, quite beautiful.

'How was he kind to you?' she asked.

'Oh, innumerable ways,' said Isabel. She shook her head, just perceptibly. 'But there was one. One I will never forget.' She hesitated. 'I don't usually run on like this. It's the wine, I suppose.' Her hand went to her neck, and she twisted the fine chain that hung there, the locket at its end. 'I had a child, you see. A son. Philip. And he died. He was eight months old, just eight months, and it was . . . They used to call it cot death, but there's another name now. Anyway, he was terrifically small, but he was . . . a person. He was already very much his own person. He had been from the day he was born, his character stamped clean upon him. But not everybody sees that, you know. You lose a child, a baby, and people think that what you've lost is hope, the promise of somebody, and of course that's true, that's always true, but . . . he was somebody already. And Valentino, when I eventually told him why I was here, not all of it, but some . . . he took my hand, and he asked me what he was like, my Philip. It was four years since we'd lost him, and for all the sympathy, all the condolences, nobody had ever asked me that question.' Isabel's finger went to the corner of her eye, and she pressed just lightly, the most delicate gesture. 'I dare say he's many things to many people. But to me . . .' She sighed. Dropped her hand in her lap. 'To me, he'll always be the man who wanted to know my son, even a little. To see him as I did, just for a moment. And I'm extraordinarily grateful to him for that.'

eighteen

VALENTINO TOOK HIS FIRST COFFEE OF THE MORNING, A *macchiato*, always from the same white cup, standing by the window in his kitchen. There was no accompanying cigarette these days, but the view was constant: the terracotta terrace, the band of sea, the white walls of the still-sleeping hotel. His villa was just behind the main building, a two-room cottage built into the side of the hill, a stone's throw from Oliviero's. Both places had been dilapidated once, windows laced with spiders' webs, bathroom taps that coughed out brown water. He'd spent three weeks gutting them, in the crackle and mist of an island autumn, welcoming the pain in his back and the splinters in his palms. Occasionally a curious local had passed by, and he'd wiped his hand on the leg of his trousers, then extended it. *Be interesting to see what you do with the place*, they'd said, and *There's good trade to be had, if you work for it*. And *What brought you here?* Back then it had seemed remarkable to Valentino that he could recount such details as the restaurant on the mainland, the need for something different, the appeal of an island existence where, outside of the busiest summer months, you could fancy yourself in some kind of exile. So did he fish? Hunt? Sail? Hike? He'd said he simply liked the views.

Perhaps, then, it was no surprise when they later saw him string his thousand lights, making his spot on the clifftop as beautiful by night as it was by day. He was an aesthete, they'd observed then. The island women had pushed back their shoulders and swept lipstick across their lips, waiting in vain for his admiring glances. Perhaps he liked men, one rumour had gone, but that one hadn't lasted. He'd never attended church, though Paolo Botta had apparently said he'd seen him emerging once from a chapel in Marciana Alta, amidst a trail of sunhatted tourists, as unlikely a figure as a rabbit among a shoal of fish. The island had embraced him, for all that its people didn't know, and he'd embraced the island. When Oliviero had eventually joined him, and gone about his work with quiet grace, Valentino had felt that things were about as complete as perhaps they ever could be.

His coffee finished, he rinsed his cup in the sink and went to get dressed. His existence was pleasingly rhythmic, made of predictable patterns. Guests came, guests went, everything and nothing changed. His heart, too, was constant; deserving no repair, he'd simply marked it derelict and shut it down. Very occasionally, though, he felt something deep in his chest, and it was less like an old wound reminding him of its existence, and more the startling sensation of contrast – as when a light is flicked on in a dark room, and one blinks, and squints, as though such a thing has never before happened. Isabel could make him feel like this, and yesterday Kit Costa had done it too: a different feeling, but a feeling nonetheless. In the evening he'd seen the two of them sitting together on the terrace: in the half-light they could have been mother and daughter. He'd wanted to go over and join them, but he felt that whatever bond was being formed, it was too delicate to test by adding his presence.

He bent to put on his shoes, and winced. He must have done something to his side when he fell yesterday. Aches and pains, pains and aches, but wasn't everyone walking wounded? As he stepped outside, the sea hit him as it always did. At that hour it was a precious metal, the sun streaking across its burnished surface, and he felt all the promise of a day's heat on the rise, as though someone somewhere had their hand on a dial and was turning it by degrees. He was in the hotel by six thirty in the morning, a commute that usually took him somewhere between fifty seconds and a minute. As he tapped in the code at the door to the reception, and let himself in, the sweet scent of Abi's hibiscus filled his nostrils. And there was coffee, too – coming from the kitchen, Oliviero probably blasting away the vestiges of a late night with shots of espresso. He was set to follow his nose and join him in a cup when he saw an envelope addressed to him lying on the reception desk. It hadn't been there as he'd turned off the lights the night before. He picked it up. His name was written in full, Valentino Colosimo, but the marks of the pen were light, the letters somewhat uncertain. He opened it, and read: *Thank you for your help today. I realised I hadn't actually said that to you at the time, although I wanted to. There's something else I wanted to talk to you about too. Perhaps we could find the time, during my stay? Let me know when you're able. With best wishes, Kit.*

He folded the note and put it in his pocket.

* * *

'I asked her out.'

Valentino split a roll, warm from the oven still, and spread it thick with butter and jam. Beside him Oliviero sliced a pineapple, quartered oranges, his eyes on the fruit, his knife, the counter top.

'Who now?'

'Kit. Costa.'

'Did you,' he said, without it being a question. Then, 'When are you going?'

Oliviero set his knife down, turned. 'I thought she'd like this concert in Marciana Marina. Neil Younger again. He's not bad, you know, that guy . . .'

'She needs to be careful,' said Valentino, his voice stiff. 'When an ankle's weak it can easily sprain again.'

'We're not going.'

'What?'

'I asked. She said she couldn't.'

Valentino raised his eyebrows.

'Are you mad at me for asking?' said Oliviero.

'Why would I be mad at you?'

Oliviero shrugged. 'I don't know, her being a guest . . .'

'If she wants to go for a drink with you, she should go for a drink with you,' said Valentino. 'And if she doesn't . . .'

'You don't need to say it,' said Oliviero. Then, 'She's had a bad time recently. I thought she might have liked the change of scene.'

Valentino saw him hesitate. He was no gossip, Oliviero. If people told him something, he held onto it in the manner befitting the spirit in which it had been given. 'She told me she'd lost her mum,' he said, delicately, 'less than three months ago. So I guess she's here on her own, trying to work, hurt her foot – it's not the best time, is it? If I could have given her a nice evening . . . you know?'

Valentino dipped his head. 'Only three months . . . Did she say what happened, to her mother?'

'She didn't really want to talk about it.'

'No.' They glanced at each other, the unspoken passing between them, as it always did. Valentino drained his coffee cup. He thought of mentioning the note she'd left, but changed his mind. There wasn't anything to say, not yet.

'I like her,' Oliviero said. 'I know you think I like everyone, but I don't.'

Valentino had spoken to her at breakfast, and once he'd asked after her ankle, how her previous evening was, if the dinner was to her liking, he brought up the subject of the letter. For a moment he wondered if it had been meant for him after all, if there hadn't been some mistake, for she'd looked away from him, her face, her whole body, appearing to tighten. Then she'd asked, *Would that be okay?* each word said so carefully, her voice taut. He'd suggested they meet later that morning. *What, today?* she'd said, her eyes meeting his, and they'd been full of something he couldn't read – trepidation, or reluctance? – leaving him a little confused as to why she was seeking him out in the first place.

'The terrace?' he'd said, attempting a casual footing.

'Maybe somewhere more . . . less busy. Have you an office?'

It was small, room enough to swing a cat, but only just. Fortuna, of course, would be slinking about somewhere, keeping out of the sun. He'd need to tidy a few things, for guests didn't normally go in there. But then guests didn't usually request mysterious meetings; most of their requirements were covered in passing, over drinks, or at the dinner table. *Could I have some more towels? Might we take a picnic lunch? Could our friends from the other side of the island join us for* aperitivo?

He'd agreed to the office, of course, and they'd planned to meet in reception at eleven o'clock. He was early; how could he not be, he'd thought of little else since breakfast. When she arrived, without the stick, a just-discernible limp, he felt a disproportionate sense of relief that she'd come at all. As he showed her in, she peered at the small wooden desk, the leather easy chair, the loaded bookshelf, the cabinet where he kept glasses and a bottle or two. It was a cramped, unadorned space, unlike the rest of the hotel. There was no window, and a lamp in the style of a ship's lantern hung from the ceiling. An Egyptian rug, bought from a market in Portoferraio, lay on the floor. He gestured to the leather chair, and offered her a coffee.

She sat on the edge of the chair, her legs crossed, one hand smoothing the material of her dress. She wore a stretchy bandage on her bad ankle, and it seemed at odds with the rest of her. She said no to coffee, then yes to a glass of water. He poured her one from a carafe, and as he handed her the glass he said that he was very sorry to hear about her mother. He saw the glass slip from her fingers, as if in slow motion, the water spilling as it tipped. It dropped on the rug with a clunk, but didn't shatter, instead rolling beneath the chair. He felt extraordinarily heavy-handed, blundering in with such a thing, and apologised twice over, as she sat quite still, pressing her fingertips to her eyes.

'Really,' he said, '*bella signorina*. Excuse me. Oliviero said, and . . . I wanted to offer my condolences. Sincerely.'

She didn't say anything. She still held her hands to her face, and he saw then that they were shaking. He stood up, took a bottle of whisky from the cabinet. It had been a gift from a Scottish guest two summers ago. Perhaps it could ease things.

'It's very early, I know,' he said, 'but . . .'

She nodded, and he opened it with a difficulty that made a mockery of his years in the trade. He poured two measures, and he realised she'd dropped her hands to watch him. When he held out a glass, she took it, and drank fast.

'Thanks,' she said, through the heat of alcohol.

He sipped his own more slowly, his eyes never leaving her.

'I'm sorry,' he said, and he didn't know if he was apologising for mentioning her mother, or for the loss of her mother, or for something else entirely, but she accepted it. She nodded. His eyes went to her empty glass.

'Too soon for another?' he said. 'Isn't it?'

'Dutch courage. Why not?'

He didn't know the saying, but he guessed what it meant. He refilled her glass, then, reluctantly, topped up his own.

'I like that phrase "hair of the dog",' he said. 'We don't say that in Italy. So I suppose that suggests something about our two countries.'

Kit clutched her glass, and he saw how her fingertips were pressing white. She took a very deep breath, as if she were about to inflate a balloon, or jump from a great height.

'Do you have a word for love child in Italian?' she said.

'Love child?' He tapped his fingers on the chair. 'You mean . . . illegitimate? *Figlio illegittimo*. Or *figlia illegittima*. Nothing so informal as love child. Nothing so romantic. Your language is . . . idiomatic. Fluid. I like it very much for that.'

'*Figlia illegittima*,' said Kit, with a near enough perfect accent.

They looked at one another. He twitched, his head moving just the slightest amount, neither nod nor shake.

'Why do you want to know the Italian for love child?'

'You were married, when my mother knew you.'

He felt a rip in his chest, sharp as a knife.

'And you broke her heart. Irreparably.'

His hand felt for the arm of the chair, something solid to hold onto.

'Do you even know who I'm talking about? Or were there so many women that she could be anyone? That *I* could be anyone?'

'I know who you're talking about,' said Valentino. Then he said it again, because the first time his voice hadn't worked, not even close. His throat had contracted, swallowing back the words before he'd spoken them, feeling their burn all the way down. Thirty years, and it still physically pained him to speak of it. He gripped his chair and stared back at the girl called Kit.

nineteen

OLIVIERO HAD SET HIS AUBERGINES TO MARINATE. HE'D LAID slices of *melanzane*, scattered chilli, garlic, capers and mint, and added a liberal dousing of olive oil. Three almond blossom cakes were in the oven. The chickens, delivered early that morning by Marco, were awaiting the juicing of lemons, the fine-chopping of shallots, the addition of grapes that were, in that moment, ripening in a bowl in the sunshine. All was in hand. He wandered outside, jumping his lighter between his fingers. He squatted in his customary spot, in the shade of the pines. He turned at the sound of giggling.

'Hey, guys, what's up?'

It was the Berger boys. In sandals and swimming shorts, their blond hair standing on end, slicked by sun cream. He could see it streaking down their arms and their cheeks, as though they were mid-application and had given someone the slip. They were peeping round the corner of the building.

'Shouldn't you guys be at the beach? You've got some serious sandcastles to make. Er . . . *Sandburg*? *Schwimmen*?'

They jostled one another, tumbling out from their hiding spot.

'Where's your *Mutti*? *Vater*?'

They said something he couldn't understand, which was more to do with the accompanying shrieks and laughter than his incomprehension of German. He heard, then, a distant voice calling. He set a hand behind his ear in cartoon fashion.

'If I give you something, you go back to your mum and dad, okay?' He waggled a finger at them. '*Warten Sie hier*, okay?'

He dipped inside, went to the cooling rack where the chocolate was just setting on a new batch of *cantucci al cioccolato*. He picked up two. He heard voices, frustrated German voices, the gruffness of Max, the whining of the boys. He got a plate, and filled it. He could always make more.

'Hey, *hallo*!'

Max was hauling the two boys away. His shorts were smeared with sun cream. He gripped the bottle, looking defeated.

'They think it's a big joke to run away,' he said, holding it up. 'My wife usually puts it on them, but she's having a morning on her own today . . . a holiday in a holiday, so . . . I'm sorry for the interruption. They shouldn't have come back here.'

Oliviero offered him the plate. 'The guys wanted to surprise you. Right, boys? To go with your coffee.'

He saw Max's expression soften as he caught the scent of toasted almonds and chocolate. He reached for one, a childish smile of pleasure lighting his face. The boys, sensing a reprieve, twined about his legs, as affectionate as puppies. As the three Bergers stood munching warm biscuits, Oliviero slipped back inside to make the father a coffee. And one for himself, too, to enjoy with his cigarette once they'd gone on their way, harmony temporarily restored.

* * *

Valentino was making his way up the back path that led only to his villa. That was the sound Oliviero heard as he stood in the shade, his second attempt at a moment to himself. Valentino's steps were slow and unsteady, and intermittent, as though he kept pausing for breath. Normally he was a bustler and a hustler, going everywhere with purpose; he didn't shamble about in the sunshine, his arms out wide as though feeling his way in the dark. Oliviero jumped up, snapping the unlit cigarette from his lips, and called out.

'Hey!'

Valentino looked about him, as if uncertain of the direction the shout had come from. Oliviero bounded over, covering the ground in just a few strides.

'Hey. You okay?'

'I'm just taking a minute,' he said. He gestured towards his villa. 'Just a minute or two.'

He looked, to Oliviero, as if he'd aged twenty years: his tanned skin had assumed a grey pallor, and there were creases at his brow. Yet at the same time, unnervingly, there was something of the child about him. His eyes were as wide as windows.

'You don't feel well?' said Oliviero.

'Not completely,' said Valentino. 'Not altogether.'

'Can I do anything?'

Valentino's hand went to his chest, and he rubbed it back and forth.

'I think,' he said, 'no. Not just now.'

Oliviero looked him over, his eyes narrowing. Valentino had had a scare two years ago. It was just before the summer season, and he was up a ladder, replacing the bulbs in several of his lights. Oliviero had seen him stretch for a garland, then

142

fall forward, doubling over. He'd thought he'd slipped and was simply clinging on to the ladder for balance. He'd sprinted over, ready to make a joke about his precarious position, when he realised Valentino was clutching his chest, his mouth gaping like a fish. Oliviero had tried to take the weight of him, to talk him down, all the while his own heart hammering. The doctor had confirmed it as chest pains brought on by a panic attack, but to Oliviero it had looked as if he was collapsing, and he'd felt fear slice through his body. Ever since, he'd been quietly watchful. He thought Valentino an unlikely candidate for panic; he was too calm, too stolid for that. But the sudden seizure of an aching heart? As unthinkable as it was, it was possible.

'Are you . . . in pain?'

He saw Valentino hesitate.

'I'm coming back with you.'

'There's no need. But I might take a moment. Just a moment. Abi is there for the guests. Perhaps you could . . .'

Oliviero figured himself to be pretty good at reading people. Valentino had taught him that the most important thing was, quite simply, to care. If you cared enough to try, you could always find a way to see what people wanted, and what they needed. The biggest thing, he'd always said, was to learn to set yourself aside. It was easier said than done to think of people only in terms of their intentions, and not your own, but when it came to Valentino, Oliviero's own wants were more or less insignificant. He didn't accept his reassurance simply so that he could go back to his day as it was before: the sweet little freedom of a cigarette in the shade, his chickens ready for quartering, the almond blossom cakes turning golden in the oven, the reverie of Kit finding the CD he'd slid under her door, with all the songs he wanted her to know, because even if she wouldn't go to the concert with him, she might enjoy the music all the same. And maybe, just maybe, she'd change her mind.

'I'm coming with you,' he said, taking Valentino's elbow, gently steering him up the path. And Valentino let him, without a fight, making Oliviero both glad that he'd insisted, and afraid of why he'd had to.

'Kit,' he said her name slowly, carefully, as if handling a delicate piece of china, 'has gone to Capoliveri. She's taken a taxi, she'll be away for the night.'

'But the festival's not until the weekend,' said Oliviero. He wanted to add, *And she's coming back, isn't she?* but instead he bit down on the thought and gestured to a chair. Valentino looked at it dimly, as though he'd seen something like it before but couldn't be sure.

They were in Valentino's kitchen. The door of the villa opened directly onto it, and it was a square space, of white stone walls and blue tiled floor and a cupboard that held just one plate, one mug, one bowl. Supermarket crockery, flimsy and functional, yet as far as Oliviero knew he'd always used the same set. When they ate together in the off season, they did so at the hotel, using the expansive white plates and weighty cutlery of the dining room, turquoise cotton napkins laid across their knees. Oliviero loved these nights; he couldn't think of any better. He'd cook a rabbit, or roast a wild duck, bring a couple of swordfish steaks back from the market. Their conversation was of the food as they ate it; where it had come from, the method of preparation, how the flavours jumped and melded with magical alchemy.

'She wants me to talk to her tomorrow, when she gets back.

She talked to me today and, tomorrow, she wants me to talk to her.'

He turned round, and gave Oliviero a look that was so stricken that something in him plummeted.

'Is this,' he said, 'about Kit?'

'What do you do,' Valentino said, 'when someone gives you something that should be . . . a gift . . . and yet you can't take it, you can't hold out your hands to accept it . . . because you don't know if you can bear the weight of it, and you're not even sure that they want you to have it, in fact you're certain that they don't, and yet they're here, holding it in front of you, and . . .'

He lost his way, glanced up at Oliviero, and found it again.

'. . . and you want to do the right thing. Above all, you want to do the right thing. But you don't know what that is. Perhaps you never did. Not by her, not by . . . anyone else . . .'

Valentino was a simple man, on the face of it, and he made things easy for those around him. When it came to life's messier bits, he'd simply erased himself. He didn't get emotionally entangled, you didn't see him pushing his face into his hands, drinking too much, fretting the marks of his existence. He didn't talk about thwarted hopes or broken dreams or awkward dates or quick encounters. He was never caught out of step. He didn't explode like a firecracker, in a vivid and unnecessary blaze of light. You took someone like Isabel, someone Oliviero liked a great deal, and Valentino behaved as though she simply wasn't for him. A shoe of so completely the wrong size there was no point even trying it on. And Oliviero had never pushed him, because he knew how it was to box something up and take it to your attic. Because that was it, wasn't it? You could never entirely remove a part of yourself. You couldn't drive ten miles and leave it on the roadside. Skip across an ocean, and expect it not to follow you.

Even when Valentino had told him the worst of himself, years ago, the man hadn't fallen apart. Perhaps, Oliviero had thought afterwards, with a philosophy that belied his years, it was because he was already broken. They'd been on the terrace, on one of those island nights when the sea beat against the rocks and the moon was eaten up by clouds and they were sitting in their heavy coats, surrounded by a thousand lights. It was the end of his second season working alongside Valentino, after a glorious summer of uninterrupted clear skies and happy guests, and he had said something praising. Something gushing, probably, what with the rich wine and the good dinner and the sense of total and absolute gratitude that descended on him every so often. That in fact never really left him. And Valentino had waved it away, as he always did.

'No,' Oliviero had said, 'you have to know, you're the one good person there is.'

He'd met with no obstruction, so he carried on, taking his chance.

'I don't just mean all the things you've done for me,' he said, his voice breaking, 'but how you are with everyone. It's . . . almost holy. It is holy. That's what it is.'

Valentino had made a sound then. A short bark of a laugh. 'Never say that.'

'I know that doesn't mean anything to you, but . . .'

He watched as Valentino lit a cigarette and drew hard on it, holding the smoke inside him then blowing it out in one sideways stream.

'There are things I don't talk about,' Valentino had said, his mouth not quite righting itself. 'Things I can't talk about. But

146

I'll say them now, and then you'll know. God knows I hate to disappoint you, but you need to see I'm not the man you think I am. That I never was.'

Afterwards, Oliviero's throat ached as he'd said, *Thank you for telling me*, then, *I'm sorry*, as intently as he could, with the full comprehension that they would never speak of it again.

In his kitchen, Valentino gripped a glass of water and stared at Oliviero. He knew, then, that this had to be a part of that conversation, that night, eleven years ago. There wasn't anything it could be but that. Then Valentino turned abruptly and threw the glass into the sink, where it shattered with a violence that made Oliviero want to cry like a child, inexplicably, unfathomably, and most of all, pointlessly.

twenty

KIT HAD TOLD VALENTINO THAT SHE WAS GOING TO CAPOLIVERI, as if she were still trying to make him believe that she was really there to write about Maria and Lorenzo. But instead she got on one of the island's blue buses, and got off it again up the road in Marciana Alta. It wasn't a deliberate deception; as she'd boarded, she'd just repeated what the girl ahead of her had said. Space was what she wanted. It didn't matter where.

I need to understand what actually happened, she had said. *Your word is the only one I'll ever have, so when we speak again, please don't lie.*

She'd told him of the deaths: her mother's, two and a half months ago; his reported own, thirty years before that. She'd spoken with brevity, and a certain pragmatism, as if she were simply communicating the details of someone else's story. She didn't tell him of the months and months of Rosa's illness, how it felt to see the one person you loved, the one person who loved you back, fade before your eyes and there be nothing you could do about it; the hanks of hair that started appearing on the bathroom floor, how the bones in her wrists had begun to stick out like blades. She didn't tell him how as a child she'd imagined bears coming down from the forest, shipwrecks, duels fought on dusty, sunlit squares – a dozen fantastic ways of dying for her irredeemably flawed father. She didn't tell him how she'd written the letters of his name into the cup of her hand, sitting on a hard-backed chair on the fourth floor of an impervious building, and beside her, her mum, her lovely mum, lying back on a thin pillow and closing her eyes, a flush spidering across her cheeks. She didn't tell him how she hadn't been able to bear the thought of causing pain on top of pain, not when it was so visible, so undeniable, and so instead of finishing what she'd started, she'd told Rosa that they could talk about it another day, when she felt better. When the drugs coursing through her mum's body weren't making her speak of things that couldn't possibly be true.

She didn't know what to say, but she knew that it couldn't be any of this.

Valentino's reaction had thrown her. It was as though she had set a great weight down upon him, and he'd reached out and taken it, his legs bending, his eyes popping, knowing there was no way he could carry it but attempting to bear it all the same. He had accepted what she told him without question, although she'd never said the word *daughter*. Just as she hadn't said *father* either. Then she'd left him, without staying for a word of his story, without hearing a thing that he might have had to say – because it was shocking, the emotion in his response, and she could only pretend that she hadn't noticed if she quit the room that very moment. So she'd told him they each needed space. That she'd return tomorrow, that they should talk then. And then she'd left his office at speed, putting full weight on her foot even though she'd felt the burn all the way up her leg and down to her toes.

As they had climbed the hill towards Marciana Alta, Kit had felt an uneasy sense of relief. The bus – swaying and jolting into every mountainous turn – was doing a very good job of bearing her away. The lush hillsides rolled out behind them, the sea spun away to the horizon. The peninsula, with the red roof of the Mille Luci, its striped parasols and azure pool, was just a dot, a smudge, and then it was out of sight altogether. The bus had wheezed to a halt and the woman who'd got on at the same stop as Kit – younger than her, with her hair piled in a topknot and the glint of a stud in her nose – had jumped off. Kit grabbed her bag and followed.

The young woman set off, striding purposefully. Kit stood and watched the bus depart in a flurry of exhaust fumes and grinding gears. She took a deep breath. Lifted her arms, and stretched her back until she heard the click, click, click of vertebrae. Then she put one foot in front of the other, and walked in the steps of the girl.

Marciana Alta was suspended high in the hills. Deep green forests fell away on all sides, in a densely woven blanket. Just below, perhaps five miles away, but appearing only the distance of a well-lobbed ball, the resort of Marciana Marina lay glistening: a cascade of red rooftops and burly-headed trees, the miniature oblongs of boats in the harbour. Alta itself felt like disappearing inside a catacomb. It was a place of narrow alleyways, sheer drops, and steep flights of stone steps, of café tables and coffee stops and the names of pizzas chalked on boards. Kit walked the streets – her ankle was holding up well enough – but what she really wanted was to be running, her feet pounding, her blood pumping. Adrenalin was in her, for something would happen now. It had to. There would be consequences to her actions.

She headed away from the stretch of cafés and into the places where people lived, where bead curtains click-clacked and washing lines hung in improbable places. It was comforting, the signs of ordinary life. To see that even on this day other people were going about their business as usual, the sky above their heads still holding, the ground beneath their feet intact. She passed a transistor radio set on a windowsill, crackling incomprehensibly, and resisted the urge to reach inside and turn its dial all the way up. To find a song, something raucous and surging, with an incessant beat. For all the kindness of her friends, she'd felt so alone these last months, stuck in a place where nobody could reach her. But he, Valentino, was there now too. She'd stretched out her hand and yanked him in. Rudely, probably, with altogether too much acrimony, but when the moment had come, she'd found no other way of doing it.

At her words, he'd seemed to age before her. His composure dismantled with one fell swoop. Once she might have imagined that she'd experience satisfaction at engendering that kind of reaction. Such had been her naivety. To think that she was here for Rosa too, as though that meant taking her mum's hurt and doubling it. Kneading this sum total between her hands until it was hard as stone, then hurling it, without a care for consequence.

She'd been right to beat a retreat afterwards, to let him process the fact of her existence. That had felt fair, perhaps even gracious. Or maybe it had been more like cowardice. In the face of his reaction, she simply hadn't known what to say next. A prickle of guilt already rising in her stomach, even as she continued to sit there, the taste of her words still in her mouth. And Oliviero. She hardly knew him, yet she felt as though she'd somehow cheated him. There was no use pretending: he'd thought she was somebody else. The kind of woman he might buy a drink for, with the hope of more to come. All those smiles he'd wasted on her. And worse, the ones she'd returned, trying to absent them of anything more nuanced than courtesy, or simple gratitude. Nothing had started – a couple of invitations, that was all, the kind he likely threw out to anyone, anywhere – but she still had the feeling that she should have stopped it. The thought of him loping across the lawn towards her, the clean lines of his face newly blurred with incomprehension and accusation, was an uncomfortable one. Maybe some part of him would think it amusing, but it was still his family in the mire, and Oliviero didn't seem to be the kind of man who was built for inconvenient truths.

The sun was high overhead, and she'd had nothing to drink since Valentino's throat-burning whisky. As soon as she acknowledged her thirst it became unbearable, and she ducked into the first shop she came across, a grocer's. She chose an ice-cold can of *limonata* while the young shopkeeper regarded her with curiosity. She felt as though she still carried traces of the scene she'd left that morning, as if she had the glow of sensationalism all about her. She called out *arrivederci* and her voice sounded like it belonged to somebody else. Standing outside in the street, the lemonade fizzing in her throat, her fingers pinching the can, she couldn't believe what she'd done. That even now he was somewhere down there, far below – her eyes squinted as she looked back towards the sea – possessed of this new information, and wondering what on earth to do with it.

When she and her mum had lived in the grounds of the manor, Kit had broken one of the windows of the big house once. It hadn't been intentional: the misthrow of a tennis ball, the unanticipated force. When the owner had come out, she'd hidden from him. He'd looked more sad than angry as he'd stooped to gather the shards of glass. She'd been eight years old, maybe nine, but as she'd watched him, she'd felt the echo of his upset. She hadn't been able to eat her dinner that night, and later, tearful in her nightdress, she'd owned up to her mum. *I saw him earlier too*, Rosa had said, *he never mentioned a thing*, which only made Kit cry harder.

She saw a tiny chapel then, and felt drawn towards it, with its crisp white walls and promise of a cool interior. Outside she paused and glanced about her, feeling a trespasser. But the street behind her was deserted, and she ducked inside.

Her eyes adjusted. It smelt of stone, and the uneven walls were printed with a decorative floral pattern in pale blue. There was an altar set with a pair of crooked candlesticks, a vase of paper flowers, an oil painting of an angel and a man in robes. Altogether it looked a little shabby, but undoubtedly beautiful, appearing almost like vintage set dressing in a London interior shop. A photograph propped in an alcove showed a man and woman leaning against one another. They were silhouetted, their faces dark. The light burnt behind them, the sea a blaze of white. The image was sun-bleached and water-damaged, but someone had leant it against a crucifix, as though it too was a precious thing.

Her mum's view on religion had been as much of a mystery as everything else. She'd never attended church, as far as Kit knew. Once, when Kit was about fourteen, they'd gone to Wells for the day. Poking about in a junk shop, Kit had come across a necklace of dusky pink beads. It was broken, and she could see no way to fasten it, but she was sure that Rosa could mend it, and knew it would look beautiful around her neck. She had spent all her pocket money on it, buying it secretly as her mum rooted through a box of old maps. She'd given it to her when they were outside. *This is for you*, she'd said. *It's for Mother's Day, but I can't wait.* She'd watched as her mum had held it up to the light and let it run between her fingers. She'd felt a thud of uncertainty, and told her that she knew it was broken and probably needed a clean, but if they could get a new clasp fitted it could perhaps be a good necklace again. *Oh mi amore*, Rosa had said, *didn't you know? It's a rosary. It's the most beautiful rosary, and I'll treasure it forever.* Kit never saw her mum hold it in her hand again. It was only as she was going through her things, a few weeks ago, that she'd found it. It had been at the bottom of a shoebox that contained a stack of Kit's baby photos, folded in a fragment of precious Italian silk.

Her hand went to her bag. Inside was her diary, and tucked into its pages were the pictures she'd brought with her. Earlier she'd looked into her mum's eyes and said, *I told him. Is that what you wanted? Is that okay? It wasn't like I thought.* She had the desire, suddenly, to take out one of her own photographs and stand it, for just a moment, in this sacred place. To ask, *What now, Mum? Whatever he tells me, what am I supposed to do with it?* And then, in a whisper, *Why is it that I feel bad? What's fair about that?* She reached into the bag, her heart thundering as if she was doing something she shouldn't.

'Hello.'

She turned sharply, and saw a woman framed in the doorway. She returned the greeting, and made to leave, for it was too small a space for two people. The moment for the photograph was gone.

'You're from the hotel? I'm Steffi.'

She recognised her then. The German woman with the matching boys and the handsome, sturdy-looking husband. Kit arranged her features into what she hoped was recognition and amicability, but without giving the impression that she wanted to linger.

'You're here on your own, aren't you?'

Kit nodded.

'That is wonderful,' said Steffi, running a hand through her hair. 'What bliss that is. I have the morning to myself. Three hours. For the first time in . . . a long time.'

She still stood in the doorway, unintentionally barring Kit's exit. Kit stepped sideways, creating space for Steffi to fully enter, but she stayed where she was, seemingly more interested in Kit than the chapel.

'Did you want to take a coffee with me?' she asked.

'A coffee?'

'I know. I have this time to myself and yet . . .' She shrugged, gave a self-conscious laugh. 'They do a good cappuccino at the café down there.'

Kit adjusted her bag on her shoulder, took a last glance at the crucifix. It wasn't for her, this place, and it wasn't for Rosa either.

'All right,' she said. 'Why not?'

Steffi Berger drank two cappuccinos and told Kit she used to be a ski instructor in the Bavarian Alps. She spoke as if this was a crucial piece of information that had to be conveyed if they were to have any kind of conversation – however idle, however passing. She then stretched out her leg, showing the snaking white scar over the ridge of her knee. Kit asked what had happened, and Steffi told her about the perfect powder day of pillowing white, rock drop after rock drop, skis parallel, falling with style, then the sudden rise of an unseen slab, the fissure in her ski pants, the pain like a flock of arrows up and down her leg. How the mountains were all that she'd loved, but now that life was gone forever. That she couldn't bear to even look at them. Kit scratched her arm, wondered what to say.

'So . . . you moved away?'

'No,' said Steffi, 'my husband still instructs.'

'Skiing?'

'Sure. It's how we met. We go away in the summer, but in the winter we live in the snow and . . . I keep my curtains closed. And the boys are very busy for me.'

'Twins must be . . . hard.'

'Twins are hard,' said Steffi. 'Very, very hard. My husband thinks they make a good distraction. For me.'

'Do they?'

'Yes. And no,' she added, with a smile that was just as mixed.

Kit imagined stating the facts of her life with such forthrightness. It was an impossible idea. What was it about her that was making people open right up, splitting themselves down the middle like pomegranates? Her mum had been like that, drawing confidences from the most unlikely sources. Bristol was peppered with people who'd told her something that no one else knew: the garage mechanic who admitted his gambling debts as he changed the oil in her car; the flower seller who'd wrapped her tulips and told her she couldn't stand the man her daughter had married. *Sometimes it's easier to talk to someone you don't know*, Rosa had said, with a one-shouldered shrug. Or perhaps, Kit thought now, for all her mum's finesse, she had something in her eyes that spoke to those who knew how heavy untold secrets weighed. Did Kit possess that same mark? Even Isabel, yesterday, who had seemed as buttoned-up a person as you'd meet, had wandered into territory so personal that it had kept Kit awake that night. It hadn't just been the loss of her child, or the quiet grace with which she had narrated it; it was Valentino too. How he had made life better for her, even for just a week a year. Kit had finally gone to sleep only to dream of a very small baby left screaming in its cot; a baby girl, whose crying was heard only by a man in a different country altogether.

'Are you enjoying the hotel?' she asked, as if to provoke herself, and immediately saw how Steffi's face lit up, as though she was once more high in the mountains on a day of speed and light. She nodded vigorously, while rooting in her bag. She pulled out a sketchbook.

'I'm a terrible artist, but Abi said to paint what I love. So I'm on an Italian island, drawing very bad pictures of mountains. But today . . .' She held up a page. 'You wouldn't recognise them, but that's my three boys. Five minutes away from them and maybe I miss them after all.'

'Abstract. I like it.'

Steffi laughed. 'I was definitely deliberately trying to be abstract.'

'Abi's paintings, they're the ones in the dining room?'

Steffi nodded. 'Too beautiful. Everybody at the Mille Luci has a talent. Did you notice that? They don't *do* ordinary.' She stuffed the book back in her bag. 'Or maybe nobody feels ordinary once they get here. Maybe that's it. Look at Oliviero. A phenomenal cook. And outrageously good-looking.'

'You think?' said Kit.

'He likes you, that's clear to see,' said Steffi, with a theatrical wink.

Kit shook her head, protesting it, a heat burning her cheeks. If Steffi noted her embarrassment she'd probably think it endearingly teenage, confirmation that the admiration was returned. How sweet and simple that would be, to give yourself away like that, the only consequence self-consciousness: a far cry from mortification.

'Really, no,' said Kit, a sharpness in her voice. 'Not at all. No way.'

'Enjoy it,' said Steffi, waving her hand dismissively. 'It's nice. As for Valentino, the man is a saint.'

Kit stirred her coffee vigorously, the spoon clacking. 'He runs a good hotel,' she said.

'Good? That's British understatement. I'm not sure we Germans are known for going over the top either, but . . . perhaps this week is making me more Italian. It's a very special place, the Mille Luci. *Himmel auf Erden*, I want to say.'

'Heaven on earth,' translated Kit.

Steffi raised an eyebrow. 'You wouldn't agree?'

'I guess I'm not religious,' said Kit.

She had a sudden fierce desire then to be on her own. No more conversation. No more pretence. A spell of oblivion before she went back down the hill. Tomorrow she would learn Valentino's version of events, after giving him a day and a night to order his words. What shape would they make? Whether the truth he'd tell turned out to be mundane, or petty, or utterly devastating, it would be all she had. No choice but to take it on, fold it into her comprehension of her existence.

She realised that Steffi had asked her another question. She asked her to repeat it, while digging in her bag for her wallet, already signalling for the waiter.

twenty-one

IN THE SUN-HEAVY HOURS OF THE AFTERNOON, WHEN THE hotel was mostly emptied of guests, Valentino tried to occupy himself with a number of incidental tasks. He took a cloth and wiped all the glasses in the bar, setting them back one by one. He went along the driveway with a basket, gathering any of the prickly pears that had fallen to the ground. He took a broom and swept the back steps, where pine needles sometimes settled when a particular wind was blowing. Had the pool been deserted he might have skimmed its surface for bugs, but Lucille was lying on a lounger, a magazine held in front of her face, while Nina swam a painstaking backstroke that didn't quite match the flash of her leopard-print costume. Valentino called out a greeting, but he didn't linger for the reply. Instead he worked his way back up across the lawn, his head bent. And then he saw Isabel. She was in her customary spot by the eucalyptus tree. She wore a straw sunhat, and beneath her long skirt her legs were crossed. She held a paperback novel on her knee, but didn't appear to be reading it. He told himself that if she lifted her head and saw him, he would go to her. And if she asked him how he was, directly, looking right at him, then he would tell her, and seek her counsel. Part of him wished she already knew everything.

'Good afternoon,' she said, waving a hand.

He walked towards her, his legs unsteady.

'I smelt an unfamiliar burning coming from the kitchen earlier. Is Oliviero experimenting with a char grill?'

Oliviero's almond blossom cakes, three of them ruined, were scattered now in the woods for the birds.

'My fault,' he said.

'You're not in charge of the food today, are you? Dear God, I fear for us.' Then, 'I always forget, you know, that you were a chef yourself once upon a time.'

'A lifetime ago,' said Valentino. He gestured to the bench. 'May I?'

She nodded, smiling, and he sat down beside her. He put his hands together, his fingers knotting.

'Do you ever miss it, the kitchen?'

He dropped his head. 'I miss a lot,' he said, 'but not that.'

Isabel knew that he'd been married once, and she knew that his wife had died, but he'd told her no more than that. She paid for the pleasure and service of his hotel, not to be an ear for its owner. So he always smiled, and clicked his heels, and whisked away plates, and asked after her well-being, and not for a moment did he take advantage of her sincerity. But today . . . today was different.

'It has been an . . . extraordinary morning,' he said.

'Happy extraordinary?' asked Isabel. 'Or . . . other?'

Valentino turned his hands over, studied his palms. Lines tracked both hands, and his skin was ridged at the base of each finger. A scar ran the length of his thumb. They were worker's hands, and they belonged to an old man.

'I think . . . other,' he said. Then, 'Can I . . . ask your advice?'

A butterfly alighted on the grass near Isabel's foot. It was a blue so bright as to be unnatural, and they both saw it, took in its presence, without remarking on it.

'Please,' she said, quietly, her eyes on the butterfly, 'please do.'

'I don't know the right place to start. I haven't spoken it out loud before. Not all of it. And not before this morning, with Oliviero.'

It had cost him, the conversation. Instead of feeling a lightening sensation, a relief at admitting it all to someone other than himself, the pain had seemed to embed itself further, twisting ever deeper. Afterwards Oliviero had laid a hand on his arm, and said all the right things, that were – Valentino suspected – also the wrong things, for his voice had lacked conviction. Then he had left him, realising that his cakes were burning to ash, about to take the whole hotel with them if he didn't get there quickly, he said. By the time he returned, Valentino had regained his composure, and Oliviero had seemed to have a different mettle about him. *You can't lie to her*, he'd said. *There have been enough lies. Haven't there?* and he'd been talking about the behaviour of Kit's mother, but Valentino couldn't help but feel an ache, knowing it ought to be for him too.

'I have a daughter,' he said to Isabel. 'A daughter I knew nothing about.'

Perhaps she was startled into silence, for she said nothing. He ploughed on.

'She didn't know about me, either. Her mother told her that

162

I . . . died before she was born. We are . . . a surprise to one another. For her, that I still exist. For me, that she exists at all.'

The butterfly was still in the grass, preternaturally motionless. Valentino, glancing sideways, saw that Isabel's eyes were trained upon it, with an expression that was impossible to read.

'Not a happy surprise, though. Not for her. I think her mother always told her that I was . . . that my death, the death she made for me, was . . . no loss. I'm certain of this, in fact. I think she came here wanting to . . . hate me. Already hating me.'

Isabel turned to him then, her brow creasing. 'To hate you?'

'I wasn't good to her mother. I behaved badly. I didn't . . .' He hesitated, then went on, 'I didn't treat her as she deserved to be treated. I made a very bad mistake.'

'It was an affair that you had with her?'

'It happened just once, and I . . . regretted it almost instantly. So many years of thinking and questioning and I still do not understand this part of myself. How I could have done it.'

Isabel's silence was drenching. He lost his way, stopped.

'This is very difficult,' he said.

'I should think it is,' said Isabel.

'She wants me to explain to her why it was that her mother hated me so much.'

A pause. 'She never asked her herself?'

'No,' said Valentino. 'I think not. And it's too late now.'

'So she only recently learned of your existence?'

'And that is why she came to Elba, I think.'

Isabel's hand went to her locket. 'Oh my,' she said.

'You know who I'm speaking of? I saw you talking to her last night. She didn't . . . mention this?'

'Not a word.'

He nodded. Said her name. *Kit*. Low, and sad, but not without wonder.

'She struck me,' said Isabel, 'as a young woman looking for something. I thought it simply to be love . . . I suppose that just shows my lack of imagination.'

'She wants to understand, I think,' said Valentino. 'Her mother is no longer here to ask. I don't know how much she knows. I think perhaps . . . very little.'

'She lost her mother?'

'Just a few months ago.'

'Her thoughts must be . . .' Isabel waved a hand in the air, her fingers fluttering, 'awry. Quite awry. So you will help her,' she said. 'Give her something.'

'But not something good,' said Valentino.

He couldn't shake from his head the image of Kit in his office. Her hands folded in her lap, her legs crossed, her ankle bandage bright white. How her eyes had flashed as she'd said *love child*, fury striking, as blinding as lightning over water. A young woman who was nothing and everything to do with him.

'I don't want to hurt her,' he said. 'That is the absolute most important thing. And I don't want her to think badly of her mother. To hurt her with that too . . .'

'She's already hurting, isn't she? She might say she wants the truth . . .'

'That's what Oliviero said.'

'. . . but, I don't know, perhaps a gentler version . . .' Isabel smoothed the fabric of her dress with her hand. 'There are always ways of explaining things, are there not?'

Valentino sank his head into his hands.

'If you tell me,' she said, carefully, 'then perhaps I could . . . I know how it is to have a thing come between two people, you see. To love someone, but to hurt them all the same. To get lost in one emotion at the expense of all else.' She laid a hand on Valentino's shoulder, and he felt the unaccustomed heat of her touch. He lifted his face, very slightly. Glanced sideways at her. 'You have a daughter,' she said, her voice choked, 'and that is, surely, amidst all else, a wonderful thing. Isn't it?'

When Kit's mother had told him she was pregnant, he'd felt sick. An instant wash of nausea that had scooped him up like a high wave and dumped him down again. She'd asked to meet him. He hadn't wanted to, but had gone all the same. She'd worn a long coat, and there was a suitcase by her feet. They were sitting at the very back of a café he'd never been to before when she'd told him. He'd felt sickness, then disbelief. *Are you sure?* he'd asked, and she'd sent him a withering look. Pulled on her cigarette. She'd looked different in that light. Brisk. Businesslike. Her coat was tightly buttoned, her lips clamped together. Seven weeks ago . . . and he knew it was seven weeks, because every single day of them he'd felt like he was outside of his own life looking in, each day feeling so falsely bright, from first waking to last light, hating the words that came from his own mouth because anything he said, even the everyday things like *pass the salt*, or *this sauce is delicious*, or *it's set to rain later*, sounded false and untrustworthy and wheedling. Seven weeks ago. And for all his deep regret, the vividness of the night had stayed with him, creeping into his consciousness, leaving him simultaneously aroused and appalled.

He'd thought of how they'd lain twisted in bed sheets, misted in one another's sweat, stupidly drunk. How they'd been noisy, although they'd tried not to be, pushing fists into mouths, swallowing their cries with urgent kisses. How she'd left bite marks in his shoulder, and a strawberry-like stain had bloomed on the side of her neck. How it had been so easy – the looks swapped, the match-strike of alcohol, the unstoppable blaze that followed – and so, so wrong. He'd left her, his mouth still stinging from her kisses, murmuring incoherent, impassioned apology, and she'd returned them, those apologies of his, and said it was nothing between them but a moment of madness. Delectable madness, she'd said, for all the tears that ran down her face. And despite the guilt that was coursing through both of them, the phrase had lodged, and he'd returned to it, in those seven weeks, found himself agreeing with it, even as he tried to shake it from his head. Now it was a new guilt that gripped him. He honestly thought he'd vomit into his hands.

'The worst of it,' he said to Isabel, 'well, no, *one* of the very bad things about it, was that Bianca had wanted a baby for a very long time. For nearly three years we'd tried, and . . . She was losing her faith in it ever being possible. She was losing her faith in me. She made that very clear. I told myself it was a strain on our marriage, over and over again I told myself that, the tension was just . . . too much. Trying to find a reason for why I walked out of our home one day and . . . turned into some other person. The kind of man who climbs into bed with another woman. That wasn't me, I tried to tell myself. I must have been . . . what? Unloved? Disrespected? Under pressure, maybe. Drunk, yes. My opinion of myself so very low that the first person who . . .' He stopped. Started again. 'But none of it was true. It wasn't. Apart from being drunk. We had problems like anyone, perhaps more than some people, but . . . I always knew Bianca loved me. And I knew I loved her.'

'How we react under stress . . .' Isabel began to say, 'we can lose ourselves, we . . .'

'No,' said Valentino. Still now, his throat burnt with shame. 'Not like this. The woman . . . She was Bianca's best friend.'

Valentino thought, at the time, that the night he'd told his wife was the worst of his life. Her face had turned white, as though all colour, all vitality, had immediately drained from her. Then, at the flick of a switch, her skin had gone red, furious red, as she'd lifted her fists to him and beaten at his chest. Screaming. The windows of the apartment shaking, the floor tipping, the contents of the kitchen disordering itself, knives raining down on them, plates smashing. The stairs slipping and scattering. The roof blown right off. That was how it had seemed to him, a vortex of complete destruction. His home and all it held, shattered.

'I have to be a father to this child,' was what he'd said. 'I need to take responsibility for my mistake.'

What had he meant? What had he imagined? Money? Every month, a postal order, or an envelope of cash. A card here and there. Gifts of stuffed rabbits and balls and paper bags of sweets. A long train ride to spend an afternoon at the park, swings and slides and sandpits, then a train back again to his other life. Never that he should leave his wife to be with *her* instead. Never that. But to Bianca, the betrayal was everything. And the particular pain of the longed-for child emerging in not just any other woman's womb, but the one friend who knew how much it had meant to her, who was now laying claim to the thing she'd wanted above all else. They'd raged at one another, Valentino professing his love, his regret, in all the ways he knew how, but the facts would not pale. Bianca had left their apartment – as it went up in flames, as it flooded, and fell – and he'd never seen her again.

'I told you my wife died, didn't I?'

'Yes. You did.'

'She drowned. She loved the sea, Bianca. And she always told her troubles to it. The Mediterranean knew more about our marriage than either of us, she used to joke.' He paused. 'She had a little sailing boat – it was hers, and she sailed with her friend. The same friend that I . . .' He passed his hand across his face, as if trying to wipe the memory. 'So, of course, she went alone, that day. Maybe it was a kind of . . . defiance. That she didn't need either of us. And Bianca, once she got an idea in her head, you couldn't take it out again. But she would never have done that, gone out on her own with the boat, sailed so far, for so long, if she wasn't so . . . if I hadn't done what I'd done, and said what I'd said.'

'Valentino,' began Isabel, 'we can't . . .'

'A storm came in that afternoon,' he said, unhearing, 'one of those storms we get along the coast in the springtime; they come from nowhere, they're vicious, really. Waves . . . waves as high as a house. Uneven winds, blowing in all directions. The boat was found in pieces, wrecked, a lot later. She would never have stood a chance.'

In his nightmares he'd heard the tearing of the sail, the thrash of water, imagined her frantic hands grasping for ropes. She'd have fought, he knew that much.

'It was my fault that she died.'

'Valentino . . .'

'No. No. There is nothing to be said. It's true. It's the only possible interpretation.'

'A tragedy,' said Isabel, 'very much a tragedy, but an *accident* . . .'

Valentino shook his head. 'It's done,' he said, 'that story. I'm not looking for . . . I know my part in it, Isabel. And I live with it. I have to. But what came next. With . . . the baby.'

The butterfly took flight at last, wheeling and bobbing across the garden, a tiny blaze of blue. Isabel watched it, her hands knotted in her lap, ankles crossed. He saw how her shoulders lifted, very slightly, as if her breath was laboured.

'And here you were,' he said, 'sitting and enjoying the shade. Perfectly peaceful, I think. I'm sorry. I should not have . . .'

'Please,' said Isabel. 'Tell me. It's a long time since anyone has told me anything that . . . mattered.'

Bianca Colosimo's death had been reported in the newspaper. A small article, squeezed beside an account of the closure of a silk factory, and the theft of ancient silver jewellery from a museum in Firenze. Her picture was included, Bianca in black and white, with the words *A keen sailor*, and in capital letters, *TRAGICO*. And of course the fact of it ran up and down the endless grapevine that connected all the villages and towns in Toscana. How the chef at Café Italia had lost his wife and gone to ruin. Grace was not to be his. Bloody-knuckled, breath foul with cheap liquor, nobody was safe from his ire, least of all himself.

Kit's mother would have seen it all, heard these things, and thought, *We did this. This was me, as much as him.* And then, *He is not a suitable father. We, together, are not suitable parents.*

'She telephoned me,' he said. 'I hadn't answered the phone for weeks, but I did that time, for no particular reason.' He stopped. 'Or, I don't know, I wanted to hear a voice. Finally, a voice. I'd pushed everybody away. People had given up, I think, and they were right to. Or perhaps I was so drunk I thought it would be my Bianca on the telephone, as if a miracle had saved her after all.' His voice creaked. 'No. Not a miracle. I stopped believing in anything the day she died, other than my own particular ability to make ruins of people.

'As soon as I heard her voice, I realised I hadn't thought about how she must have been feeling, her own guilt, her sorrow, how she had lost her friend too. Instead of going to her, the one person who might have understood a little bit of what I was feeling, I'd run in the opposite direction. And, Isabel, I hadn't thought about the baby once. Okay? Not once. She must have been hurt, so hurt, and she told me that she was sorry . . . and I don't know whether she meant for Bianca or for . . . I don't know . . . because then she told me she had lost the baby.'

She'd delivered the news in the same manner that she'd told him the child existed – factual, unemotional, without the painful detail – but then she'd fallen very quiet, and Valentino, holding the phone at his end, had sucked in the same silence. Life, and loss, had washed between them. The pointlessness of it all.

'I think,' said Valentino, 'I know, now, that of course . . . it wasn't true. But even at the time, a part of me wondered if she'd just said it to . . . to try and make things better. To excuse me from having to live with something, with someone, when I'd lost the person I really wanted.'

He rubbed his face again, his palms crackling against his stubble.

'Or perhaps she had heard what I'd become and desired no part of it. Or maybe her own guilt was too much. I don't know. I wouldn't have blamed her for anything. But . . .'

'But . . . ?'

He looked at Isabel, full in the eyes for the first time. He saw how they brimmed with tears, and in reply he felt a heat behind his own. He gritted his teeth, determined not to permit them. 'If it was written up there in the stars that she would lose the child, why was it not before she decided to tell me she was pregnant. *That* was the pathetic thought I had. And I saw it as a punishment, by the might of God knows who, to make me feel – with all my bones – that the only thing I was capable of creating was pain and loss. All around me, whatever I touched. Destruction.'

'So,' said Isabel, 'when Kit's mother told you that she . . . had lost her, it only made everything worse?'

'She would not have known that. I could barely speak. She would have thought I didn't care, that I was relieved, even, to be spared this . . . I was pathetic enough, God knows. But for me? Yes. After everything, it just made it worse.'

Isabel was quiet, and Valentino edged a look at her. They were side by side, yet it felt to him as if he was peering round a corner, not brave enough to step right out. She shook her head, and his throat ached. It was as if he'd been opened right up, and as he looked into her eyes he felt a little of the tension running out of his body. He gave a heavy sigh. He couldn't look away.

'Valentino,' she said, and he didn't think he'd ever heard anyone say his name like that. 'All this time, for thirty years, all you've had is . . . loss, and yet now, here, is a young woman who didn't have to seek you out, who could have lived forever making up her own answers to whatever questions she had, and wouldn't that have been easier, wouldn't that have been simpler, in so many ways? But she came anyway. She came for herself. She came for her mother. But perhaps she came for you too. I call that very brave.'

Valentino wanted to take Isabel's hand and hold on to it. Lift it to his lips. Press it to his face. Instead he blinked, mute with gratitude. He looked away, past the pear trees, where somewhere down the coast there was his daughter. Waiting. Wondering. Angry as an axe, and broken-hearted too. He steadied his breathing. Nodded, with something like resolution. After three decades of wilful desertion on his island, it felt as though a boat had appeared on the horizon. He was not the kind of man to wave his arms and send up flares, but if it were a mooring she sought, he would do his best to offer her one.

twenty-two

OLIVIERO WAITED IN THE HALLWAY OF THE ONLY GUEST HOUSE in Marciana Alta. His hands were in his pockets, and he rocked on his heels. It was ten o'clock at night, and the cautious proprietor had regarded him over the top of her spectacles as she asked after his business. He'd called her *signora* with utmost respect, then complimented the wallpaper, the religious painting he could see halfway up the stairs, the smell of someone's dinner that drifted from the back kitchen – bolognese, unmistakably – and explained that he was a friend of Kit Costa, her newest guest. She disappeared up the stairs, her wide bottom cloaked in a flowered skirt, muttering his name as she went, whether to remember it or admonish him, he wasn't sure. She returned a moment later. Too quickly, Oliviero thought, as though she hadn't knocked at all.

He smiled widely, affecting optimism. 'Okay?'

'Okay,' she said. 'To the top of the stairs, the room on the right.' Then, pointing a finger at him, 'No funny business.'

It was down to one of the guests, Steffi Berger, that he was there at all. She'd called him over to her table to praise the chicken, and as her husband was checking on the boys, she'd poured another glass of wine and toasted Oliviero. *We were talking about you today,* she'd said, *another guest and I.* Her tone was unusually playful, and she'd gone on, *The young British woman, Kit. She was wandering the streets of Marciana Alta looking like a sheep who'd lost the rest of her flock.*

As soon as service was over, he'd sought out Valentino. He'd been aware of Valentino's every move that evening, watching how he'd attempted to be his customary self – sharing patter with the French women, indulging the elderly sisters, as he poured wine and set down plates and flitted between the tables – but he knew the effort it took. *Will you turn out the lights for me tonight, at midnight?* Valentino had never asked him to do that before.

Oliviero had spun up the mountain road on his motorbike, past the towers of eerily outlined trees, into the glinting mist of fireflies. He'd felt a tingle of excitement, not knowing if he'd be welcomed, but certain of his mission. When he got to Alta, the roar of the bike was audacious in the quiet streets. He left it in the first space he found, and carried on by foot. With the tourists all but gone, by night the village was like an emptied stage set. Anyone who was left went quietly about his or her own business. The leather worker who sold his wares from a table outside his front door would have his head bent over a plate of *ragù* in his tiny front room. The barkeepers, mixing sweet cocktails for amorous couples, one eye on the television in the corner perhaps, following Serie A. The sharp-elbowed children who slept with their footballs, their bedroom windows open to the moonlit hulk of the Capanne. And somewhere, Kit.

He creaked up the stairs of the guest house and paused at

her door. It was just ajar. With caution, he poked his head in.

'Hello?'

She was standing by the window, and was in the process of pulling on a cardigan. Her arm was stuck, and as she turned, she looked curiously stunted. He saw that underneath she wore a gauzy dress, a nightdress, even; it was light, certainly, for he could see the shape of her thighs through the fabric. He quickly adjusted his gaze, and met her eye. He'd expected a cool reception, but if she was annoyed by his intrusion, it wasn't in the look she gave him. She seemed more embarrassed, and as if she were so wrong-footed that she could barely stand.

'I was ready for bed,' she said, smoothing her cardigan. Then, 'What are you doing here?'

He ran his hands over his hair. 'A messenger.'

'But how did you know?'

'Steffi. At dinner. She was talking.'

'I mean *here*. This place.'

'There's nowhere else to stay in Alta.' He shrugged, offered her a smile.

'I wanted,' said Kit, not quite taking it, 'a night away. To give us all space.' She took a deep breath. 'To breathe,' she said. 'I needed to breathe.'

'I understand,' he said.

'Do you?' then, 'I'm sorry, Oliviero. I'm sorry I didn't say anything to you.'

He relaxed, then. Leant against the doorway, but that felt too jocular, so he shifted again.

'Why would you? You had to speak to him first. It's okay if I come in?'

She seemed to be thinking about it, as if it wasn't a straightforward question, with a straightforward answer.

'Or we could talk downstairs?' he said. 'If there is a lounge, or a . . .'

'Okay,' she said. 'Come in.'

There was a desk in the room, bearing her laptop, a couple of notepads, and the remains of a meal, though it was a stretch to call it that: the cellophane wrapper of a pre-made sandwich, an unopened bag of crisps, a half-drunk bottle of wine. She perched on the edge, pulling her cardigan across her chest. He noticed her puffing a lock of hair from her forehead, the sheen at her temple, for the room was holding all the heat of the day – even he was feeling it. The window behind her was open to the night, and beyond he could see the squares of shutters, the orange tint of the building opposite, lit by wrought-iron street lights. He closed the door behind him, but as the only place to sit was the bed, he stayed standing.

'You know . . . you might not feel it, you probably don't, but . . . you're lucky. You are. That's what I came to say.'

'Right,' said Kit. 'Lucky.'

'I don't mean . . .' His hand went to his head again; he rubbed it back and forth. 'Sorry. You know I don't mean *lucky*, not with everything that happened, but . . .' He hesitated, felt shy suddenly. 'I can see him in you, you know.'

'Really?' She shook her head. 'I don't think so. You, though. You look like him. I didn't think so at first, not at all, but . . .'

'Maybe when people spend a lot of time together, they begin to grow alike.'

'So there's hope for me yet, you mean? Somehow I don't think I'll be sticking around.'

'That's sad,' he said.

'That's sad? *That's* the sad part?'

'It is for him,' he said. 'And for you, I think.'

She slipped from the desk and went to the window.

'Did you know? I mean before, years ago, did he tell you? Is that why you're . . . taking all this in your stride?'

'I knew a little bit, but . . . not everything. Not about you.'

At first he thought she'd broken into inexplicable laughter, her shoulders bouncing up and down.

'Don't cry,' he said. 'Please. He's a good man. The best.'

He laid a hand on her shoulder, and felt her stiffen. He quickly withdrew it. She turned round slowly, and faced him. They'd never stood so close before. He could see the startling blue of her irises; her pupils were the size of moons. A tear rolled down her cheek, followed by another, another, and she just let them go. He lifted a finger, gently touched it to her cheek.

'Don't cry, *signorina*.'

'Please don't do that,' she said, catching hold of his hand.

'Excuse me, I . . .'

She didn't let it go, not at first; she just held his hand, and he held hers. Then she dropped it fast.

'You should go,' she said. 'You were kind to come, but . . . I want to be on my own.'

'You're sad. I can't go. I'll go when you're okay.'

She shook her head at him. 'That'll be a long wait.'

'Listen,' said Oliviero. 'I came here for Valentino, but . . . for you too. I thought of you up here, alone, and . . . I want you to know that you have a friend.'

'A *friend*,' said Kit, and there was something in the way she said it that seemed, to Oliviero, as though she didn't just distrust it, but felt it was insufficient.

There was no music playing in the background, no drink to offer her, none of the understood props and stage settings. And from the way she was looking at him, he knew that what he said next would matter. That she would take it to heart. He hesitated. Then he told her, because of these reasons, not despite them.

'Okay,' he said. 'Maybe more than a friend. If you wanted.' Then, almost to himself, as an afterthought, 'Though I don't know how Valentino would feel about that.'

She looked astounded, her sadness blown away by something else. Shock? He couldn't say. Maybe it had been the wrong time to tell her anything, but now that he'd started, he had to finish.

'You're beautiful,' he said, as though that explained everything.

She pushed him in the chest with both hands, and he stumbled backwards, not expecting it.

'Oliviero, you're my brother. My half-brother.'

He looked at her, dumbly. Wanted to laugh. '*Fratello?*'

Then comprehension slowly dawned. The things she'd said, the things he hadn't, the faulty sense they made, when mis-assembled.

'No,' he said. 'No, I'm not.'

The restaurant's few tables were mostly empty. A couple leant into one another, murmuring, laughing quietly. An elderly man sat with a coffee cup in his hand, a small dog asleep at his feet. There was a trellis of vines running up the wall behind, twisted with fairy lights; a meagre string compared to theirs, but weren't they all? The waiter, Piero, a sallow-faced man in a white apron, shook Oliviero's hand as he extended it, but said without hesitation that they'd stopped serving.

'Come on, man, just a couple of pizzas.'

'Try your luck with Luigi if you want. Be my guest. He's in a bitch of a mood tonight, though. *Signorina*,' he said, bowing to Kit as he switched to English, 'forgive me. Can I offer you a drink?'

When Oliviero went into the kitchen, swinging through the door and shouting out a greeting, he saw that Piero was right. But wasn't Luigi always like that? They weren't exactly friends, but they'd passed the time of day before. He clapped his shoulder.

'It's not too late to make a beautiful woman and, er, me a pizza, is it?'

The response was in Oliviero's own language but nonetheless required a degree of translation. A more colourful version of *If you want a pizza at this time of night, you'll have to make it yourself.*

'No worries,' said Oliviero. 'In fact, that's even better.'

'I've got a date,' said Luigi. 'I need to be gone.'

Luigi's chef's whites were grey, and his T-shirt was damp from standing too close to the oven and the physical effort of kneading dough all night when you were too many pounds overweight.

'If she has any sense, so does she. Before you get there,' said Oliviero.

'Yeah, yeah, funny guy. Leave this place as you found it,' Luigi said, throwing him a key.

He caught it one-handed. 'What, really? I figured I'd clean it up a bit.'

Luigi barrelled out, giving Oliviero the finger as he went. Oliviero picked up a piece of dough, stretched it between his hands and made a disparaging sound. He spun round, orientating himself. He located the flour, the yeast, the salt. He threw it all together with a splash of olive oil, and kneaded it forward and back, over and under, with fast and practised hands. Then he balled his dough, set it in a bowl, and went back to Kit, feeling about as much anticipation as he'd ever felt in his life.

They ate his *pizza fritta* leaning on the kitchen counter. He'd fried the base golden as she watched, while the tomato sauce, just enough for two, was bubbling in a pan. In the cavernous fridge he'd found burrata and he cut indulgent slices of it, scattered basil leaves, crunched black pepper. He liked that she made no attempt to eat delicately. There was tomato sauce on her lips and her fingers were sticky with oil.

'It's one of my favourite things,' he said, '*pizza fritta*, to make and to eat. Valentino always says . . .'

She set down her pizza. 'Sorry, but . . . can we maybe not talk about him?'

'You don't want to?'

'Not tonight.'

'Okay.'

He smiled at her, she smiled back. She lifted her pizza, then paused.

'But you called him Papà,' she said. 'The day that I came. Why did you do that?'

'So you do want to talk about him?'

She shook her head.

They walked back through the deserted village streets, their footfall echoing off the crumbling walls, the snaking alleyways, the rising hillside. In the half-light cast by the street lamps, they couldn't see each other fully, which was perhaps why he said, *You asked me why I called him Papà.*

Earlier, in the guest house bedroom, then in the restaurant kitchen, they'd laughed, drunk, cooked and eaten with immoderation. She seemed different, the Kit who no longer thought his name was Colosimo. It was as if she was walking high on a tightrope, her arms flung wide, so elated at her feat that she gave no thought to the ground below. He didn't want to say, or do, anything that might disrupt this balance. So when she'd asked him how he'd come to Elba, he'd been both brief and vague. But now that the night was all around them, and they were walking so near to one another that their intentions were no less clear for being unspoken, it suddenly felt essential to Oliviero that here, on this strangest of nights, he be honest. That amongst all she didn't know about her mother, or her father, she knew something important about him.

They were standing by a wall, the dark hills falling away from them. Their elbows were side by side, their legs just touching. Oliviero desperately wanted a cigarette. He wanted to turn his lighter in his hands, and draw smoke into his lungs, to tap the ash against the dry stone. But she was so close to him, he daren't move a muscle in case she did too.

'Somewhere out there,' he said, nodding into the black, 'is the Isola di Gorgona. You can't see it, not in the day either, but if you climb to the top of Monte Capanne, you see it then. It's . . . a prison island. That's where my father is.'

'A prison island?'

'Yeah. Like in *The Count of Monte Cristo*. You know? Or Alcatraz.'

'God. I'm sorry.'

'No need for sorry. He was a bastard.'

'What did he do?'

'It's what I did,' he said.

'You? What did you do?'

'It's not a good story. The last girl I told, she didn't like it very much.'

'Not a great chat-up line?'

Valentino was the only one who knew about Eva, although it seemed to Oliviero that even he sometimes forgot it, when he asked Oliviero why he didn't want to stay with any woman for longer than a summer.

'Well, it was twelve years ago, so I was eighteen. But I was an old eighteen, you know? Too old. She was my girl-friend, Eva, my best friend too, had been all through school, and I was going to marry her. But after this . . . this story . . . she changed her mind about everything, so . . . yeah . . .' He took a breath. 'But I'm not talking about that. This is about *mio padre*.'

He told her how his father had been borrowing money, too much money, how he was getting hurt, and he was hurting their family too, just like he always had. Oliviero, using all his courage, had told him he needed to face up to his responsibilities. He'd meant for his father to go to the police, to report the men who were ruining what was left of him. But when the sharks next bit, his *padre* went to bite them back. He'd left one man dead, and another in hospital. He'd come home shaking, blood-soaked, the knife still clutched in his hand, and Oliviero's mother had wept, then run a bath to wash him, and set a fire to burn his clothes. Oliviero had known it wouldn't end there, that when the doorbell next rang, it wouldn't be a man in uniform with a badge in his hand, but somebody seeking a different form of retribution. That was how they worked, that was how it always went. So, eighteen and skinny with it, his poor broken heart banging in his chest, he had reported his father. He'd seen him taken off without fanfare, no sirens or flashing lights.

'I thought I was doing the right thing,' he said to Kit. 'I thought he'd be safer there. Honestly? I thought he deserved it too. But my mother . . . she couldn't forgive me for it. I mean, he used to beat us, me and my brother, and she always found a way to forgive him for that. But betraying your family? Well, apparently not. Then five months later, five months when she was pretty much in hell every day, a car hit her. I thought it was revenge. But it was just some young guy who had recently passed his test. Wrong place, wrong time.'

Caught in his story, he hadn't noticed that Kit had moved a step away from him. Now, when he did, Oliviero patted his pockets for his lighter. He stuck a cigarette between his lips. So it went.

'I came to Elba, and Valentino saved me. That's why I call him Papà. Because I wish he was. Because sometimes, when everything's going right, it feels like he is. Kit, you know how people like to picture Italian families? Everybody eating together, all the generations, all the happy faces? It doesn't exist like that, not for everyone, never for me. But it's what we have at the Mille Luci. Truly, it's what we have. That's what Valentino made.'

He looked at her. 'I don't know, maybe it sounds weird to you. But . . . I know about the worst things that people close to you can do. Maybe I've done them myself. Eva thought so, anyway. I wanted to tell you because . . . I don't know . . .'

Kit took his unlit cigarette from his lips and kissed him. Just once. Then she handed it back to him, as if he'd somehow dropped it. *There you are*, she said.

* * *

The key to the guest house stuck in the lock, but then they were in, creaking up the stairs, Kit first, Oliviero following. At her room, she stopped and turned.

'Are you here because you feel sorry for me?' she asked.

'Here? At this door?'

'Yes,' she said.

'No. Why? Do you feel sorry for me?'

'That's not why I'm here.'

Oliviero opened his mouth to say something, but she cut in before he could. 'I'm sick of it all, feeling so sad, so lost, so . . . I just want to feel something different, and at last, at *last* my mind's giving me a break, because ever since you said you weren't who I thought you were, all I've been wondering is what it would be like to . . . kiss you.'

'You already did that.'

'That wasn't a kiss.'

'It wasn't?'

She pushed open the door and took his hand, led him inside. He heard it shut behind them. He couldn't take his eyes from her.

'Oliviero, you have no idea how much this amazes me. How what a complete and utter . . .' she searched for the word, '*holiday* it is, to feel like this. And I know it's not going to last, this feeling. I know that other things, far more complicated, important, far more *real* things, probably, are going to come back with a vengeance, and they have to, but for now . . . just for now . . . because it's been so long, since I even . . .'

She didn't get to finish, because his lips were on hers, pressing, parting, so soft and so warm that everything was already dissolving except for the kiss. Then her hands were inside his shirt, flicking the buttons, dropping to find his belt, his zip, and then they were falling back onto the bed, clasped to one another. It creaked beneath them, and he thought of the woman downstairs, *no funny business*, and wanted to laugh, to tell Kit, because he figured she'd laugh too, but he was afraid of the moment going, of the things she'd talked of crowding their way back.

'Are you sure?' he said, whispering into her ear, his voice already breaking. Then he felt her hand on him, guiding him in, and he emitted a low moan. He closed his eyes, then opened them again. Their two bodies pushed together, desire rising and rising until it flooded them both, and they clung to one another, their gasps swallowed by kisses. Slowly, lingeringly, they found their way back to the surface, a place that was brighter than when they'd left it.

twenty-three

KIT WAS SITTING ON A BENCH, WAITING FOR THE BLUE BUS. IT was early, but already the heat was everywhere. She tipped her head back, and behind her sunglasses she closed her eyes, letting the warmth suffuse her.

It had been an unanticipated night. She'd experienced oblivion, certainly, but also a hyper-awareness, every part of her vital with feeling. Oliviero had slid from beside her at first light, giving her a rueful smile, for there were guests at the Mille Luci needing breakfast, he'd said. She'd watched him as he got dressed, as he buttoned his jeans and pulled on his shirt. One shoe had been kicked under the bed and he dropped to retrieve it, stretching, as loose-limbed as a big cat. She wanted to reach out, touch him again. To her, his body seemed immodest even clothed, and she revelled in the novelty of being permitted to think this. After the second time, they'd lain on their sides, facing one another. His eyes had travelled the length of her. He'd touched a finger to the tiny ring in her belly button.

'I've had that forever. One of those teenage things and . . . I kept it.'

'I like it,' he'd said.

'I'd made my peace with where I came from,' she said. 'That's why I got it. I was eighteen. My mum was everything to me.'

'So you got your belly button pierced?'

She'd laughed. 'I know, right? And she hated it, my mum. The irony. What is it?'

He was looking at her, his head tipped. *So much beauty,* he'd said, and she'd rolled onto him, pressed her hips to his, her lips to his.

Would it happen again between them? She didn't know. But as he'd stood at the door, his hand on the handle, he'd said, *What about the concert?* Then, with a grin, *Maybe you've changed your mind about that too?*

She hesitated. 'Well, things *are* different now . . .'

'Very different.'

'I haven't listened to the CD yet.'

'No?'

'But I will. I brought it with me.'

'Really? You did?'

'I did.'

'And so you'll come tonight?'

'Yes.'

The bus wheezed into view, and Kit stood up, flinging out an arm to stop it. She took a seat just behind the driver. It lurched forward, then was off, taking the twists and turns with the same bravado as on the way up. Perhaps it was the only way to drive a perilous road like this. Inching forward, peeping around corners would never get you anywhere.

Before Oliviero had left, she'd asked if she could show him

a picture, and he'd said, *Yes, yes, please*, as though he already knew of whom she meant. She'd had the same photograph in her bag as she spoke to Valentino, but it would have felt like a betrayal to bring them face to face like that. Suddenly, before he went back down the hill to the Mille Luci, Kit wanted Oliviero to know her mum, even in the sparest fashion. It was a liberty, she knew, a provocation in its own way, for Rosa would surely have flinched to be subjected to his gaze, the Italian man who just moments before had been entwined with her daughter. She would have disapproved in all the obvious ways, and probably some Kit couldn't even imagine.

'That's your *mamma*?' he'd said.

'I don't know why I want to show you. But I do.'

He held it carefully, and she noticed that.

'I don't look much like her, do I?'

'She's *bellissima*. So yes, I think you look like her. What was her name?'

'Rosa. I can't begin to tell you how much I miss her.'

She'd felt his arms around her, holding her tightly.

'When are you talking to Valentino?' he asked, in a low voice.

'Later. I don't know.' Then she said, 'He will tell me the truth, won't he?'

'The truth? It's all he has.'

She could have asked him more, but she didn't want to. She hadn't before, and she wouldn't now. What she wanted was for him to be the man on the motorbike who'd made her desire something she had near enough forgotten all about. After he'd gone, she'd stood in the middle of the room, looking at the shipwrecked bed, the strewn sheets, and felt a ripple of absurd pleasure. When she'd told him she wanted to breathe, she'd meant it. It just turned out that that she hadn't meant breathing alone.

She got off the bus first in Marciana Marina, delaying her return. She saw the stage in the piazza being readied for the concert that night, a poster with the skinny shape of Neil Younger clutching his guitar. She smiled to think of their date, the unlikeliness of it. For all her trepidation about what the day might have in store for her, the night held the prospect of enjoyment. Winding through the alleyways, she thought she recognised Nina and Lucille ducking into a boutique, their hands already full of shopping bags. She peeped in as she passed and saw Nina holding up a vivid kaftan, Lucille nodding approval. They'd loved shopping together, Kit and her mum. The clothes had been the least of it.

She wandered along the palm-lined front, past the fruit-bowl-coloured buildings, the old men sitting on benches, reading their newspapers over the tops of their spectacles. When she reached the water, she clambered across the rocks, a brown paper bag of peaches in her hand, and took a seat on the furthest one she could reach. As she dangled her legs, the waves slapped and pulled at her, splashing her dress, the breeze whipping spray up into her face. She ate the sweet peaches and let the juice trickle down her bare arm. She squinted at the sun, felt it tingling on her shoulders, her chest.

She thought of Rosa. Or, more precisely, she thought of *not* having to think of her, the unsought liberty of not needing to consider how her mum would have viewed her actions. The mess of her emotions as Oliviero had stepped towards her, looking at her in that way. Then the naked thrill of realising he wasn't who she'd thought he was, and how swiftly she'd succumbed to this new, possible person, almost as if it had been bound to happen all along; how the information had travelled to her brain, when her body had already seemed to have made its mind up anyway.

For Rosa, things were always either right or wrong. People were either good or bad. She hadn't believed in the existence of grey areas, much less chosen to inhabit such spaces. It hadn't always been easy, being a teenager under her mum's watch. Kit's emotions, her body, her desires had all been unruly. She'd looked at her peers and hadn't felt exceptional – they too had seemed to be similarly possessed – but when she'd tried to picture her mum at the same age, all she could think of was somebody unrelentingly controlled; supercilious, with sleek hair and dewy skin, intimidatingly righteous. On one occasion the teenage Kit had come home swaying, too many bitter apple ciders drunk in a barn at sundown, desperately trying to arrange her hair to hide the marks of a village boy's clumsy kisses. Her mum's look of disappointment had sobered her instantly, but she was sick anyway, all across the kitchen floor. Rosa had set a coffee pot on the stove, making Kit drink a double espresso while explaining the importance of *la bella figura*, of presenting yourself in the right way, of people thinking well of you; an ineffably Italian lecture. Inexplicably it was still a good memory: the two of them in the cottage kitchen, the hiss of the coffee pot, a plastic bucket balanced on her knees, Kit feeling more *brutta* than *bella figura*. She had always felt acutely that she was the only person her mum had; she couldn't bear the thought of not being enough.

Much as Rosa had been unforgiving of others, she'd held herself to an even higher account. She'd loved food, but never ate more than was sensible. She'd adored flamboyance, designed her dresses accordingly, but always, herself, remained as controlled as a pirouetting ballerina. She hadn't stood for the ravages of time, barely of disease, and had been immaculate almost to the last. *She's extraordinarily brave*, the doctor had said to Kit more than once. And she had been. Faced with the same, Kit feared she would crumple, inside and out. Her mum's force of spirit had been, in part, made of lack of compromise; she was capable of adjusting her receptors so they didn't pick up anything she didn't want. For all her romantic cynicism, she had never permitted outright sorrowful talk. She'd turned off the radio whenever the news had come on.

Before Kit had left the room, she'd listened to the album that Oliviero had given her. She'd filled that small space with 'Only Love Can Break Your Heart' and every line had cut her. It was Rosa's song, perhaps even hers too. But, she'd thought, as she'd played it over again, perhaps only something in working order could break. Was life with her mum worth the pain of a life without her? The answer had to be yes. With Valentino, there was no such equation. No exactness to account for how she must think or feel, now that the fact of him could not be denied.

It was afternoon by the time she returned to the Mille Luci. She found Valentino in the grounds, and they fell into step as if it had all been planned.

'You're okay to walk a little?' he asked. 'Can you manage it, with your ankle?'

'It's fine,' she said. 'I'd prefer that.'

They went into the olive grove beside the hotel. The ground was dusty underfoot, and they followed a rough path through the silver leaves and twisted trunks to a bench. The sea was at their feet, the sky all around them. The air was full of the warm scent of rosemary.

'I built this bench,' he said, 'when I first came here.'

'It's a nice spot.'

The breeze took Kit's hair, blowing it across her face. She pulled it back, quickly twisted it into a loose plait. She wanted to look and feel composed. She crossed her legs tightly. She was aware of all the details, and their faint imperfections: Valentino in a cotton shirt, creased at the back; her dress blue cotton, with the stain of spilt sun cream at the hem that she'd only noticed as she'd followed him across the terrace. Her throat stung, as though the age-old anger on behalf of her mum was rising, reasserting its presence. He said her name: *Kit*. He asked her to look at him, so she did. The dent in his chin. The darkening of the skin beneath his eyes. The iron-coloured stubble that marked his cheeks. His dark lashes, long for a man, and almost a kind of frivolity in such a rough-hewn face. She saw nothing of herself in him. She met his eye, and was grateful for the sunglasses pushed down over her own.

'Imagine,' she said to him, 'that I know nothing.'

He nodded. 'Okay,' he said. 'Then . . . first, this. I do not blame your mother for the decision she made. I don't.'

'Which decision?'

'To tell you that I was dead. Because, you see, the last time she spoke to me . . . I might as well have been. Honestly, I probably wanted to be. I think . . . she only wanted to do the best thing for you.'

He rubbed his hands together, shaking his head as if to clear it.

'Okay,' he said, 'from the beginning.'

Kit listened, as still as a painting. Loose strands of hair blew about her face, sweat pricked at her armpits, but she didn't move. He spoke of the wife he'd fallen in love with at first glance. The child who wouldn't come, and how that absence became an inescapable presence, an invisible but constant weight. The mutual friend whose support and compassion had become something else, and the drink-fuelled night where the two of them had crossed a line he hadn't even known was there, because when you've never before been tempted, you don't see the line, you don't need to. He stopped. Reached for her hand.

'None of this is any good,' he said, in a creaking voice.

Kit let her fingers be lifted by his, for one second, barely that, but it felt too long and she pulled her hand away. Her fingers were hot, and she spread them like starfish against her dress.

'My mum did that to her friend?' Her voice was shot with disbelief – not her irreproachable mum, so refined, so controlled – but inside she was making mental adjustments. Rosa's steely talk of self-reliance, her absence of meaningful friendships – perhaps it made sense, for she'd seen up close how some women could be: in fact, she knew better than anyone. Wouldn't Kit have preferred to have heard this truth from her mum, to feel a sense of Rosa's own culpability? No daughter sought a morality tale, but growing up she'd felt what she'd presumed to be the weight of Rosa's wronging, and at times had staggered beneath it. She was hit by a pang of outrage, fast as a punch. Never before would she have imagined that she'd believe Valentino so quickly, but what reason could he have to lie?

'Did you even know that she was pregnant?' she said, her lips tight.

'Yes. I knew.'

'That she was pregnant? That I was yours?'

'Yes,' he said.

He was telling the truth, he had to be, for it was the un-wanted answer, wasn't it? The harder one to give, and to receive – it would have been so easy for him to plead a kind of ignorance. She glanced at him, and he seemed to be about to say something, but was hesitating at the edge of it.

'What is it?' she said. 'Tell me.'

'I told my wife about . . . the baby. After doing . . .' his hand went to his head and he rubbed it, 'the wrong thing, I wanted to do something right.'

'And what was that?'

'To take responsibility. For her to know what I'd done. And . . . to be a father to . . . to you.'

Kit shook her head. She felt something dangerous growing inside her, like the start of a flame, just a flicker, but one that could jump in height, lick its way out of her.

'My wife. Bianca. She died. That same night. And to this day I hold myself responsible, I *am* responsible, for her death.'

The fight, the boat, the storm. As he spoke of such things, it was hard to look at him, and Kit's hand went to her mouth. For all the heat of the day, she felt cold. He talked of how, afterwards, he was broken in all the ways it was possible for a person to be. How at last he'd answered the ringing telephone, and it was her mum, telling him that the growing baby was no more.

Kit stayed quite still. 'She told you that she'd lost me?'

Perhaps Valentino had noted the look on her face, for his voice was thick with reassurance. 'She was protecting you,' he said. 'I'm certain of it. I was a bad person to be around, so angry and so sad . . . After Bianca died, I wrote your mother a letter, just a few lines, saying I couldn't see anyone, couldn't talk to anyone, and that included her, and that I was sorry I couldn't be more . . . gallant. Is that the word you'd say? I don't know. I don't think there is a word, for that situation. Perhaps I didn't acknowledge how bad she must have been feeling herself, and the strain of the pregnancy added to that, and . . . that was unforgivably selfish. She made the decision that she felt was right. For herself, and for you.'

Kit stayed quite still. How were you supposed to think coherently when the things somebody was saying cleaved you down the middle? *There are two sides to every coin.* That was something she never heard her mum say, in English or Italian, in thought or in deed. Until the very end, Rosa had always thought she was right, painting herself – surely, even just with her few words, her reluctance and pained expression whenever Kit so much as tiptoed near the subject – as the wronged woman. Guilt, then, almighty guilt, for it was not one lie, but two, even three, seeping in with her illness and contaminating her just the same. Forcing the words out of her. *He didn't die, Kit.*

'Your mother had always been a good friend to us both. And she was . . . a fine woman. A principled woman.'

Kit made a small noise of derision, and Valentino blinked fast.

'She made a mistake, just as I made a mistake, and . . . The storm kept raging after Bianca died, that storm at sea, whatever forces had brought it on us . . . it took me, and she saw that, she felt it, so she saved herself the only way she knew. I never heard from her again, and somehow that felt right.'

'But she told me you broke her heart.'

'Broke her heart?' He shook his head. 'I don't know how

she felt about me. All I knew then was that everything I touched I ruined.'

'She wasn't just collateral, though, was she? She was part of it. Just as much to blame.'

'For how I was with her afterwards, when Bianca died, she was right to hate me for that. All I cared about was what I'd lost, and my part in it. Her feelings, they . . . did not figure, and that was unforgivably selfish. She told me that I'd never hear from her again, and, honestly? I was glad. Well, not glad, nothing could make me glad, but . . . I didn't do anything to stop her, you know. I told her, in fact, that it was the right thing. I've always been very sorry, for that. Perhaps . . . despite what I'd said about wanting to be a father to you, she knew I would struggle to do that, even if I tried, because I would never be able to look at her without thinking of what I'd lost because of the two of us . . .'

'And because of me,' finished Kit.

She saw the colour of his eyes change, the blue grow darker. She dipped her head.

'So she was right, wasn't she?' she said.

She felt a very light touch on her chin, tipping her back, turning her to face him. It was so barely there, it could hardly be called overfamiliar, for it was gone, the touch, as soon as it had come, and she was left looking at him. Looking *for* him.

'Your mother deserved better. She did. I hope she found it.'

'We were happy together, just her and me,' said Kit. 'Maybe we shouldn't have been, but we were.' She glanced down at her hands. When she tried to speak, her voice fractured. 'I'm sorry,' she said. 'For your loss.'

'And I'm very sorry for your loss too,' he said.

Although his sorrow was apparent, Kit knew better than to

imagine it was for her mum – the worst of friends, the catastrophic start of it all. It was for another woman altogether. What would it have been like for Rosa, to carry that burden down the years? Was it her shame that stopped her ever telling the truth, holding on to the fury of the forsaken wife, as well as her own for being so swiftly abandoned? The two lapping over one another, melding, ever intensifying.

She thanked him, quietly, and wondered what – if anything – they were supposed to do next.

'Whatever you think of me,' Valentino said, 'I'm glad you're here.' Then, haltingly, cautiously, as if losing his confidence in his command of English, 'I'd like to get to know you. If you'd let me.'

Until he said it, she didn't know how much she'd wanted to hear it. The rush of gratitude, of relief, was flooring. Perhaps that was why she heard herself asking him one last question, as though it was an ordinary day, with an ordinary night to come.

'There's this concert, and Oliviero's asked me to go. Why don't you come too?'

Kit put on a yellow dress. It was the colour of the butterflies that flitted across the Mille Luci lawn. It was the colour of the door of Deer Leap, when she'd come home from school one day and found her mum in paint-splashed overalls, triumphant at the vibrancy she'd brought to their tawny cottage in the woods. Whatever Kit hadn't known about her mum's life, she'd known *her*. And she was sure that Rosa really had loved Valentino. That their one night together would have been the culmination of a long time wanting, wondering, fighting with her own conscience and morality code, and that before it had been the worst thing to ever happen to her, perhaps, however wrongly, it had been the best. She hadn't told Valentino that her mum had, as far as she knew, never gone near another man for the rest of her life. And that she'd never had another best friend either, except perhaps for her own daughter. That much had seemed unnecessary; there was enough wreckage. Even though their story wasn't hers, Kit felt somehow part of it. She *was* part of it. She was the minuscule, unconscious catalyst, whose very being had been a bomb. His translation, *figlia illegittima*, was far more fitting than love child, for even if her mum had fallen for him, Valentino's own descent had nothing to do with *amore*.

She turned in front of the mirror, looking at the shape of herself in the dress. It was loose on her, but less so than before she came, when she'd tried it on in the empty bathroom of the Bristol flat, surrounded by cupboards still full of pots and packs of pills that had been good for nothing in the end. She'd looked like a ghost in a party frock, then. Now, even in just a few days, the Italian sun had browned her chest, her frame had filled a little. She tipped her chin, pulled back her shoulders. She wished her mum had found a way to tell her the full truth, to acknowledge her part; wouldn't it have armed Kit better, to grow up knowing the wild ways that life could work, how even a true friend could lose their compass and spin off course – everywhere the boundless possibility for loss, so hold fast, *amore mio*, keep your nerve? Wouldn't that have been a valuable lesson?

That night, Kit was determined to stand in a town square, among a crush of people. To hold a drink in her hand and listen to a boy from Milano sing songs like Neil Young. There would be a man beside her who was not, after all, an ogre, nor was he inconsequential, but someone who, much like Rosa, had got things wrong and been devoured by the consequences. Someone who, despite him telling her the most important facts of her life, she still felt she scarcely knew, and certainly not enough to call him *Father*. And Oliviero, who she barely knew either – unless you counted the shape of him, the feel of him, the sounds he made in the night – he'd be there too. Oliviero would be surprised, perhaps, to have his beloved Valentino along with them, but probably not unhappy. Had she done it, in part, for him? Asked Valentino along because he'd told her she was lucky, and she wanted to show him that she was ready to believe in the possibility of this perhaps, one day, being proved true?

She eyed herself. The thought that Rosa would never know about any of it was unimaginable. Surely, just surely, she'd have to make herself heard? An invisible thread had always connected them; either could pull, and the other would feel it. A small tug of uncertainty as Kit made a redoubtable decision. A sense of surety, like the snap of a rein, as she embarked upon something with her mum's blessing. But here, in this place? Nothing. She had no sense of anything.

twenty-four

AFTER KIT HAD LEFT THE OLIVE GROVE, VALENTINO STAYED. HE leant forward, dropping his chin into his hands. He'd talked more about himself in the last two days than he had in thirty years, and it had left him feeling scattered. Other people now carried little pieces of him. It wasn't that he didn't trust that their hands were safe, only that it was odd, to live this way in the world again. For that was how it felt. When you walked about buttoned up with secrets, your heart unknown, your existence was less patent. Now, when Isabel looked at him across the breakfast room, she'd see a man with cracks in his facade, the unstable foundations within. Could their exchanges ever be normal again? If he remarked on the heat of the sun, the sweetness of the strawberries, asked after her plans for the day, would his words have lost their easy currency? Oliviero had known much already, but not about the baby. He'd winced as Valentino had told him, as though it was a story he hadn't wanted to know. And Kit.

Kit Costa. His flesh and blood. What a strange thing it was, that a moment of madness between two people who should never have got that close could result in a whole new person. Arms and legs, a head and a heart. It shouldn't be that easy to make somebody else.

She was a young woman – whole, complete – and he'd marvelled at her. She was unknowable, but imaginable; and what he'd missed was, paradoxically, tangible. He hadn't carried her about the world, told her the names of things, nor scooped her up when she'd fallen down. He hadn't seen his whole life in the palm of her hand, the lobe of her tiny ear. He hadn't seen the pearl-white glint as her first tooth had pushed through. No legs finding steps, or tiny footprints left in beach sand. Scraped knees and elbows, chickenpox, a day spent in pyjamas with a doll under each arm. Pasta sauce stains on her cheeks. Satchels and storybooks. One sock up, one sock down. Loopy handwriting in jotters. Poems, love letters. Legs getting longer, skirts getting shorter. Lips too bright. When kisses on lips became cheeks became hugs became quick waves, already on her way out. Perhaps being a parent was a lifetime of small goodbyes. From the days when you were essential – life itself – to a thing to be navigated, negotiated, tolerated. He would never know these things; he could only guess at them – vividly, sorrowfully.

Valentino stood up, and felt his bones creak. He was sixty-three years old, and a father for the first time. He felt ancient, yet a novice. She hadn't taught him how to be a father. They hadn't found their way together, hand in hand. She had never needed him, so now she probably never would. But perhaps they could be friends, or something like.

Costa. Her mother must have married, for that hadn't been her surname when he'd known her. He realised, then, how few questions he'd asked Kit. How the shock of her existence had blitzed away all sensible thought. When she knew she was pregnant, Kit's mother had moved away, keeping in touch with nobody, but how had she ended up in England? Had Kit been born there? Valentino wound his way back through the olive grove, the dust settling on his shoes. He'd been insensitive, he could see that now. Was it illness that had taken her mother? Or an accident, a sudden swipe? He hadn't even asked. She was grieving, and all he'd been able to think about was his own loss, one so old that it should have found its place by now, as a small hollow in his chest, or a scar that ran the length of his body but was no longer raw.

Bianca and Kit, much less Kit's mother, could not be held in the same thought. They were inextricably linked, but they should never have existed together. That was the bare fact of it. When he'd said he wanted to get to know Kit, he'd meant it, but it was more complicated than that. Opening himself to his daughter felt like closing a part of him that belonged to his wife.

Valentino walked back towards the hotel. The sun was full on the walls and they shone white. The silken-headed palms bobbed and swayed in the breeze. It was so solid, and had been his home, his absolution – if there existed such a thing – for nearly thirty years. So why did he feel as if the ground beneath it was shifting, cracking? As if it might all slide off the clifftop and into the sea, the tangles of lights coming down behind it. Sinking. Air all but gone.

When Kit's mum had laughed, she'd tossed her head, and the black of her hair had shone like a blackbird's wing – blue and gold. She was clever, and used words he didn't understand, darting over them in conversation like they were no big thing.

When she and Bianca were together they'd made a formidable pair, and he'd enjoyed the sight of them, but never before too much. He'd always thought her impressive, but perhaps a little impervious too. Then she'd showed a side he hadn't known existed: a willingness to listen, a sympathy for what he, Valentino, was feeling. He'd stepped outside of himself, told her of his deepest worries, but she'd reassured him. Her company had felt simple, and it had made him feel good. Powerful again. Attractive, even. How pathetically easily he'd been intoxicated by these things.

When she came to tell him about the baby she was expecting, her nails had been painted deep plum; he'd noticed them because she'd drummed her fingers on the table as she spoke. He'd been struck, then, by her independence. Perhaps her guilt had shaped her that way, but she'd made no obvious demands of him as she wrapped her coat tightly over her not-yet-rounded stomach. Except he'd said, *I want to do this right*, and she'd blinked at him. *Really?* she'd said, and she'd given him a smile that was full of complication, for she knew that doing it right meant telling Bianca. He'd seen then that she hadn't expected that from him, and as he'd said it, and witnessed the pleasure it brought her, the fear too, the no little sorrow, he'd realised that he could perhaps have escaped after all. But it was done now. Too late. And he knew his own conscience could not have tolerated it any other way. Later, as he'd prepared himself for telling Bianca, a small thought had reared itself. *It means I work down there, at least*. For that had been a fear, had it not, that for all their trying, he wasn't good for it? With a flicker of what he knew was stupidity, he'd wondered if it might, in some way, be a strange kind of comfort to her. That their time would surely come too, unless it was Bianca who had the problem. In which case it only made everything worse. That her traitorous friend, so brazenly fertile, could open her legs just once and come away with a baby.

It was no good. If he tried to think of it, it just led to pain. The kind of pain that creased him over. Had him pound the walls of his villa, willing it to go away, knowing that it never would, and it never should.

He saw, then, the boys from Torino, ambling down to the pool. One dribbled a beach ball across the lawn, flicking it with his heels, laughing as he fudged it. Another had an inflatable lounger, as yellow as the sun, tucked beneath his arm. The third trailed, intently tapping at a phone, perhaps swapping messages with a girlfriend back home, or stoking the fire of a new romance. Would he want to be them, exchange what he knew for that which they didn't?

'Hey, excuse me!'

Ricardo, angular as a stork, darted over, his lilo bumping his side.

'Tonight, could we bring some dates to dinner? Would that be okay? For us to be six this evening?'

Valentino was endlessly accommodating, but he said, 'Tonight? Ah, tonight could be difficult.'

'Oh.' The boy looked immediately crestfallen. He rallied. 'What about just for drinks then, before?'

Valentino hesitated.

'It's just we've been talking about the hotel, and they've never been, and it's much nicer than where they're staying, and . . .'

'Of course,' he said. 'For *aperitivo*.'

They shook hands, Ricardo thanking him profusely, then bounding back to his friends, already sharing what he considered to be good news. Valentino felt a prick of guilt. They were decent boys, not so cavalier. He should have let them have their dinner guests. He walked on towards his villa, his head bent, and for all he had to think about, it nagged at him, this pointless denial of their pleasure. It wasn't his way. He stopped at the door, his chest aching for the privacy that lay beyond the walls. It wasn't that he hadn't wanted them to be happy, these careless youths. It was because, as the boy had veered towards him, his face full of expectation and enquiry, Valentino had felt suddenly phenomenally tired. It had been the simple dread of being asked for something when he had nothing left to give. His hand on his door, he sighed. He turned and walked back to the pool.

'Hey, boys!'

Their red plastic ball smacked the surface. The water was so blue, dancing with sunlight. They turned hopeful faces, and he told them that it was his mistake: it was okay for dinner after all. Three guests would be no problem. No problem at all.

It was cool in the cottage. He ran a glass of water and drank it quickly standing at the sink. Then he crossed into his bedroom. It was a small, simple room, as unadorned as a monk's chamber. Uneven whitewashed walls, a hard wooden floor, and a window that looked out onto nothing but the sea. He went over to the wardrobe and reached into the back of it. Past the shirts, his thick winter coat, a tartan scarf he'd bought once in the depths of a Venetian winter. His hand closed around a tin. When was the last time he'd opened it? Years ago. Seven? Eight? No, he knew exactly when. Six years ago. After he'd spoken briefly to Isabel, saying Bianca's name out loud for the first time since Oliviero's arrival. Afterwards he'd felt the need to hold his wife again, even just the two-dimensional, unbearably unreachable version of her. The feeling that possessed him now was different to that. As he opened the tin, he realised that he was looking for permission, and the idea was so pathetic that he almost closed it again right then, but he'd already caught a glimpse of her hair, a strand caught by beach wind, the perfect heart of her face, the flash of her smile. He took out the photograph, and held it delicately. Then another. Another. If he was looking for a blessing from her, he wasn't finding it. If he was trying to find a new way to say sorry, he'd run out a long time ago. And if he was trying to make himself feel better, it wasn't working.

The rest of the afternoon slipped away, and he hadn't realised that he was crying, and certainly not out loud, until he saw Oliviero's face peering around the corner of the door.

'Sorry. I'm so sorry. I heard . . . you, and . . .'

Oliviero slid inside the room, as if trying to make his presence as subtle as possible.

Valentino rubbed his face with both hands. His cheeks ached. He gathered his pictures, placing them back into the tin with less care than he would have wanted. He felt like he'd been caught in the act of something illicit, his tears the least of his shame.

'I didn't want to intrude,' said Oliviero, his eyes still wide. 'I just came to see . . . You're usually out by now, people are asking after you, and . . .'

The boy was floundering.

'I'm coming,' Valentino said, a little sharply. Then reset himself. 'Of course. No problem. I'm coming. I'm sorry.'

'Are you okay?'

He nodded.

'And Kit, is she . . .' He stopped. 'Is that . . . your wife?'

Valentino glanced up and saw Oliviero gesturing to the tin.

There weren't any framed photographs about the hotel, not even in the private spaces of his villa. He'd never slid a faded snapshot from his wallet, passed it to him saying, *This was my Bianca*. It was their wedding picture that lay on top of the tin, and as Oliviero came closer, Valentino held it up to him as if to say, *See what I had, see what I lost*.

He could remember everything about that day, and the night that had followed. To him the photograph was like the postage stamp on an envelope, when the letter inside contains all the deepest secrets in the world. They were kissing to order, the photographer instructing them as he looked for his shot, and consequently there was caution in their posture, a stiffness in their limbs that was familiar to neither of them. Rice had been thrown, and their guests had their hands full of sugared almonds; wishes for good luck and long life and fertility had been all about them. Of all the pictures in the tin, it hurt to hold this one perhaps the most of all. Bianca had looked into their future that day, and seen all the children they'd have together. They'd set to work that night, certain that nine months on they'd recount to their firstborn how they were made of so much love. And then the things that they wouldn't tell – that confetti was still in their hair, that their breath had been sweet with wedding wine as they'd murmured *vita mia, vita mia*, and how they'd peeled off each other's clothes as if strange and delicate fruit had lain beneath. Oh, but he had let her down in all the ways he could.

'Yes. That's her.' He fastened the lid of the tin and took a deep breath. 'Shall we go?' Then, 'We have a date afterwards, do we not?'

Oliviero's discomfort was obvious. 'Are you sure,' he edged, seeming almost to squirm before him, 'that you want to go? That it's the right thing?'

The invitation had been unexpected, it was true: first Kit's cautious delivery, then Valentino's awkward acceptance, as though, if only they could see it, it was a natural thing for the three of them to do.

'She asked me,' he said, 'so I said yes.'

'You don't feel like you need to talk some more? There must be so much to say, to . . . unpick. It's been a shock, that's all, for both of you, and . . .'

He was pacing, his face choked with what, to Valentino, looked like guilt. He only remembered then about the lights. He'd woken at three o'clock in the morning and they had still been blazing. *Turn them off at midnight*, he'd told Oliviero, and he'd never before let him down. But for Valentino, after the day he'd had, such an oversight was inconsequential. Oliviero had no need to feel bad.

'If you're concerned about last night,' he said, 'it's nothing, it doesn't matter.'

Oliviero stopped. He looked more culpable than ever, which made Valentino wonder if he wasn't thinking about something else. At breakfast he'd observed, for all the thrumming inside his own head, that Oliviero had had a particular lightness about him, but also that he was attempting to contain it, as if he hadn't thought it appropriate. He had looked, thought Valentino, almost as if he'd been holding onto the string of a particularly spirited helium balloon, his feet tripping, heels lifting. Was Kit the reason?

He knew he had no right to think, or say, anything where she and Oliviero were concerned. He must know that.

'*Andiamo*,' he said, clapping Oliviero's shoulder, affecting ease. They'd done this so many times, and tonight, the first part of the evening at least, need be no different. '*Aperitivo*. Dinner. Everything business as usual.'

twenty-five

KIT WORE A YELLOW DRESS, AND OLIVIERO MUSTERED A LOW
whistle as he met her at the gate after dinner.

'You don't mind that I asked him too?' she said.

When he leant in to kiss her on both cheeks, he noticed that
she held onto him for longer than was necessary, and despite
everything, he was glad of that. He'd wanted to greet her
differently, pull her into a proper embrace, tell her that he'd
been thinking about her all day, but when it came to it, he
couldn't.

'Are you okay?' she asked, her head tipped, appraising
him.

'Me? Sure. Are *you* okay?'

'Yes,' she said. 'I think . . . yes.'

Valentino appeared then, wearing a white shirt and navy
linen trousers. He looked crisp, but informal. He grinned, and
said *buonasera* benevolently, expansively, and almost as if the
three of them were convening for the first time.

'They say it's going to rain later tonight,' he said, 'but I
think we'll be lucky.'

With one hand on Oliviero's shoulder, and the other somewhere near Kit, he led them to the car.

'Is this strange?' said Kit, as they sped into the dark turns, headlights flashing. 'It is, isn't it?' and she laughed, shrilly, and Oliviero heard Valentino gamely joining in, so he turned up the music, and it was 'Harvest Moon', lilting and lifting and jangling, but here, more than anything else, putting a stop to more conversation. He saw Valentino's fingers tap against the steering wheel, and he wished they could keep on driving, giving him an extension of this moment, this rhythm, this *hope*. He saw Kit stare out of the window, her shoulders lifting with a sigh, and he felt more tenderly towards her than one night, surely, gave him a right to. Already, perhaps, he was imbuing their time together with the particular tint of nostalgia that only an impending sense of the end can bring.

Earlier, for the first time in a long time, Oliviero had prayed. He'd knelt and clasped his hands together, begun with *Padre nostro, che sei nei cieli*. If he'd had time, he would have taken his motorbike back up into the hills, and gone to the tiny San Francesco chapel in Alta, or to the church of Santa Chiara in Marciana Marina. But the guests were already assembling on the terrace, Abi popping corks and pouring Prosecco. His antipasti still needed to be plated, and there'd been a tray full of grissini just tipping their prime in the oven. And Valentino, Valentino was circulating, seemingly restored, and his rallying seemed to make it all the worse. If Oliviero hadn't found him bent over his tin of photographs earlier, awash in a sea of all that he'd lost, he wouldn't have needed, quite so urgently, to place his hands together in prayer. They could have tripped out together as a trio, some kind of fragile but optimistic bond between them. The inevitable day would have come, but at least they could have had that night. God hadn't helped. Or, rather, He'd told Oliviero what he already knew; that he had no choice but to tell Kit and Valentino the one thing that neither of them would ever want to hear. The yearning strains of a harmonica filled the car and Oliviero stared out of the window, trying to work out how he could possibly do it.

With its temporary stage and throngs of people, the town piazza was dressed for a summer's night. There, the heat that had hung heavy all day was like a *forno*, contained within its walls and ragingly consistent. Oliviero had spotted the boys from Torino among the crowd, looking as though they couldn't believe their luck as they draped their arms around the girls they'd brought along. Theirs would be an effervescent night, and the songs they heard would be the soundtrack to their anticipation. He steered Kit and Valentino to a different area, before anybody recognised them.

They stood shoulder to shoulder, glasses of cold beer in their hands, as the skinny boy from Milano wandered on with his guitar around his neck. He perched on the edge of a stool and cocked the microphone towards him. He spoke in rapid, staccato Italian, but when he began to sing, it was as if some-thing else opened up inside of him, and a different person altogether emerged, with a Western drawl and a nasal tip and songs of sweetness and sorrow. You might be able to do a good impression, Oliviero thought, but you could never really know what it was like to be somebody else.

He was feeling an old, familiar pain: unwanted knowledge. It was like juggling a fearsome object from one hand to the other, knowing you had to rid yourself of it but not wanting to pass it on. Not to Valentino, not to Kit, even if it belonged to them and them alone.

He glanced at Kit and saw her face shining, her lips just parted as she listened to the music and travelled to other places. She wasn't there beside him, she was somewhere else, but then he felt her fingers lace into his and he squeezed them back. He'd wanted this night with her. And the next, the next. He'd wanted to take her to the Festa dell'Innamorata, where they'd stay awake until the light pooled in over the water and the thousand torches were all burnt out. He'd wanted to bake her *baci di donna*, biscuits of sweet almonds and bitter chocolate, bring them to her as they were warm and just-melting. He'd wanted to show her the beach he knew where there were rainbow-bright shoals of fish, and hardly anybody ever came, so you could lie in the sun with your skin quite bare, and when the fireworks of sunset exploded you could go up on to the rocks and watch from there, hands pressing all over one another, bodies following, until you had your own light and magic. But more than anything, he'd just wanted her to be happy. He hadn't thought Valentino being her father was an impediment to any of these things.

And what of Valentino? Just to his other side. Standing with his hands in his pockets, rocking on his heels. He looked as though he too was lost in the music, and maybe he was. Perhaps he'd begun to believe that life could be as simple as a song. That you could find your way back from something, and make it all right, after all.

Oliviero thought, then, of just dissolving away. Kit would think he'd gone to buy more drinks, and Valentino would imagine he'd followed the flight of another pretty girl, and the two of them would be left just with one another. They might talk together then, talk and talk, and maybe it would come out naturally, this thing he knew. Maybe they'd stumble across it themselves. He didn't have to be the one to break their hearts.

As if on cue, the boy on stage struck up the best and worst song of all. 'Only Love Can Break Your Heart'. Oliviero reached for Kit's hand, Valentino's too, and pulled the pair of them back through the crowd with him. They must have felt his intensity, for they went without protest, just as the crowd was swaying, tipping their heads and singing along.

'I can't stand it,' he said, in Italian, and Kit looked at him quizzically.

'Come,' he said. 'Come to the water. It's the only place where there isn't anybody.'

It was true. Everybody was in the square. Save for a girl wheeling a bicycle, the seafront was empty. Palm trees stood like sentries. The night sky was smudged with clouds, and stars were scattered thinly. Oliviero headed for the beach, Kit and Valentino following. They scrambled over the rocks, Valentino stooping to use both hands, Kit careful with her ankle, Oliviero jumping ahead, his every movement shot with nervous energy.

'You can still hear it here,' she said, a lick of breeze catching her hair, her dress fluttering. 'Is that what you wanted? It sounds great. I love it.' He wished it were only that. Silver water, and the drift of music.

He rubbed his face with both hands, trying to erase last doubts. He'd spent all evening working out where to begin. The words he'd rehearsed – written down, scribbled out, meticulously checked against his English dictionary – were all he had. His eyes went to the sea, then back to Valentino and Kit.

'I know what it's like,' he said, 'to hurt people you love,

when what you're trying to do is protect them. And I know what it's like to regret something, to live with it every day, not knowing if you did the right thing, or if it all would have gone to shit anyway.'

He saw Valentino reach unconsciously for Kit's hand, and he saw how she let him take it.

'I know what it's like to know something you don't want to know. And I'm sorry, I'm so sorry . . .'

'Oliviero . . .' Valentino began.

'You talked to each other today,' Oliviero went on. 'But . . . you only talked, didn't you? You didn't look at any photographs, or . . .'

He shook his head at their blank looks. He felt sick. Maybe it would have been easier if he'd spoken to Valentino on his own, tucked in the office or in one of their villas, shutters down, doors locked, but that would have felt like a betrayal to Kit. It had to be both of them, together.

'I don't know how it's possible,' he said, 'but . . . Kit, your mum, and Valentino, your wife . . . Rosa Costa and Bianca Colosimo . . . they are the same woman.'

twenty-six

NOBODY SAID ANYTHING. NOBODY MOVED. THE MUSIC DRIFTED on regardless, and at their feet the water lapped; gentle, pleasant sounds, befitting night-time strolls and passing pleasantries. Whispered professions. Not this.

Kit let out a quick huff of breath. 'How could you even say a thing like that?'

'Because,' Oliviero said, quietly, 'you showed me your mum's photograph. And then, just earlier . . .' he glanced at Valentino, 'I saw Bianca.'

'Don't do this . . .' said Valentino, his voice so low it was a rumble.

'I've never seen a picture of your wife before today,' Oliviero said to him. 'I'm sorry, I . . .'

'You were halfway across the room,' said Valentino, '*basta*.'

'I would not make this up.'

'*Sei pazzo*,' he said, and Kit didn't know what it meant but his anger was obvious, and it prickled at the bottom of her stomach, made her legs unsteady.

She reached into her bag. Her diary was in there, with the

two photographs pushed inside it. She drew out the older one, taken in the garden at Deer Leap. It would have been maybe two years after Rosa had left Italy. She'd have looked like the woman Valentino knew. His wife's best friend, who, perhaps enough to confuse Oliviero, bore a striking resemblance to Bianca. As a mistake, it wasn't inconceivable. But Kit's hand shook as she held the picture, and she kept it turned towards her.

'She wasn't married,' she said, 'not ever.'

Valentino's hands stayed in his pockets, and he stood hunched over. He looked like he'd been sucker-punched but was braced now, as if he wouldn't let it happen twice.

She held up the picture.

'It was always just me and her,' she said. 'Me and my mum.'

Valentino had sat in his office, said the words *figlia illegittima*, and then told her that he knew exactly who her mother was. He'd looked like a man whose past had engulfed him; Kit had seen in him incomprehension, confusion, even, though she hadn't known it then, swooping sorrow. But not horror. Not this . . . implosion. She watched as his face turned to granite. He reached to take the picture from her, and for a moment she refused to give it up, feeling that as long as she held on to her mum, she would stay who she was. But if Rosa slipped her grip, if she let this man with the face of sliding rock take hold of her, then, however impossible it was, something fundamental would shatter.

'Please,' he said, and her fingers lifted.

He looked at the picture, and the picture consumed him wholly. The square of glossy card, its muted colours, its approximation of a person – two people, really, for Kit was there too, round and unknowing, in a red velveteen romper. How long was it possible to look at a thing for, to see all there was to see, and yet still be searching for more? Her raven hair, falling sharply, the sweep of fringe. Eyes like jet, with curling lashes. The white blouse, a triangle of tanned skin, a thumb-deep clavicle. A pair of bell-bottom jeans, darned at the knee; long bare feet in leather sandals. A laburnum tree blazing yellow behind them, and a strip of pale sky. A child on her lap, who was laughing at who knew what, her hand closed around a rattle. Valentino looked at it all, and it seemed to break him, deeper and deeper, until she wondered how he was still standing. And then he wasn't; he was sinking before her. She saw Oliviero dart forward, reaching for his shoulders. Valentino dropped to his knees.

'Bianca,' she heard him say, and no one had ever said anybody's name like that.

Only it couldn't be. No one could be two people. No one could die and live again. There was nothing of a ghost about her mum. She'd been rock solid, ineffably substantial. She always had. But when Valentino looked up at her, Kit knew that whatever he said next, there could be no disbelieving him.

'She drowned,' he said.

'Yes,' said Kit, 'yes.'

'But . . .' said Valentino.

The whole world turned on the word.

How must they have looked, the trio on the rocks? Castaways from the square, where the crowd were still in thrall to the boy from Milano, singing someone else's songs of breaking hearts and damage done. A picturesque threesome, the first to catch the breeze as it came off the water, to spot the fizzing flight of fireflies in the light cast by the street lamps. They were arranged like figures in a painting, a Caravaggio, maybe, a man on the ground, his head bent, a younger man reaching down to him, a girl with her arms wrapped around herself, her face a pale, unreadable heart. A tableau depicting the moment when two people realise that life is not what they thought it to be, and a third who can do nothing to make it right.

'They never found her body,' Valentino said, his voice eerily calm. 'They only search for so long, then they stop, and they let the sea do its work. But the ocean is too big, isn't it? There is much we don't know. And she . . . she was never found. I asked, I said, "What if? What if there's a chance?" but they looked at me like I was . . . hoping for the impossible. Showing myself as the madman they all thought I was.'

Kit stared at him, entranced against all will.

'But we waited, I insisted on that, and then we had the funeral mass. We buried a . . . picture. A photograph.' He paused, passed his hand across his mouth. 'That was what went in the ground. She had no family, she'd lost them all, over the years, but a few friends came, and . . . I threw the first soil. It . . .' he made a scattering gesture with his fingers, 'it missed. It didn't cover her. She was in there, looking at me, still. A picture of her at the beach, that was what I chose, because she did love the sea, she did, and it was the happiest picture I had of her, the . . . most free.'

He stopped. Slumped again, with Oliviero kneeling beside him. Valentino made no attempt to shake him off; it was as though he wasn't there at all.

'As she walked out the door, she said she never wanted to see me again. That was what she said. She wore her sailing jacket. Her hair was tied back with a ribbon. She told me that she hated me. She hated me, and she never wanted to see me again.'

He looked up at Kit, as if noticing her for the first time.

'But you,' he said, 'what did she tell you?'

Isn't it more or less the same for everyone? Maybe there are photographs about the house – a bride and groom dappled with confetti, perhaps, implausibly high heels, an amusing moustache – but don't most of us almost believe, in that childish way, that our parents' lives began as we were born? There is no requirement to stitch together the past and wrap the sum of it around ourselves, like a patchwork quilt. Her mum's past, particularly, had never been a topic for easy discussion. So at eighteen Kit had got a ring pushed through her belly button, and never asked about her father again. Rosa had said to her once, *Don't ever get stuck,* mi amore. *It's not true that you only get one life. You can have as many as you want.* It was the day of her graduation, and Kit was distracted, thinking only of the night ahead – the club they'd cram into, the white dawn she'd see in. She'd kissed her mum quickly on the cheek then flown out the door. It was only later that she'd thought about her words again, as they swam up to meet her in the delirium of drunken sleep, and she'd remembered the look on Rosa's face, how fiercely intent she'd been. An unwelcome intrusion, for although her mum had always preached liberty, there was also the burdensome sensation that it came from experience hard won; but she had never wanted to talk, and Kit had been afraid, and unwilling, to press her. *It's not true that you only get one life.* Perhaps, Kit thought now, her whole childhood had been peppered with unrecognised hints. Dropped pearls. Rosa's entire story chopped up and scattered over thirty years, until, at the last, *Valentino Colosimo*, laid in the palm of her hand.

'We didn't really talk about it,' she said. 'Not like that.'

'You knew nothing of her life in Italia?'

'Not quite nothing.'

'Then what?'

'Just . . . bits. Pieces. Not much.'

She faded under his stare. Surely *this* wasn't the incomprehensible part? That Kit hadn't demanded a history. That Rosa hadn't proffered one, not until the very end.

'It wasn't up to me to ask. That's not how it works, okay? You can't understand that – how could you? She was my mum, and so she told me what she wanted and that was it. It wasn't up to me.'

'As a child, perhaps, but as a woman . . .' he persisted.

Her chest burnt; she felt like a teenager, full of easy embitterment.

'I think,' said Oliviero, stepping between them, his hands out, 'that this is a shock. A crazy shock. I think, maybe . . .'

But Valentino's eyes were still on her, and amidst the hurt, and the fear, and the sensation of it all, she thought she saw something else in there too: accusation.

'I don't have to defend anything about our life,' she began, stepping past Oliviero, 'so don't even . . .' She took a shuddering breath. 'She hated you, okay? She *hated* you. And now I understand. Now I get why she never, ever spoke about you. Her life in Italy was over. *Over.* What you did, I mean . . .' She felt a surge of emotion; it swamped her. She fought through it, like a desperate swimmer pushing back to the surface, breath choking. 'She didn't have anything left, did she? You took it all from her. You took her *whole life*.' Tears were coursing down her cheeks, and she rubbed them away, angry at their insistence, angry at everything. 'So she made a new one. And you know what? I'm glad she did.'

She knew it wasn't her words that did it. It was the culmination of everything, surely, her response just tipping him, but later, when it was just her and Oliviero left, she wished she could have said something different. Or nothing. Nothing at all would have been better. Because, really, what did she have to say? What possible sense could she bring to the nonsensical? She'd pointed her finger as she'd said *you took her whole life*, and he'd reeled back. Then he'd picked himself up, shaking off Oliviero as he went, and staggered away across the rocks. As she watched him go, moving like a wounded animal, a boar full of arrows, she suddenly had the distinct feeling that she would never see him again. She took a step forward, as if to follow, but Oliviero held on to her.

'Don't,' he said. 'Let him go.'

twenty-seven

THE THOUSAND LIGHTS WERE BLAZING. AS HE ROUNDED THE hill, taking the bend faster than he ever had, the road spooled away before him, and his hotel beckoned at the end of it, garlanded in luminosity.

Valentino had found the idea for the Mille Luci at the bottom of a bottle. People said nothing good came that way, but it was just how it was. A piercing sense of clarity that cut through all else, that was clearer, even, in that precise moment, than the pain that had consumed him for months and months. And it was still there the next morning, emerging through the thud of his ever-present hangover, a small thing, rather like a gem in a pile of rubble, a tiny gleaming piece of hope. Or, perhaps more accurately, salvation.

Make the happiness of others your sole purpose. Create a place of eternal sunshine. Cast no shadow ever again.

A lifetime ago they'd holidayed in Paris, Valentino and his Bianca. Before they were married, before anything else. They'd stayed in a once-grand old house on a narrow street, and to them it had been a palace, with its tall rounded windows and mansard roof, its goose-down linens and roses in the bathroom and roundels of baguette spread with apricot jam and bowls of good strong coffee and at dinner steaks that left blood on your plate with a sheaf of *frites* and a salad that tasted like spring. *I'm so happy here*, she'd said. *It's like life, only better.* And as they'd left, climbing into a taxi, watching the hotel recede through the rear window, with its fluttering flag, its name spelt out in stacked letters, she'd said, *Is there anything better than a good hotel?* and he'd wanted to say love, and sex, and food, and wine, and beauty, and conversation, and kindness, and generosity, and, and, and . . . but hadn't their stay been full of such things? All of life lived out in simple, defined spaces: a microcosm of pleasure and comfort.

Much later, when Bianca was gone, and most of his reason for existence along with her, his grandmother – a woman of high principles and, it turned out, some considerable wealth – passed away in her sleep. She was nearly ninety, and it was the way that people should go, their pillows soft against their heads, a delicate descent into a long, sweet slumber. Her money had gone not to his parents but to him, an arrangement cooked up in a Firenze town house by elderly people who knew that it was possible for the living to be dead also, who wanted to lift their dear Valentino up off the floor and didn't know how else to do it. *Do something*, his father had said, *something meaningful*. Money wasn't everything, a long way from it, but an inheritance had felt different – it came with responsibility, and duty. Valentino had been a chef, a decent one too, fast with a knife and sure with his flavours, and being an hotelier felt like a fuller, more complete version of that endeavour, a tending to mind, body and spirit. He was afloat in the hard, sharp waters of grappa when he realised that this could be the thing: *like life, only better*, as Bianca had once said.

It was a meandering path that he took, but in the end it had led to Elba. He'd been there only as a boy, squeaky-voiced and short-trousered, walking the rooms of Napoleon's villa, marvelling at such a prison, with its azure waters and white-sand beaches. An island appealed to Valentino. Perhaps unconsciously he sought the surrounds of water, the resting place – if it could ever be called that – of his wife. Consciously it felt like exile; a long way from anyone. A summer holiday season, then an emptying: boats unmoored, villas vacated, cafés shuttered, Elba reclaiming itself, the smoke and mists of autumn shrouding the island. Winter hibernation: a time to draw in, and gather strength, and, above all, be alone. He'd found the place, and immediately seen it for what it was: an unloved house – big and rangy, falling down and forgotten. It had crumbling stonework and a rusted iron gate, boarded windows and scattered tiles. The gardens were choked and overrun, but enormous, and raucous with vegetation. Altogether, it was a mess to take on. *This is for me*, he'd thought. *This is right*.

He'd wanted the thorns in his hands. The back-breaking work. The betterment of something that others had written off. His elderly father had visited from the mainland, on a rare frost-bitten January morning, when the ground was hard and fissured, the sky granite. *It's too much for you*, he'd said, which, by Valentino's reckoning, made it just enough.

The last job had been to string the lights. Garland after garland. When locals saw the name go up, Hotel Mille Luci, they knew the legend it came from, the torchlit beauty of Innamorata. The Thousand Lights Hotel. Nice for the tourists, they thought, and such a blaze on the hillside was welcome, a brightening sight. That first night of light, Valentino had stood in the garden all on his own. The sea was dark at his feet, and the palms threw jagged shadows. Everywhere there were pinpricks and starbursts. His hotel behind him gleamed.

'So,' he'd said. 'Now, this.'

He walked across the deserted terrace. Above, the skies had broken and the pool, usually as still as an ink drop, was pockmarked with rain. The parasols were folded and stowed. Guests were tucked away or sleeping; only the lights shone on. As he crossed the paving, the soles of his shoes made no sound. Or was it just that his ears were filled with roaring, blasting out all else? Rain, too, that which had threatened, that which he thought they could avoid, now lashing down. He stopped, and turned, wincing at the glare that surrounded him. His head ached, and what had been a dull, deep-set pain now shot spears into him. He closed his eyes, pushing his fingers into the roots of his hair.

He'd thought home was where he needed to be; to return to a place that made sense to him, where he knew who he was, and who other people were too. But seeing it all now – the folly of the bright-painted shutters, the terracotta pots of pink and yellow hibiscus, the vine-twined pergola – it seemed to him to be a mere stage set. A place of artifice, built from sorrow, run on guilt. Twenty-eight years of welcoming people in and out, hello and goodbye, the pointlessness of it all. Thinking he was finding his feet again, providing small measures of happiness summer after summer that might, in the very end, add up to something worthwhile.

Life was handed to you, and it was up to you to figure out what the hell to do with it. If you slipped, if you fell, if you knowingly threw yourself headlong into disaster, what could you do but try to clamber back up? Lay down apology, and face the consequences of your actions? When he'd told Bianca, he'd understood that meant that everything with her could be over. He would have accepted an existence of loneliness, regret, a one-room apartment in a nowhere town. He'd have called himself a savage and a fool, and understood her non-forgiveness. He'd have taken that. And he'd have spent the rest of his life trying to earn her esteem once more.

But she'd died.

Only she hadn't.

It was the kind of miracle that, once, he might have prayed for.

Bianca. She'd never felt the need to explain herself. It had always been one of the things he'd admired about her, her self-belief, her verbal economy. When they'd swapped cards on birthdays or Christmas, he'd always tried to plumb the depths of his heart for that small space, but she only ever wrote *Love Bianca*, and that was enough, because they'd each known what that word meant, and all that it encompassed. Their first date – him filling the spaces with talk of this and that, and her sitting there, composed, a feline smile at her lips. When had her quiet become something more shuttered? In the last couple of years they'd had together, certainly. She'd take the boat out, and maybe she shouted it all into the wind, her best words settling at the bottom of the ocean. Her impetuosity had turned to ill-temper those last years too. She'd always made decisions at the snap of a finger: *I'm painting the house raspberry pink! A midnight walk, in the ice of winter. Make love to me this moment, now, this train, this carriage, this one-metre cubicle, rattling on its tracks*, but her quick intent, her lack of consultation, had made her seem to Valentino like a woman who'd stopped believing in the capability of the man beside her. Was it any surprise that when he failed her utterly, she fired off all on her own?

What use was this, trying to find reason where there was none? It was an unthinkable thing, this trick of life after death. A dirty sort of magic.

At the time, he hadn't been able to deny the facts. The smashed hull of her boat in one place, the busted mast in another, the shredded mainsail, tangled with weeds, washing up along the coast. Lost and drowned, she had to be. But now? It was unfathomable that she might have lived another life, and yet it was true. He'd seen the photograph, and he'd felt it in his bones.

He hadn't spoken at the funeral mass. He hadn't been able to find the words. Grief, and regret, and culpability had taken them from him, along with just about everything else. They'd sung 'Ave Maria', and although he'd moved his lips, he'd had no voice. He thought, then, of everyone they knew. The other mourners, their faces drawn and sorry, dabbing eyes with handkerchiefs and gathering round the excuse for a casket. Were they complicit? Was there someone, just one man, or one woman, who knew? Who allowed themselves a small, grim smile as the pathetic cheating husband tried to say goodbye to a body that wasn't there?

The rain was rolling down his cheeks, soaking his shirt. He didn't care. It could pour, it could storm, for all the difference it would make. He went to the outhouse where they kept the garden equipment. He pulled out the shears, and swung them like a rapier. They were satisfyingly heavy in his hand.

What of Kit? Bianca must have been carrying her inside her

as she ran. Did she know it then? Was it all part of it, fuel to the fire of revenge, to take their baby with her too? The child that had been the thing they'd talked about from the very beginning, as a symbol of their commitment, the strength of their love, this desire to bring another life into the world. *I'd like seven children*, she'd said, laughing, on only their second date, *maybe eight*. Over the years, the number had gone down. *A boy and a girl, the perfect pair*, until, at the end, *One, just one, one isn't too much to ask, is it?* and her eyes had been skyward then, not on Valentino at all. Then the telephone call from the other woman – Mia, Mia, the name he hadn't been able to bring himself to say out loud; Mia, who'd moved away and severed all contact – her quiet, faltering voice, telling him of the baby lost: there had been no lie from her after all. The *figlia illegittima* had never been born. Kit was a love child all right, but in a different sense; the daughter of a man and wife, however ruptured. Kit was his. Kit was theirs.

Valentino dragged a metal ladder across the lawn. His feet skidded, but the shears were secure in his hand. The roaring in his head seemed to spread throughout his entire body, and his limbs jumped with a manic energy.

Bianca.

How could the thought of her having lived be more terrible than her death?

And what did that make him, worse than ever before?

He didn't just want to extinguish the lights; he wanted to hack, and split, sending everything blacker and blacker with every stroke. He wouldn't stop until he'd killed them all, lights tangling in strawberry bushes and choking the necks of palms. He snapped the ladder out, and leant it against the wall. Took a first step, then another, his feet slipping on the wet rungs. He climbed onto the roof, and stood there, panting. Only then did he realise the depth of his own breathlessness, and feel the spread of pain in his chest. He sank to his knees, still clutching the shears. He squeezed his eyes shut, and let the soaking darkness take what was left of him. Which was not much at all.

twenty-eight

KIT SAID SHE DIDN'T WANT TO GO BACK TO THE MILLE LUCI, not that night, so Oliviero had called around, and found her a room in a quiet hotel a few streets back from the seafront. It had no view, and the only lights were those illuminating the hotel's name. She stood on the steps, her arms wrapped around herself. She'd barely spoken since Valentino had left, and Oliviero couldn't shake the feeling, one that was as persistent as a migraine, that their suffering was by his hand.

'You should go to him,' she said now.

He wanted to touch her. Hold her. Bury his face in the waves of her hair and say, *I'm sorry, I'm so sorry for everything.*

'It's worse for him,' she said. 'It is.'

'But I don't want to leave you alone with this,' he said.

'I shouldn't even have asked you to stay this long.'

She kissed him on the cheek. He caught her hand, and drew her closer, but she shook her head. He felt a drop of water, then another: the heat that had been building and building until it had nowhere left to go had finally broken. They stepped sideways and watched it come down. At first fat raindrops spotting the pavement, then sluicing it. It seemed to roar.

'I'm worried about him,' he said. 'I'm worried about both of you.'

'Oliviero, it's okay. Really. Go.'

His fingers sought hers, and found them. They stood together as rain splattered the tips of their shoes. He felt her shiver beside him, although the night was warm still.

'You should go inside,' he said. 'Stay dry.'

Kit squeezed his hand hard.

'Thank you,' she said. 'For everything.' She lifted his hand to her lips, and kissed it. A girl had never done that before. 'I think I'm going to say goodbye now,' she said. 'I think it's best.'

'*Buona notte*, Kit.'

'No, I mean . . . *goodbye* goodbye. I'll go back to get my things tomorrow, but I might miss you then, and . . .'

'You're leaving?'

'Well, I can't stay.'

He set a hand on either shoulder. She looked up at him; her eyes – the colour of Valentino's, that same sky blue – were clear, windows onto a mind made up.

'Oliviero,' she said, 'I was leaving on Sunday anyway. I'm just . . . bringing it forward. I can't be here. It's the last thing he's going to want.'

'But you,' he said, 'what do you want?'

He had no real idea what her life in England looked like. She could have a great band of friends waiting for her to fall into their embrace, to draw her back into their landscape. To agree that the Italian venture was crazy, and to help her forget it had ever happened. Who needed a father anyway? Who wanted this . . . *shit*? Maybe she had a cat that would wrap itself around her legs and tell her she was home. Another job lined up, her next assignment, to the palaces of St Petersburg or a Thai dream beach. Maybe she had a whole world waiting for her, and this was just a strange foray in a spacecraft, into the unwanted infinite.

She smiled then, and it was one of the saddest smiles Oliviero had ever seen.

'I just want my mum back,' she said.

And he understood it. He did. Because remembering someone as you wanted was perhaps the only privilege the grieving could ever be afforded.

The rain cascaded down the sloping streets and gushed from the tops of awnings. People turned umbrellas like spinning tops. Children up past their bedtime ran fast through puddles, shrieking with glee as they skidded in their sandals. Throughout the course of an Elban summer it rained just a handful of times, and the flash and flurry of it was a novelty. Oliviero was glad of the drenching. He bent his head as water ran down his cheeks, making no effort to brush it away, and unless you were right up close to him you couldn't tell it wasn't rain. He'd wanted to pick her up the next morning. Or make her promise to find him when she returned to the Mille Luci. Or drive her to the port, if it had to be that, let him see her onto the ferry – at the very least. *He needs you more*, she'd said, and although he figured it to be true, he wished he could divide himself, half to him and half to her, knowing that, really, he was no good to either.

He'd seen it in Valentino, the age-old hurt. That was the sum of it – the grief, the regret, the blame, you balled it all up and it became one great pain, tightly knotted and inextricable.

Perhaps Valentino thought he kept it buried deep, locked away in some place he only accessed on rare occasions, but if you knew him well enough – and Oliviero was probably the only one who did – you could see that he wore it about him every day. It was in the small things he said, and the big things he didn't. The set to his shoulders. The dark scoops beneath his eyes. It was as though, Oliviero had always thought, he didn't believe he had a right to happiness. He was generous, gregarious, the perfect host, but as personally impenetrable as a hilltop fort. He'd built a beautiful place, and he tended it every day. He was good to everyone, and enjoyed great pleasantness in return. He'd even, perhaps just lately, felt a lightening of the spirit, for Oliviero had noticed the way he spoke to Isabel, how he seemed to smile without realising he was doing it when she was around. And then Kit, who could have been this remarkable thing for him: a chance to have a different sort of life. And now . . .

Oliviero was eighteen again, surveying the hopeless wreckage of his family, and the pain of his own part in it. He ducked into a dark alley and leant his hands against the wall, pressed his forehead to the cool stone. His steady tears turned into a single shuddering sob. Then, after no more than a few seconds, he rubbed his face, took a breath, and splashed back out into the rain.

He hitched a lift down the coast road with a young Austrian couple in a red Mercedes. They'd been at the concert too, and they wanted to sing, belting out 'Old Man' as though it wasn't any kind of a sad song at all. The car was a convertible, and the rain hammered on the fabric of the roof, adding a relentless beat. Oliviero was crammed in the back, his clothes sodden, his chin bent to his knees. They took the turns like locals, sending him queasy for the first time in his life. He asked them to drop him by the bus stop, despite their protestations. With perverse superstition, he didn't want to tell them where he was going.

As soon as the car sped off, he broke into a run, his path down the hill sketched out by moonlight. The rain had brought out the scents of everything: the scrubland with its wild rosemary and lavender and thyme, the soil, even the dust on the road itself, smells he would normally have revelled in, but all he could think of was where he'd find Valentino. Sunk in the chair in his office, working his way to the bottom of a bottle. In his villa, a snowdrift of torn photographs blocking the door. At the beach, even, looking out over the water, trying to find some kind of explanation in it. Would he want to talk? What could Oliviero even say? Perhaps just being there would be enough. That was what Kit had said. He saw the hotel, and skidded to a stop. Its lights were blazing. Then he heard a bang. He began to run again.

As he rounded the corner, Oliviero saw that something was different: a stretch of darkness where there should have been light. He raced forward, and fell suddenly, his foot catching in something. He got up, rubbing at his knees, taking in the tangle of broken lights that trailed the lawn. Then he heard a shout.

Valentino was up on the roof. Clambering. Slipping on the wet tiles. Oliviero saw the sheen of metal as the light caught the shears.

'No!' he yelled. 'Stop!'

There was a ladder up against the wall, and he threw himself at it, feet skidding through the rungs as he climbed.

'Stop, Valentino! Don't cut anything! Don't be crazy!'

As he neared the top, he could see Valentino hacking at

another string. Below Oliviero the lights jumped and jerked, rustling the palm trees. The rain kept coming.

'Please, please stop!'

Giving up on the shears, Valentino yanked at the cable with his hands, pulling it from where it was fastened. Oliviero was almost at the top of the ladder. He yelled again, but Valentino couldn't hear him, for water roared in the gutters and sang off the tiles, and he was grunting with his own exertions, hauling, pulling, then falling back as the string finally gave. The lights snapped out instantly, and in the drenching dark Oliviero didn't see him fling the cable to one side. But he felt it. Exquisitely. As it hit the metal ladder, a shock ran through his body, and he convulsed. The noise he made was entirely involuntary, the strangest sound. His hands were stuck fast as the current kept on bolting through him. He pushed back, with an incredible effort, freeing himself from the ladder, kicking away from it. There was the briefest moment of limbo, a sensation of weightlessness, almost time to think, *I did it, I'm free*, then he felt the full slam of the ground. An instant and all-consuming whoosh of pain. Then nothing.

twenty-nine

KIT ROLLED OVER, RIDING THE LAST WAVE OF A DREAM, A SMILE at her lips. She opened her eyes, and squinted. She'd neglected to close the shutters, and early sunlight, fragile but determined, filled the room. She brought her knees up to her chin and wrapped her arms around them. Closed her eyes again, seeking the embrace of her dream.

The lines were blurred, so blurred that she wasn't sure if it was, in fact, a memory, one that had surfaced in the night, sent to her by some unknown force. It was her mum, and Kit as a tiny girl, and they'd been standing together in the sea. Crystal clear, the picture had been, sensationally real; her mum lifting her skirt, the shape of her calves, the water pulling at Kit's ankles, the feeling of the retreating sand running between her toes. *We begin in water*, her mum had said. *I did, you did, it's always the start of everything.* Kit had kicked at a wave, and the drops were diamonds in the glare of the sun. Her mum had sent it splashing back, their laughter criss-crossing.

She opened her eyes again. There was no going back. Only forward. She would be at the port before the morning was out.

Stay, Oliviero had said. *You need each other.*

But how could she face Valentino? How could she ever explain that for all its dreadful absurdity, to her it made a sort of sense? That all the mysteries of her childhood, from the minuscule to the mighty, were, while not solved, rendered a little more understandable. For her mum to have told Kit anything would have been a betrayal of her own self. Whatever resolutions Rosa had made, she'd stuck by them impeccably, until almost the end. All her life Kit had believed herself to be born of a moment between two people that had not been destined to last. That, at least, remained true.

She pulled herself out of bed and went over to the window, pushed it open. The skies were clear, the air was fresh. She took a breath, filling herself right up. What should she be feeling? That she didn't really know her mum? Maybe for the first time, she realised that she understood her perfectly. For all the shocking implausibility, there was undeniable fact. The kind of contradiction that had been inherent in Rosa. Perhaps even in Bianca, too.

Her mum had liked to go to bed early, apart from when she wanted to stay up all night and watch the sky turn pink in the east. She wouldn't listen to music for weeks and weeks, then Kit would catch her dancing in the kitchen. She told Kit she should strike out on her own in the world, without ever looking back over her shoulder, but then she followed her to her university town, telephoned her when she knew she was travelling, sewed her unasked-for dresses and folded them in tissue paper, sent them in padded envelopes. She'd never wanted to talk about the country she'd left behind, said she'd never go back, yet she baked polenta cakes from memory, sat at the kitchen table pinching bow ties of farfalle. Only when she told Kit to never trust in love was there no discrepancy. None at all.

The street below was deserted, puddles of rainwater enjoying their last moments before the sun was upon them, the beginning of another broiling day. Kit could see the bus stop at the end of the road, and she'd be waiting when the first bus came along. For all the devastation of the night before, she couldn't imagine anything except them carrying on as usual at the Mille Luci. Valentino in a new shirt, freshly shaven, determined to face the day and whatever else it might bring. Looking tired about the eyes, maybe, or perhaps showing an uncharacteristic testiness when the little German boys grew shrill. Because what on earth else could he do? There was no rulebook reaction to a story like theirs. And Oliviero. In his kitchen, maybe baking another strawberry focaccia, because he felt they all needed a reason to smile on a morning like this.

She'd slip through the grounds without seeing anybody, and go to her room for the last time. She'd pack her bag, then leave a note for each of them. Neither would be long, but both would be difficult to write.

Kit crunched across the gravel, trying to tread lightly, moving quickly. She wore her dress from the night before, and her hair was damp from the shower. It wasn't yet seven o'clock, and the hotel was still sleeping. She noticed a bike propped up against the back wall, and recognised it as Bernardo's, the boy from the kitchen. It was early in the day for him. There was a movement by the doors to reception; it was Abi, darting out, seeing Kit, going back in again just as fast. Then Isabel hurried out and came towards her. She was wearing an apron. Her eyes were rimmed red. She stopped. For a brief second they looked at one another, and Kit realised then that she knew this moment. It was the phone ringing in the middle of the night. It was the doctor leading her to a quiet room. Her hand went to her mouth.

'Oh darling girl,' Isabel said, as she opened her arms.

The taxi to Portoferraio, a paint-chipped Fiat, was flying like a racing car. It was early in the morning still, the roads not yet clogged with holiday traffic; the driver had the windows wound down, his shoulders loose as he spun them from turn to turn. *Okay, signorina*, he threw back to her every so often, but without ever making it a question, and Kit was glad of it. She sat in the back, her hair blowing across her face, flinching as one of the rambunctious blue buses thundered round a bend to meet them, or a piece of island vegetation smacked through the open window. She pressed her hands together in an attempt to stop them shaking. She'd drunk a coffee, a strong one that Abi had made, and she felt it agitating inside her now, working her up.

At the port, the ferryboats would be in a line, gleaming in the sun. The first passengers clattering up the tall metal steps, and she might have been among them. Elba disappearing in the churn of the wake. Eventually Bristol. The bus to Clifton, the so-familiar streets, the click of her key in the door, the futile call of *I'm home!* Instead, she was here.

She tried to order her thoughts. She'd always been better at writing what she meant than saying it out loud. But the writing paper in her room at the Mille Luci remained untouched, along with all of her belongings. Her dresses still hung in the wardrobe. Her laptop and notebooks were still laid out on the desk. The last thing Oliviero had said to her was *Please don't go.* She hadn't thought to say it back to him.

It was Isabel who'd found them. Oliviero flat on the ground, Valentino bent over him. She'd heard a scream – *or, I don't know, not a scream as such, but the strangest, most awful sound* – and the shout of despair that had followed it. Her room, she'd told Kit, with the kind of detail that the shocked took refuge in as they tried to piece together the broken sense of events, was the only one in that corner, her bedroom window looking down on the paving where Oliviero lay. She'd run down in her nightdress, her feet squelching in the grass as she went to them. It was Isabel who'd phoned the ambulance, and away from Valentino her voice had turned falsetto. As she returned to him – *they're on their way, they're on their way* – she saw how he had mud across his chest, striping his cheek, and how he gripped Oliviero's hand in his. She had knelt down beside him and held onto Oliviero too. *He looked so young, lying there*, she'd told Kit. *No more than a boy. And with his eyes closed, he looked* – she'd stopped, righted herself – *he looked just as though he was sleeping.*

Kit stood looking up at the hospital. It was the colour of beach sand, the building, and hemmed by palm trees and sprays of bamboo. The windows had bright white metal shutters, and the sky above was blue. Altogether it looked more like an uninspiring hotel than a hospital. Perhaps, she thought, hospitals in holiday towns were different. There would be deft hands applying aloe to sunburn. Minor injuries incurred from slipping on pool tiles, or tumbling from scooters; the kind of incidents that could later be embellished over dinner, when you asked the waiter to sign your plaster cast and said, *Yes, extra ice cream definitely helps the pain.* Ankle sprains from running in dark woods, and a bowl of lemon ice brought to your room by a man you didn't want to be your brother? That too.

She willed herself to go inside, to ignore the familiar flutter of dread rising in her stomach. It would be different, she told herself, so different from the Bristol hospital. The place whose scent lingered so deeply on her skin that the last time she'd left it she'd stood under the blast of a shower for an hour or more, sinking to the ground, curling up there, only startling when the water ran freezing. Hospitals didn't have to be the end.

She squeezed her hands into fists, wishing she was wearing something different, her dress from last night so foolishly bright, too flimsy to be adequate armour, her bare toes in her sandals feeling frivolous and exposed. But as soon as she'd spoken to Isabel, she had given no thought to changing, no thought to anything except getting to where she knew she had to be. Now she walked through the revolving doors, keeping her eyes straight ahead. She went to the front desk, where a mustachioed man in short sleeves said something she didn't understand. She faltered, realising she didn't even know Oliviero's last name.

'Colosimo?' she tried instead, and his fingers tapped in the name disinterestedly, as though it meant nothing. Eyes on the screen, he shook his head.

Behind her, a voice, so low, so full of sad music, said, *Kit?*

thirty

PERHAPS THAT WAS HOW IT WORKED. WHEN A FRESH HORROR struck, it eclipsed the existing one.

They'd told him to go home, the doctors, for there was no more that he could do. He'd stayed awake the whole night, first propped up by coffee from the machine in the hall, plastic cupful after plastic cupful, that somehow managed to taste both nasty and of nothing at all. The mud from the lawn was still on his clothes from where he'd slipped down the last rungs of the ladder. Mud had still been on his cheeks too, until he'd gone to the bathroom, stood beneath the fizzing strip lighting and washed his hands and face, letting the cold water run over his wrists and down his neck. He hadn't realised that he was gasping out loud until the door behind him opened then promptly shut again. What did it matter? The hospital was full of people with their lives stripped down to nothing, their distress peeled back for all to see. Whimpering relatives, cries of discomfort, everywhere the hiss and whine of machines, the squeak of trolleys in the halls, the relentless hive of pain and the tending to it. He'd always hated hospitals. Never having had the joy of becoming a father in one, the scales were tipped only towards suffering.

He looked again in the mirror. Took in his quivering mouth and bleary eyes. His hair raked upward. He hated the sight. They were only here now because of his loss of control. Up on the roof, intent on destruction, he'd been in a place where rational thought had counted for nothing. As he'd first climbed the ladder he'd felt an immense pressure in his chest, and at the top he'd dropped to his knees. He knew the shape of a panic attack, knew he had to ride it out, but this time he'd half willed it to be the other thing. He'd knelt, his head hanging, his breath coming short. Then rage had enlivened him, and he'd got back up, wielding his shears. As he'd flung the cable, all he'd wanted was to be rid of it, for the last of the sparkle to be extinguished for good. Then he'd heard that inhuman cry, and seen Oliviero convulsing. Valentino had lunged forward, an instinctive quickstep, the kind of footwork he hadn't used since his long-gone days in the ring. He'd kicked the cable away, pulling muscles and straining sinew, at much the same moment as Oliviero had pushed himself free. He hadn't saved him, nowhere close. In fact as Isabel tried to console him, all he could say was *I did this, I did this*, over and over, as though a shock was bolting through his own body.

He set his hands either side of the basin, breathed slowly in and out, willing himself back. He repeated the words that Isabel had said to him. Then he patted down his hair, and went out.

There was an all-night café along the street, and Valentino fetched espresso for anyone who wanted it: the gruff fellow on the front desk, the strung-out mother with her arms full of a sleeping child, the teenage boy who sat curled in a chair, his headphones emitting a relentless tinny beat. When dawn came, he headed for the nearest *forno*, and returned with paper bags full of *cornetti* that he passed around the waiting room. They tasted nothing like Oliviero's but were better than anything the vending machine could dispense. When the man beside him, a thin-faced guy in a dirty shirt, offered him his crumpled cigarette packet in return, he was about to say *no, grazie,* but he was there waiting on his own, the man, and Valentino saw there was barely any light left in his eyes, so although he hadn't had one in ten years, he said *sì*. They stood beside one another outside the hospital doors, smoking quietly. Valentino watched as rose light ebbed into the sky.

Oliviero had been a little boy lost when he'd first turned up, full of righteous honour, and lazy beauty, and the saddest eyes Valentino had ever seen outside of a mirror. Hovering at the Mille Luci gates, with a rolled-up sleeping bag in one hand, and a flimsy bag of market produce in the other. *They said you'd show me how to cook*, he had said, and it could have been any one of the old boys in the village who'd sent this waif his way; only days later, he wished he'd known whom to thank. When had Oliviero become a son to him? They'd simply rubbed along together, as if they'd always been side by side; occasionally Valentino would catch himself looking at the boy with heart-stopping pride and no little fear, and thinking, *You've got your whole life ahead of you*, then, *I hope you spend a little more of it with me*.

'Who are you here for?' the man beside him said, as he tossed his cigarette end to the ground.

'My boy,' said Valentino.

'It's the waiting, the not knowing that's the worst part, isn't it?' the man said, then nodded that he was going back in.

Valentino murmured *sì, sì*. He stooped to pick up the

dropped cigarette butt then followed him inside, coughing at the abrupt change of air.

As day was breaking, he'd phoned Isabel from a payphone in the corridor, dialled right through to the phone in her room, and she answered straight away for the second time that night. As he heard her voice again, he found, suddenly, that he needed to sit down. He stretched the cord, sank into a plastic chair. He closed his eyes as he talked, and rubbed his head with one hand.

'For breakfast,' he said, 'I'll make a call, perhaps a chef from the Europa or the Bella Vista could come, and . . .'

But Isabel told him that Abi was already on her way, and that Bernardo was coming in early too, that between the three of them they'd have it covered. She gave a low laugh, gently said that she'd attempted to recreate enough Mille Luci breakfasts at home in England to have some idea as to how to go about it. He moved his hand across his mouth. Thanked her.

'And . . . Kit . . . if she returns . . .'

'*When* she returns. Don't worry, I'll tell her. Valentino?'

He nodded. Realised he needed to speak. 'Yes?'

'You're all right, aren't you? The doctors, they're taking care of Oliviero, but you . . . you're on your own, and . . .'

'I'm not on my own,' he said, gratitude threatening to take his voice. 'I'm talking to you.'

Valentino heard his name, and started. He must have dropped off. He could have missed it, for it wasn't called out with any authority. Rather it seemed full of hesitation, trepidation; a bad-news voice. His chest tightened as he stood up.

He saw her dress first, before he registered anything else.

The waiting room was full of people wearing whatever they'd been in when disaster occurred – beach shorts, a tuxedo, chef's trousers – and she seemed to shine amongst them.

'Kit?'

She turned. She opened her mouth, but no words came.

The first time that Oliviero had called him Papà, he'd said *Sì?* without thinking. He'd gently pointed out that Oliviero still had a father, but the boy had shaken his head. *He never did what he was supposed to,* he'd reasoned. And maybe he was right. Valentino had never thought of himself as a widower, for hadn't he lost the right to 'husband'? The most important titles had to be earned.

He saw her eyes fill, and he felt his own do the same in reply. He'd thought he'd known all there was of remorse, but here he was again. He wouldn't let it take him, not this time.

He said her name again, and opened his arms wide.

They sat side by side on plastic chairs, a little distance from everyone else. A window gave a view of the car park, palm fronds and the glinting roofs of vehicles. Their eyes kept straying to it, as if it was easier to look out than in.

'They're doing . . . tests.'

'Tests? What kind of tests?'

'He hit his head, there's a . . .' his hand turned, seeking the word, 'concussion.'

'But he's all right, I mean . . .'

Valentino nodded. 'A broken ankle. A rib, too. With his head, they need to check that . . . everything is okay. It will be. It will be okay.'

He edged a look at her. He felt shame burn in his chest, and the back of his throat.

'You saw Isabel,' he said.

'Yes.' She blinked, wiping her cheek with her knuckle. 'She's got Bernardo frying sausages. And Abi's a dab hand at rolling pastry, it turns out. She also just about managed to stop Francesca and Veronika from coming in the taxi with me. I think they're a little bit in love with Oliviero.'

He appreciated her attempt at levity, but he had to say it. 'Isabel knows what happened. The only one who does.'

'All of it?'

'Most of it.'

He'd phoned her, once the doctor had told him what she was able to. Once there was nothing left to do but wait. He'd given her the explanation that she hadn't asked for as they'd knelt beside Oliviero, as ambulance lights swooped across the Mille Luci lawn, revealing the destruction. There was nothing she could have said to make any of it better, but somehow she'd managed it.

'I was going to go home. Not once I knew what had happened to Oliviero, not then, I wouldn't have just . . . gone. But before . . .'

'You were leaving?'

'I thought I should never have come.' She tracked her nail across the paper coffee cup. She said, 'I know how to be without a father. And since she died . . .' she hesitated, glanced at him, a brief shake of her head, 'I've been finding a way to be without my mum, too. I'm not very good at it yet, but . . . I'll get there. And you, you were okay before, weren't you? When you first met me on the lawn, when you showed me your hotel, you seemed proud of it. You seemed content. If I hadn't come . . .'

They didn't notice the approach of the doctor until she was standing right over them. She wore a large pair of glasses, and behind them her eyes were serious. When she said, *Signor Colosimo, è possible vederlo ora*, Valentino took hold of Kit's hand. It wasn't until they were halfway along the tunnel-like corridor, bustling to keep up with the doctor's fast strides, that he realised they were each yet to let go.

thirty-one

WHEN OLIVIERO WOKE, HE HAD NO IDEA WHERE HE WAS, OR how he'd got there. Fear and pain came at him then in almost equal measure. He tried to sit up, but the effort was futile. The noise he made as he sank back down brought a nurse swiftly to his side, pushing back the blue curtain. His eyes were full of tears, but the smile she gave him sent them down his cheeks, and even that hurt, the crying. His mind rolled this way and that, unable to form a coherent question.

When the nurse left him to get the doctor, Oliviero wanted to reach out to her, to say, *Don't go,* because the room wouldn't stay quite still, nothing would, and he was worried that he'd slide too. The plastic of the curtain flapped behind her, shining like it was wet. He held onto the sides of the bed, and closed his eyes. Why all the pain, and where had it come from? His thoughts struggled against one another. Was it his dad, getting his justice at last? Or had it not come to that; had he, Oliviero, fed the sharks instead, offering himself up as bait? His brother? Had he been able to get there first, and broken Danilo's fall? Would he appear at any minute, swiping aside that slippery curtain, beaming with chemical delirium? Or his mum, as the car came at her, had he thrown his arms around her, then turned to stop it himself? Everybody's pain was his, and he felt it now, all of it, running up and down his body, but mostly right in the back of his head. The spinning sped up, and he opened his eyes, hunting for something to fix on. He retched, and was almost glad of it, the burn in the back of his throat, the splatter it made, because at least it felt real, and like something he might have done before.

Later. How much later he couldn't say, but the ghosts of his family receded, the spinning slowed, and his startling white pain dulled to an imprecise ache. The light that filtered through the blind was no longer the neon slivers of street lights; it held the promise of day. And he knew where he was, if not exactly why. *Decembre, Novembre, Ottobre, Settembre, Agosto, Luglio*: he could recite the months of the year backwards. He could reach out and touch his finger to the one the doctor held up, and then bring it back to touch his own nose with what was, apparently, acceptable speed and accuracy. He could tell them that he lived and worked at the Mille Luci, and had done for twelve years. That he was supposed to be taking Kit to Marciana Marina to see the kid who thought he could sing like Neil Young, and you know what, he'd seen him last year and he wasn't bad.

'You don't remember the concert?'

He went to shake his head, but it hurt. His hand went to touch it, and that hurt too.

'Oliviero, what is the last thing you remember?'

She was nice, the doctor; she reminded him of a schoolteacher he'd had once – stern, but well-intentioned. He wanted to give her the right answers to her questions. He wanted to see her place a tick on her chart, or whatever it was she held on her clipboard. He tried to think. He closed his eyes.

Kit. He remembered leaving her that morning, his whole body basking in the afterglow of pleasure. How for the first time in his life he'd wished he didn't have to make breakfast at the Mille Luci, and how he'd taken the turns back down the hill thinking of the glint of silver at her belly button, how her mouth had tugged at his earlobe, and their immaculate intensity as they'd moved together. He remembered how Valentino had been on edge all morning, and he'd felt guilty for having only just left her, hating the thought of doing anything that might hurt the man who, for all Kit's mistake, was a father to him in all the ways that mattered. When finally Kit had appeared, crunching up the gravel in the heat of the afternoon, Valentino had turned to Oliviero, his face somehow full of both dread and wonder. He had gone to shake Oliviero's hand before he went out to meet her, a peculiarly formal gesture, as if he was sealing a pact, but Oliviero had pulled him into an embrace instead, said, *It'll be okay*. But these things weren't for the doctor, and beyond them? Beyond them he had nothing.

'All right. Can you remember what you served for dinner last night?'

He almost laughed. Always. But when she gently pressed him for specifics, he found that his kitchen was empty.

The doctor had listed off his injuries as though a waitress recounting daily specials. A broken ankle, a fractured rib below the shoulder, bruising to the back. *I'll take the broken ankle, thanks*. A bump on his head that would eventually go down.

Several hours of lost time that would, she said, return in fragments that he'd have to piece together. *That sounds a bit fiddly; I'll have the bump while it's fresh.* She'd told him he was lucky, and it seemed hard to believe.

Then Valentino and Kit walked in, and he felt his fortune then. Their familiar faces, in the astounding strangeness of the hospital, were each, in that moment, beloved.

They looked exhausted, the two of them. Swimming blue eyes and drawn expressions. Standing side by side, as formal as chess pieces, uncertain of their next move. He smiled, wanting to reassure them. Did he look that bad? Maybe he should ask them why he'd been up a ladder. Had they even gone to Marciana Marina?

'*Ciao*,' he said, and pretty brightly too, he thought. They came over to him, Valentino bending to kiss his cheek, Kit laying her hand on his. Both of them were crying, and both trying not to, and both failing.

'*Perchè stai piangendo? Sto bene, sto bene.*'

He saw them exchange a look.

'*Sollievo*,' said Valentino. 'We're crying from relief.'

thirty-two

THE BEACH WAS CALLED LE GHIAIE, AND WAS ONLY A FEW minutes' walk from the hospital. It had bright white shingle, and the water was the vivid blue of a lido. Who came here, wondered Kit, amongst all the happy holidaymakers and sun-kissed locals; who else shook down a towel or slid into the water? When visiting hours were over, was it the wrecked and the restless, the hopeful, the hopeless? Was there ever anybody like her and Valentino?

The doctor had told them Oliviero needed to rest, and that they should do the same. *Are you hungry?* Valentino had asked, and Kit had nodded, following him out into the brilliant day, where, on the hospital steps, they'd each unconsciously paused, and turned their faces to the sun.

'He's okay,' murmured Valentino. Then, barely audibly, and to whom she didn't know, he said, '*Grazie.*'

As they cut down through the streets, Kit saw Valentino's steps slow, and how he stopped to mop at his brow. It was too much hurly-burly, with the growl of traffic, the snapping walks of other people, the clamour of shop windows.

'Are we near a beach?' she'd asked. 'Could we eat there?'

Now they settled down beside one another, a pizza box between them, and stared out at the never-ending blue.

'It's the Sirocco,' he said, quietly, 'the wind. When it comes from the south it makes the sea as clear as crystal. Today, today it's perfect.'

She wanted to tell him not to blame himself, not for Oliviero. An accident, she wanted to say. But how could she speak about what had happened without talking about everything else too? Earlier that morning, as she'd waited for the taxi, Isabel had caught her hands, squeezed them tight, and said that no good ever came of blame. That perhaps of all emotions it was the most useless, and the most destructive. She had told Kit how when life became intolerable for her, she'd made it intolerable for her husband too, as if he wasn't already with her in grief. Her great shame, she'd called it. He was married to someone else now, and had two children.

'Isabel told me that . . . you thought he was gone.'

'Gone?'

Valentino picked up one of the beach stones, and rolled it between his palms.

'Oliviero. When he fell, when he was knocked out. She said you thought he was dead.'

'I couldn't tell if he was breathing,' he said. 'Isabel came and . . . She was so calm. She pressed her fingers to his wrist, and here too,' he touched beneath his jawline, 'and she said it was okay. Me, I was . . . useless.'

'But you got to him. You saw what was happening and stopped the electric shock. His injuries are from the fall, not the shock. You saved him.'

'I don't think it counts,' he said, 'if I was also the cause.'

He threw the stone and it fell just short of the water.

'Well, you saved him twelve years ago. I know you did.'

'He told you that?'

Kit squinted. There was barely a line between the sea and the sky. The wind he spoke of was rippling the surface, refreshing, enlivening. She took a breath.

'They were for my mum, weren't they? The lights.'

He kept his head bent. Picked up another stone.

'Not for Maria, or Lorenzo,' said Kit. 'They were nothing to do with the legend. They were for Bianca. For your love, not theirs.'

Still he said nothing.

'I didn't really come here to write an article,' she said. 'You know that. When I said I didn't believe in that kind of everlasting love, I meant it. But now . . . I don't know . . . now maybe I do.'

He looked up at her. His cheeks were dark with stubble. He seemed like a man who hadn't slept for days, not hours.

'I lit those lights every night for twenty-eight years,' he said.

Kit nodded, picking up her own stone, passing it from hand to hand.

'I liked the ritual of it, the routine, you know? Other people, maybe they visit a gravestone, or say a prayer. But praying wasn't for me, and . . . the ground . . . I never felt like I'd find her there.'

He gestured out over the water.

'The sea,' he said. 'To be surrounded by sea. I wanted that. For my own . . . *sentence*, is that the word? If you can call it that. But also . . . because she loved the water. Once, she loved it.'

Kit could picture her. Hair dark as oil, seawater slicking

down her back. Towelling herself off before striding up the beach, not permitting herself so much as a backward glance. Was that how people walked out of water? Was that how it went?

'She did. She used to take me when I was small. We always played a game, the first one to spot the sea would win a prize.'

They'd catch the train, then take a bus to the wind-battered north Somerset coastline. Rocky stretches and grey water, gorse that tore at your knees. They'd sit side by side with their hoods up as they took their cheese sandwiches out of their brown paper wrapping.

'What was the prize?'

'I don't know, I never won,' she said. She dropped the stone, picked up another, tracing her thumb across its smooth surface. 'Do you think . . . when her boat was wrecked, do you think someone saved her? And then, I don't know . . . you hear about amnesia. Memory can be crazy. Oliviero's lost nearly everything from yesterday, and maybe she forgot who she was, and . . .'

He shook his head, was kind, probably, in his response. 'I think she wanted to forget,' he said, 'and that's a different thing.'

Perhaps he knew as well as she did that if anyone could rise from the sea it was her mum. That for all the fabulousness of it, they could both see her shaking the water from her ears, brushing the sand from between her toes, and declaring herself new. Briskly onward, with absolute certainty. The practical matters would have been the least of it for a resourceful, determined woman. But the leaving? The deletion of what had been an entire life? No one erased anything quite so ferociously unless it had, once, meant the world.

'I can't speak for her,' said Kit. 'I wouldn't even want to try.

But for her to do what she did, I think . . . only love can do that to a person.'

'I think hate can do it too.'

'Can you ever hate without once having loved? I'm not sure it's possible. You know, outside of me, she never let anyone get close to her. Not men, not women. I always thought it was because she didn't need it. But . . . I think maybe she'd had love. She didn't want it again, because she'd had all there was of it.'

Kit was conscious of him then, watching her. She felt as though she was holding a piece of him, and if she didn't handle it carefully, it would break.

'What you did,' she said, 'other people have that happen, and they don't do what she chose to. They stay, or they go, or . . . that's it. Those are the options, right? If someone I loved cheated on me, I wouldn't . . .' She paused. 'But I'm not her. No one's her. She did this to you, and to herself.'

He gave a small nod, a cautious, guarded gesture, but Kit saw how his eyes brimmed with gratitude. She nodded back.

'It was all for her,' he said, after a pause. 'The Mille Luci. Or because of her. I don't know. The lights were . . . only part of it.'

'You really lit them every night?'

'Every night.'

'Even when the guests were gone?'

'Every single night.'

'And everyone who comes thinks of Innamorata, don't they?'

'Of course,' he said. 'It has to be that way. And it was because of the legend, you know. That was how it began. I came to Elba, and I heard the story. But it didn't mean a lot to me, not so deeply. The new couple, just married . . . of course they loved one another. Of course you think a love like that will last forever. But . . .' he hesitated, gathered himself, 'the man in the story, the Spanish nobleman who lives alone and lights the lights, because he's so moved . . . it was him who made me stop. I thought, why? Why was he so affected? What losses, what shame, had he endured? He makes something beautiful out of something sad. Light from darkness, you know? I wonder if those first lights of his were for Maria and Lorenzo, or if they were for someone else. Or for some part of him.'

'What happened to him?'

'In the story?'

'In the story.'

Valentino rubbed his face. 'He left the island. He moved to the mainland, and met someone. Lived happily ever after.'

'That's a good ending.'

'It is.'

'Would you ever leave, do you think?'

'No.' Then, 'I don't know where I'd go.'

'I was leaving,' said Kit. 'This morning I was ready to go. It was only because Isabel saw me, and told me what'd happened, and . . . I didn't think you'd want me to stay.' She blinked fast, glancing skyward.

'Kit.'

She bit her lip, the faint taste of metal.

'I'm not going to say that knowing you your whole life would have made me a different man, a better man. I'm not going to say that, because I don't know if it's true. But I do know it would have given me some . . . happiness.'

He held her hand lightly but firmly. His thumb smoothed her palm, as if he was tracing her lifeline.

'I lost the right to a lot of things when I betrayed your mother. But I don't think . . . I don't know . . . perhaps I shouldn't have lost the right to that.'

Kit let her tears roll unchecked. Of all the ways she hoped she was like her mum, she no longer wanted her extreme self-control; her ability to think one thing and say another, to be one thing and be another. She wanted to tell Valentino that perhaps it wasn't too late, that maybe amidst the wreckage there was something that could still be salvaged. That her mum had given her everything she'd ever wanted, was impeccable in that way, except . . . she'd never given her him. And she hadn't realised how much she'd wanted him until the moment she thought she'd lost him. When he was walking away, across the rocks, and she was left standing, feeling more alone than she'd ever felt, the bitter taste of her ill-meant words in her mouth, and in her hand the picture of a woman called Bianca. She vowed to tell him all these things, but for now, she just leant in to his side. Together they sat, shoulder to shoulder, looking out over all that infinite blue.

Their pizza had been cold by the time they'd eaten it, but it was still good. So good that Valentino insisted on calling into the pizzeria on the way back and picking one up for Oliviero. *His* pizza fritta *is amazing*, Kit had said, and Valentino had looked puzzled, said, *We haven't served that this week, have we?*

When they returned to Oliviero's room, he snapped open his eyes, filled his nostrils. Then he grinned. 'Anchovies . . . olives . . . it's Napoletana.'

'*Un professionista,*' Valentino said to Kit.

The doctor had taken them aside and explained that with concussion a patient could easily feel confused, upset even, so if there were any circumstances surrounding his accident that might prove – she'd regarded them over the top of her spectacles – distressing, they should keep it to themselves until he'd recovered. They'd agreed not to talk about Rosa being Bianca; it didn't feel like subterfuge, more a re-establishment of the status quo. And it was the rainstorm that had brought down the lights. Valentino had insisted that, if Oliviero asked, his part in it was not to be omitted: that it was his foolishness in being on the roof that had prompted Oliviero up the ladder. They'd tell him the real story in time, show their gratitude for his part in revealing it, how he'd laid the truth in their hands so gently, so carefully, and the courage it must have taken to do it that way, before it leapt out at them, or crashed down from a great height. And if Oliviero asked how the concert had been, they would say that when Neil Younger sang 'Only Love Can Break Your Heart', the whole crowd, including them, had lifted their voices: they all knew the words.

Kit and Valentino took a taxi back to the Mille Luci. It followed the same route the bus had taken when Kit had arrived six days ago. They sat in the back as the driver fiddled with the radio, chattering out football commentary, the broken segments of banal pop songs. They both gazed out of the windows, lost in their own thoughts, but every so often they turned to look at one another.

Valentino told her how, when Oliviero fell, it became the only thing that mattered: not Bianca, not Rosa, only that Oliviero be okay. Kit thought of her mum's own descent, how in those last days of her decline nothing she'd said, even *he didn't die*, mattered as much as the life that she was trying to hold on to. The life that Kit could see was slipping her grip.

'I don't think she ever would have told me, if she hadn't been dying,' she said to Valentino. 'I think one thing had to happen before the other could, you know. I wouldn't be here, if . . .'

'No,' he said, slowly, carefully. Then, 'Were you able to . . . say goodbye to her?'

'Yes,' said Kit. 'But . . . not really.'

They'd had plenty of chances to say the things they'd wanted, as they'd sat with knees drawn up on the sofa, cups balanced on their saucers. Or as they'd walked along the rim of the Downs, taking slow steps, stopping to admire the first bursts of crocuses amidst the winter mud. But they hadn't taken them. It was easier to remark on the sweetness of the bergamot in the tea they drank. The hot-air balloon whose wicker basket skimmed the tips of the trees as it looked for a place to land.

'At first, I suppose I didn't want to acknowledge it,' she said. 'And then, well, she got worse very quickly, in the end. And she knew. I'm sure she knew. But I . . .' Her words ran out. 'I don't think you can ever really say it, you know, *goodbye*. Accept that you're not going to see someone ever again. Not me, anyway.'

She realised what she'd said, and darted a look at him. She thought of her mum as Valentino had described her, dressed in her sailing jacket and heading for the door. Would she have known then? Or was it opportunism, a spontaneous act in a moment of chaos? The fact that they'd never know didn't feel, to Kit, like an insurmountable thing. It was a fact. A fact of unknowing. For Valentino, it would remain miraculous, and terrible. Between herself and him there would always be this chasm, she knew that much. Simply, they had loved two different people. And for all that Kit mourned her, Valentino was holding onto the life of her. That she was dead now, finally, was, to him, compared to all else, an unremarkable thing.

He gave a sad smile, and nodded. They swung through the Mille Luci gates. She saw him crane forward to peer through the windscreen. He checked his watch. *Mamma mia*, she heard him say. The guests were gathered on the terrace, just as they were every evening at this hour. Abi moved among them with her tray of sparkling drinks, Bernardo, in a white shirt several sizes too big for him, holding up platters of antipasti. And then Isabel, rounding the corner, wiping her hands on an apron. They saw her bend and whisper something to Bernardo, and he yelled out, *Tutti a tavola!* To which the whole terrace erupted in applause.

thirty-three

EVERY SUMMER, ON THE FOURTEENTH OF JULY, A GROUP OF
guests from the Mille Luci crossed the island to attend the
Lovers' Festival at the beach of Innamorata. This year was no
exception. They watched the groups from Capoliveri, all in
their traditional dress, racing boats across the bay. The re-
enactment of Maria and Lorenzo's story, the celebration of
everlasting love. Maria herself, played by a girl with hair to her
waist and hoops in her ears, a tattoo of a star on her ankle.
There were crowds of locals and visitors drinking pink wine
and glasses of fizz, the air full of the sweet scent of rosemary
and roasted meats and sugared nuts. Everyone ate ice cream.
There was dancing on the sand. A thousand burning lights.

Nearly all of the guests had come. Francesca and Veronika
were there in their bright-painted shawls and black dresses,
leaning on one another for support. The Berger family, the
boys wide-eyed and chaotic, Steffi and Max wandering behind
them, their fingers just touching. Nina and Lucille, in heels and
showy frocks. Valentino had spotted them doing each other's
make-up earlier, and smiled to see it. Isabel, too. Of course,

Isabel. Though after her time in the kitchen, she'd somehow crossed over, from guest to . . . something else. She'd even seemed piqued when he told her he'd hired another chef. *Just for a week or two*, he'd said. *Oliviero wouldn't like it for any longer.* She'd never attended the festival before, but then nor had he.

'I think,' he'd said, finding her in her usual spot in the shade of the eucalyptus, 'that we should go this year.'

'We should?' she'd said, with an arch smile, for the plural personal pronoun was as surprising as the suggestion itself.

Now he saw her talking to Nina, and felt a rush of tenderness. She wore a dark red dress, her locket glowing in the moonlight. Her skin had taken on the bronzed look it did at the end of every week she had with them. Her silver hair shone. Amidst all the strangeness of the last few days, Isabel had proved herself a true friend, a tower of strength; now something in her, and between the two of them, had shifted. He knew that when she came back next summer, if she did, they'd pick up in a slightly different place. Perhaps that was how the years would now unfold between them, small increments of change, as welcome as they were disquieting.

Oliviero glanced over to him, and Valentino was sure he saw him wink. Usually, released from formal duties, he'd be off among the crowd. Not this year. He stayed close to Isabel, to Valentino, to Kit. He'd been discharged from hospital only that morning; he should have been resting, but he'd said he wanted to come to the festival this time more than ever. Valentino, with fatherly authority, had advised against it, and Oliviero had sulked, so Valentino had relented, on the condition that he leave his crutches at home and they find him a wheelchair for the night. Oliviero only agreed when Kit had offered to push it.

Kit. There she was, barefoot and in a true blue dress, the lights flickering shadows across her skirt. She'd told him, tentatively, that her mum had made it, as if she were uncertain whether these sorts of details were wanted. He'd asked her to turn slowly, admiring the cut of it, but also thinking *mia figlia, mia figlia, mia figlia*. And he could picture her, Kit's mum, as she might have been just a while ago, a pair of glasses pushed up on her head, needle in hand, stitching. Her lips apart in concentration, the fabric running like cool water through her hands. He could see the ring she wore on her middle finger, a rose-coloured stone, and the way her dark hair was cut in a neat bob. He could see the lacings of grey at her temple, the wrinkles at her eyes and where she smiled, because she was grown older – not old enough, not nearly enough, but older nonetheless: a whole lifetime older. He knew these things from Kit's photographs, and the stories she'd told because he said he wanted to hear them, and now he could imagine her without feeling a desperation that those days had been taken from her. Taken from him, but not from her, and what were our lives if not our own?

The night before, after they'd returned from Portoferraio, he'd dug out his precious tin, and Kit had slipped her pictures from her diary.

'I hide them, I suppose,' he'd said. 'I didn't feel I had the right to display any, not even one. I didn't think she would have wanted it. But one week a year, I leave a picture in the chapel up in Alta. The only time I step in any place religious.' He'd looked at her, given a small smile. 'It's this week. Always this week.'

'Is this the week she . . . left?'

266

'No. Maybe because of the festival, that's why I started to do it. But this year, for the first time, I . . . picked one of us together. I haven't done that before. We're dark in it; you wouldn't know us, I think.'

Kit had told him how she'd been there, how she'd seen it propped in the alcove, against a vase of paper flowers, a crucifix. How she'd had no idea who they were, those silhouetted figures in front of a too-bright sun. He'd shaken his head in rueful disbelief, as though his capacity for wonder was now boundless, and she'd smiled in reply. He'd laid out his pictures on the table, and Kit had pored over them.

'I thought I had her whole life here,' he'd said.

Kit had seen her mum as a girl, smiling through the crescent of a watermelon on a beach of gilded sand. Sultry, one night in Rome, in a dress that she recognised the pattern of in so many of Rosa's creations, pinned to the mannequin in the upstairs room at Deer Leap, and in the Bristol flat.

'I've never looked like her,' she had said to him, tracing her finger along Bianca's outline. 'We were different in so many ways, Mum and me; appearance was the least of it.' Then, 'I don't really look like you either,' she said, 'do I? Except the colour of the eyes, maybe . . .'

'That's a good thing,' he'd said. 'A good thing for you.'

But she'd told him she'd have liked it, to bear the print of the two of them, outside as well as in.

Now, at Innamorata, for all the hurt, Valentino could feel a new sensation pushing up from his core. It was unfamiliar, but it felt something like appeasement, or liberation. Perhaps it was both. For the loss of Bianca's life, the particular life she'd lived with him, had been her own decision. He would always regret his betrayal, but he'd come to realise that he would never regret telling her, and attempting to take responsibility for the child he thought was to be his. He might have railed before, on his sorrier nights, bemoaned the fates that took the baby anyway and made all the suffering for naught. But he would never have wanted a child of his in the world and it not be part of his life. Kit had made him realise that.

'Hey,' she said.

His daughter, taking his arm. Just lightly, a press at the elbow, a touch that he felt from the tips of his fingers to the ends of his toes.

'*Ciao*,' he said, '*ciao, cara.*'

She was leaving tomorrow. At least, that was what it said on her booking form, and a couple from Antwerp, the Hausmanns, were due to take her room. She hadn't mentioned her departure, and nor had he, and it didn't seem to matter. There would always be a room for her at the Mille Luci.

'I want to give you something,' she said. 'I've been waiting for the right time, but I've decided there probably isn't one. Or,' she swept her arm, took in the blaze of a thousand torches, the water spliced with colour, the star-laden sky, 'as moments for this kind of thing go, maybe this is it. Maybe this is exactly it.'

She held something in her hands, and his eyes went to it. A tiny tin. A sweet tin; lemon yellow, the name *Leone* in curlicue writing.

'Mum never went back to Italy,' she said. 'But I don't think that meant she didn't love it.'

He nodded. He saw more and more of him, and her, in Kit. And the more time he spent with her, knowing what he knew, the more the years fell away. An old man dreaming, of course, but maybe our lives were altogether more fluid than we gave them credit for. In the last day and night, images of Bianca had returned to him. Of the happy days, the good days, the days of promise, and possibility, and unbridled joy. Midnight feasts at the stove, sucking inky spaghetti from each other's forks. Picnics beneath the pines, winey kisses and drowsing in the shade, wrapped together, limbs tangled. And the blissfully ordinary things, full of the everyday magic of a life shared. Walking side by side down a street in sunlight. Choosing a new set of sheets. Glancing out of the window and turning, one to the other, to say, *you know, I think it might snow later*. The things that bound our lives together, if only we could see it.

'And Elba, you said she never came here, but I think she would have thought it beautiful. Don't you?'

'Yes. I do.'

'I brought these with me,' she said. 'Thinking I'd find the right place. I think . . . I think the right place is with you.'

She passed him the tin, and his fingers closed around it.

'I went back to the house I grew up in,' said Kit. 'I scattered her ashes in the garden there. But . . . I saved some. Just . . . not much . . . but for Italy, in case when I was here it felt like the thing to do . . .'

'I can't. It's not right.'

'It is,' said Kit.

'She wouldn't have wanted it.'

'I want it,' she said. 'It's what I want. I was going to throw them from the ferry, just toss them out, wildly, so the wind would take them and blow them all over everywhere. But then I came here. And . . . it's right.'

He bent towards her, and kissed her on the forehead.

'I don't know what to say to you,' he said. 'And I don't know what to say to her.'

'Goodbye,' she said. 'You just need to say goodbye.'

* * *

Valentino stood on the shoreline. A little way up the beach, away from the party. From there he could see the lights, and the flickering shapes of people as they moved among them. The indistinct but definite sounds of merriment, and celebration, filled the air. He walked a little further still, on towards the darkness. Then he removed his shoes, and his socks. He waded out, the water swilling around his ankles, as warm as a bath. The tin was in his hand, and he clasped it tightly. There was so much he wanted to say, yet when the moment came, he found himself lost for words. He simply let her go.

thirty-four

IT WAS THE FIRST DAY AFTER THE LAST OF THE SEASON. THE Mille Luci was empty. The guests had gone. Abi too, to her sculptor in the hills, and Bernardo had washed his last dishes. Oliviero moved through the stillness of the kitchen, the dining room, out onto the terrace, enjoying the quiet but feeling the absence. When the final guests went, they took something indefinable with them. And for all the satisfaction he felt at the season's end, after six months of long days and nights, there was always a sense of loss. There would be no deliveries arriving at his door, no boxes of courgettes and swollen *melanzane* and sheaves of lettuce. No lengths of fish draped over ice crystals, and buckets full of *gambini*. No bartering and bantering. No sizzle and flame. No too-hot plates and searing burns and mad dashes to send it all out not just right, but perfect.

He took a seat on the bench beneath the eucalyptus and lit a cigarette. He'd get on his bike and go to the market later. He'd fill a string bag with just a few things, but he'd have chosen each of them, and they'd be the best there was: the first tastes of an island autumn. He stretched out his legs. He'd been off his crutches for a few weeks now, his ankle fully healed and his rib getting there. Yesterday he'd had a farewell kick-around with some little kids from Amsterdam. He'd scored a goal past the seven-year-old keeper, with his left foot too, and he could tell by the looks on their parents' faces that they considered his celebrations to be somewhat over the top. Daft as it was, he'd wished Kit had been there to see it.

She'd written the piece about the Lovers' Festival after all, and sent them the pages of the magazine when it was published. It had ended up being less about Maria and Lorenzo and more about the man who'd first lit the lights, what they'd meant to him and to everyone who saw them. She hadn't mentioned the hotel, of course. There was no review, as Isabel had once wondered. It was simply a story of love everlasting, in all its imperfection. He'd read the piece aloud to Valentino in the kitchen, one night when dinner was done. At the last paragraph his voice had cracked, and when Valentino had taken it from him and tried to carry on, his had failed too. It had read:

For every story like Maria and Lorenzo's, with a date in the calendar, and revellers until dawn, there are the unsung songs, the words written on water, the narratives that are known only to the people who appear in them. Such stories are no less extraordinary for not containing pirates, or ghosts, for having no obvious heroes and villains. Nor are they any less celebrated, for the people to whom they belong mark out the passage of their days by them. They are learning to live not in their shadow, but in the light that they give. And while the endings of these unfamed stories might be fluid, as yet unwritten, they are nonetheless full of hope and promise, as all living things must be.

Kit had told them she'd been commissioned for more pieces

after that, and on the money she'd earned, she'd paid her way around the country, writing as she went, up and down the Boot from top to toe, all summer long. British people liked stories of Italy, it seemed, and she had a particular way of telling them: she wrote as though she was seeing it all for the first time; she wrote as though she belonged. She travelled on her own, but Valentino had joined her for a few days in Roma, and then Firenze. He'd come back glowing, told Oliviero how he'd shown her the house he'd grown up in, the restaurant he'd worked in, the apartment he'd once lived in with Bianca, where now a bicycle was upended on the balcony and scarlet geraniums sat in cracked terracotta pots. He hadn't told her as much as he could have, and she hadn't asked as many questions as she might; they were, after all, still feeling their way. But she'd taken his arm as they'd walked across the Campo de' Fiori, and once, just once, he'd overheard her speaking to a waiter, and at the words *mio papà* he'd felt a swell of pride and joy, the like of which he'd never quite known before. A passing of the baton, Oliviero had decided, when Valentino had recounted this to him, for he'd stopped calling him that, of course. It hadn't felt right any more.

Oliviero had gone to meet her too, just once, in Venice, leaving his crutches behind for good. He'd thought to take her on a boat on the canal, lie back like one of those tourist couples and kiss beneath the Ponte dei Sospiri, but they only had one night, they didn't know if they'd ever have another, and she'd wanted to stay in their tiny hotel room, and that had been fine by him. Pizza slices from the bakery across the alleyway, wine from the bottle, and the sights they'd marvelled at were all their own.

Oliviero drew on his cigarette and leant back, sunshine

warming his face. He let his mind drift, imagining all the things he could have cooked for her had she stayed for the Tuscan autumn. A risotto with wild porcini. Truffle oil on their venison steaks. Wild boar stew. What about the olive harvest, too? The oil pressing? Winter would have rolled into spring, and spring into summer. He could have baked her a *torta mimosa* with the first yellow blossoms, a frittata with courgette flowers. Food and flowers, flowers and food. He'd never been much of a daydreamer before he'd met Kit. Now he found it to be a pleasurable, if self-indulgent, pastime.

The other thing Oliviero sometimes imagined was considerably less of a pleasure, but it was proving itself to be, every day, a little more essential. The contours of a faraway island, appearing slowly from the mist. Before Kit had left for her travels, she'd said that there was a corner of Italy she'd one day like to visit, a place where people could quietly resurrect themselves, untouched by the rest of the world: the prison island of Gorgona. *It's not my place to go, though*, she had said, *but if you wanted to, some time in the future, I'd go with you*. He'd asked her if she meant to write an article, because it would make for a good one, he was sure – not his father, but the place he was in – but she'd said, *No, no article, just for you*. He didn't know how he felt about it, the idea of going; he didn't know if he ever could or would, but that she had suggested it? For him? That did something to his heart that he wanted to hold on to.

His cigarette finished, he ambled towards the pool. Normally the covers were on it by now, but someone was turning lengths, with as languid a pace as befitted the day. The drone of honey bees. The silent basking of geckos. The occasional thump as a prickly pear fell to the ground. She paused when she saw

Oliviero, and threw up a hand. He waved back. Isabel was embarking on a new life of her own. She wore her locket, always. She wrote occasional postcards to her former husband and his second wife. But she'd taken an open-ended sabbatical from teaching, and for the rest of the summer she had made her home on Elba. She'd continued to help in the kitchen, and Oliviero was knocked out by how much she knew about Italian food, what a willing apprentice she still was, and the things she taught him in return – like how to bake a batch of scones, and a vast and cushiony thing called a Yorkshire pudding.

Of course he'd heard all about the breakfast she'd done when he was stuck in hospital, the dinner that night too, and how she'd mobilised Abi and Bernardo, the three of them making the *cucina* their own. None of the guests had minded that their main course had been lasagne that night, and when he later tasted her *ragù* – for a teasing Abi had set some by for him in the fridge, thinking he could learn from it – he understood why. Likewise the crumbles she'd served for dessert had been much praised, earning several mentions in the visitors' book. She'd filled them with pears from the hotel garden, and the accompanying custard had been made with eggs laid by Bernardo's mother's chickens. *Hardly Italian, I know*, she'd said, apologetically, then, with a twinkle, *but you always say there's no such thing as Italian food. So perhaps my crumble originates from the Mille Luci region?*

The temporary chef hadn't lasted long; he had too big a pair of shoes to fill – Oliviero hadn't the heart to tell him they were Isabel's striped espadrilles. It was hard to believe she'd come so close to leaving. She'd stood with her case at her feet, the day after the Lovers' Festival, and taken out her purse to settle her bill, but Oliviero had heard Valentino say that they couldn't accept her payment, because she'd worked for them. That they needed her. That . . . he needed her. When Oliviero had glanced across, as subtly as he could, he'd seen Valentino passing her room key back to her, and from where he'd been standing, it had looked as though they were holding hands.

'I'm going to the village,' he called out now. 'Do you want anything?'

Isabel shook her head, mouthing, *no, grazie*, before flipping on to her back and stroking the length of the pool.

Oliviero had turned to go back up to the house when he saw Valentino coming towards him. The two met on the lawn. The loungers were stowed. The parasols rolled up and put away. It was just a sweep of green.

'Yes,' said Valentino, as if they were picking up on a conversation they were already in the middle of, 'I think we will have the lights back next year.'

Where once the garlands had hung from tree to tree, the branches were now bare. Instead Oliviero had strung some fairy lights along the terrace, looped them through the balustrade; pretty, for sure, but more of a twinkle than a blaze. If guests had seen pictures and asked what had happened to the lights, Valentino had just smiled, said it was only ever figurative, there were never really a thousand, and if they truly wanted a light show, they should go to Innamorata in July.

'Do you miss them?' asked Oliviero, with mild surprise.

His memory had returned, in fragments, just as the doctor had said it would, and it was Valentino who'd helped him piece it all delicately together. Valentino had been fastidious in acknowledging his own part, but his voice was sturdy as he did so. When Oliviero and Kit were in Venice, they'd talked about it too, wrapped in each other's arms, his respect for her multiplying and multiplying. To Oliviero it had all seemed tinged with unreality, but once or twice he'd woken sweating in the night, remembering with astounding precision the feeling of seeing Valentino up on the roof. And the comfort that lulled him back to sleep? Never before had he known a sad story to end happily.

'The guests miss them,' said Valentino.

And it was true. People had always written about them in the cards they sent, the thanks they gave. They said they were welcoming, and joy-bringing, but also radiant with hope: the darker the night, the brighter the lights shone.

'And I do too,' he added. 'I think, perhaps, they're part of who we are.'

'Okay,' said Oliviero, 'something to keep us busy this winter, then,' but Valentino was looking past him, towards the pool, towards Isabel.

'You should join her,' he said.

Valentino made a small noise of amusement, and clapped his shoulder as though he'd told a joke. But when Oliviero walked on up the lawn, and glanced back, he saw him standing at the edge of the pool. Isabel's face was turned towards him, and she was laughing, beckoning to him, and it looked for a moment as though Valentino might actually dive in.

thirty-five

SHE WALKED BACK FROM THE COACH STATION, HER RUCKSACK on her shoulders. Up the far-fetched slant of St Michael's Hill, through the cultivated streets of the university district, weaving among students as they moved like fish in unthinking shoals. On into the pale-stone terraces of Clifton, where dusk was falling, people's homes lit by lights inside and out. At the edge of the park the chestnut trees stood burly, their spiked shell casings scattering the path. Two tiny girls in ballet skirts skipped in the wake of their fast-striding father. A motorbike slowed beside her, its rider jogging up the steps of the next house she passed, a pizza box in his hand.

Kit's feet were cold inside her sandals, and the sound her soles made on the pavement seemed to belong to somebody else. She had a disquieting sense of insubstantiality, of not being as present as she should be. She was tired, that was it. Wrung out from never staying still, crashing now that she was nearly home. *Because* she was nearly home.

In Italy she'd found her mum everywhere she went. She was in a piece of piano music drifting from the open window of an apartment in Rome. She was in the inky espresso shots knocked back at the counter at the stand-up bar in Naples. And she was in the warm swell of the Adriatic as Kit had waded out in Rimini, duck-diving under the waves, flipping onto her back and blinking at the wide-open sky.

Now she turned into her mum's street, half expecting to hear her name called out, to look up to her window and see a vivid scarf, a sweep of dark hair.

She opened the door to the flat gingerly.

'Hi,' she said, quietly, 'I'm back.'

She dropped her rucksack in the hall and stood quite still, absorbing the quiet as it washed over her. She went through to the kitchen. The calendar was still on July, a splashy painting of sunflowers in a vase. She hadn't marked her day of departure on it. She hadn't marked anything at all. She turned over two pages, to another empty month. On the counter she fanned out the mail. She thought she'd told everybody who needed to know, even those for whom it meant no more than the updating of records, a simple deletion, but there was a catalogue from a fabric supplier, a couple of charity circulars. And a postcard, addressed not to Rosa Costa, but to Kit. She picked it up, held it like it was treasure.

There had been a rack of them in reception, free for guests to take. One had been in her room when she arrived, with the word *Benvenuta!* written in an extravagant scrawl, propped against a bottle of sparkling island white. It was the Mille Luci at sundown. The sky was still blue, just, and the lawn a sweep of green, the bougainvillea at its apex of pink; the night was yet to steal any colour, but all the lights were lit.

She turned it over. The text got smaller and more cramped

the further down the card it went, as if the sender had realised they had more to say than they had originally thought. It was only legible because she knew the handwriting. She began to read.

I'm happy. This is such a strange and unexpected sensation that I had to record it. I'm here, and I'm HAPPY. The question is . . . am I still? If I'm reading this, it means I – it means you – went back to England in the end after all. You're not really the kind to turn things upside down because of how you feel in a single moment – that much is not your inheritance – but to remember the clarity that such moments afford? Perhaps you can do that. I can't guess how you feel now, but . . . I know how I FEEL NOW. So let me just ask you this: are you where you want to be, Kit?

She held the card to her chest, and went into her mum's bedroom. Next-door's silver birch caught the light from somebody's window, its leaves lent an ethereal glint. *Not my style to fade away*, Rosa had said, two weeks before she died. *I'd rather be gone in a flash.*

Kit sat down on the edge of the bed, smoothed the covers with her hand. So many cups of tea drunk in this room. Delicate sunlight. Books read aloud. The burble of the radio. Other people's words, to fill the spaces between their own.

She couldn't imagine the last passage of her mum's first life – how much was premeditated, or a decision taken in a moment and sustained for as long as she lived. But she knew that Rosa Costa was as much made of bluebells and hawthorn as cypress and oleander. She was mud in the lane and the bright tail of a pheasant and foxes barking at night. She was lengths of vintage silk and pins between her lips and bright, bright underskirts beneath a dress of cotton lawn. The Rosa that Kit knew was no less real, but she'd made sense in Italy too. And, Kit had found, so had she. She'd written, and written, filing article after article. Her skin had darkened as she travelled, and her spirit had lightened. She knew the summer had changed her. That she too was capable of embarking on a new life of sorts. It didn't mean that the old one had ceased to matter. In fact it was the opposite of that.

Perhaps everybody was made of such metamorphoses; Valentino certainly, Oliviero too. And Isabel, who she'd thought of while standing with Oliviero in a square in the middle of Venice. They'd seen a mother with a child, a pudgy boy with a head of blond curls, not a mewling newborn, but not yet a toddler either, and they were laughing at one another, laughing so hard, as though they were sharing the grandest joke in all the world. Kit had thought then of Isabel, how you could hold on to someone with all that you had, how you could give them everything, and still they could be taken from you. What delicate threads bound us to one another, how weak our grip really was. But maybe that was the point of it. All you had was the moment, and the hope of more to come. Perhaps there had been something in her face as she watched them, because Oliviero had said to her, *Do you think some day you want to have a child with someone?* And she'd replied without hesitation, even though she'd never thought that way before. *Sì.* She could picture herself one day with a baby in her arms. Perhaps she'd rock them to sleep, tell a story that was just fantastical enough to be true, of open water and new lives made and old love never dying. She'd found herself saying to Oliviero that if she ever became a mother, she'd want to be like her own in as many ways as possible, and could he understand it, a thing like that? He'd smiled at her, laid a kiss clean upon her lips, and even though he hadn't said it, she knew who he'd want to be like if he was ever a father. And she understood that too.

She'd forgotten about the postcard. She'd written it in Portoferraio just before she got on the ferry: a self-conscious sentimentality, yes, but also the preservation of a crystalline moment. It had more power than a diary entry or a note slipped inside the pocket of her rucksack might have done. The card had travelled, just as she had, and remained intact. She went over to the mantelpiece and propped it against the clock.

It was nearly eight o'clock. The three of them would be having their *aperitivo* now. Candles on the terrace. The sparkle of bittersweet drinks.

A Tuscan autumn, Oliviero had said to her, *there's nothing better*.

Except, perhaps, said Valentino, *an Elban winter*.

The spring, said Isabel, *it's the spring I can't wait to see*.

Their faces had been as hopeful as children.

Through hilltop towns and Roman ruins, through marble, dust and salt water, Kit had imagined returning to Elba. To Marciana Marina perhaps, renting a tiny apartment in the Cotone, one painted the colour of the fruits in the hotel garden, sun-sweet berries or just-ripe peaches. Or up the hill in Alta, where her memories were of *pizza fritta* and a creaking bed. And the Mille Luci. She'd thought of walking through the marine-blue gates again, gates that, Valentino had said, would always be open to her. *Ciao, Papà*. She'd first tried it out in front of a mirror in a hotel room in Pisa, and it had been easier to say than she had ever thought it could be.

Yet she'd gone home. Because her life was here, wasn't it? England. Rosa's choice.

She stretched to turn on the lamp, and watched it slowly warm the space around her. The green silk scarf hanging on the back of the door. The rolls of fabric propped against the wardrobe. A picture of the two of them posing on Carnaby Street, hands on their hips and looking as insouciant as starlets; it had been taken by a passer-by, who'd never know the value of what he'd given them. The window had become a black oblong, reflecting the room back at her. Beyond was darkness, an unsettling place; no matter that she knew the stretch of gardens, the gallant oak where the blackbirds nested, the Downs beyond where she'd run in all lights. She stood up to draw the curtains, securing her cocoon. How did you ever know that you were in the right place? Was it because you'd stopped thinking of any others, or simply that you could do so without burning inside?

She slipped off her sandals and lay back on the bed. The way the light was falling, the postcard on the mantelpiece appeared to glow. And when she closed her eyes, she could still see it. She could see it all, and it was incandescent.

epilogue

Deer Leap, 1986

SHE WALKS DOWN THE LANE, AND IT'S MORE LIKE A TUNNEL, with the hedges rising above her head, and grass tufting in the middle. This is England. An English autumn. It's green and brown and the air is wet, but they're nowhere near the sea. Perhaps water will always follow her about now. Perhaps that will be her fate.

She stops, and peers down into the pram she pushes. She kisses the tip of her finger and presses it to her daughter's forehead. Her miracle girl. Her sea sprite.

'It's you and me now,' she says, 'just us,' and she wonders if this small girl of hers will ever forgive her.

She thinks of all the people she's left behind, even the ones who came into her life only at its end. The fisherman who pulled her from the water in the middle of the storm, wrapping her in a blanket as she coughed up half the sea. His dear wife, who let her take their narrow wooden bed, made her bowls of soup, and stroked her back as she wept. Who later handed her

284

a newspaper, where, seeing her own face staring back at her, the word *TRAGICO* written across the page, she read of one way that her story could be told. The idea came to her then, a flash of blinding light. Perhaps for the first time in her life she found herself truly believing in signs. And she knew that she could do it. After all, wasn't some part of her already dead?

It was a resolution from which there could be no return, and the practicalities gave her a grim sense of momentum. How easily it all came to pass, once she'd channelled everything she had into becoming someone else. She contacted a man who'd once known her father – bad men, both – who'd promised if she ever needed anything he would be her servant. She'd always sworn she never would, but now she went to him and asked for a passport, some money, and his silence – and he helped her as though she'd given him a last gift before dying. She took the maiden name of her great-grandmother, Costa. Her mother had always said that theirs was a family of women and women alone; well, she was continuing the tradition. And Rosa? Because roses had a strength that belied the serenity of their appearance, and if you mishandled them, then by God they'd cut you.

Rosa Costa had to go somewhere, so she chose England. Because a neighbour had once travelled there, and said how strange it was to be in a country where people kept themselves to themselves, where four generations didn't routinely cram around the table for lunch, and where they were so polite they'd sooner die choking on a fish bone than cause a scene in a restaurant. Because she'd learnt the language at school, and had been good at it. Because she loved Audrey Hepburn in *Vacanze Romane*.

Anywhere but Italy would have done.

She thinks of her friends. Marina and Luca and Arianna. How they'd have told her that they would see her through this, without realising that 'this' was her whole world, and now that it was gone, she had no choice but to build a new one. But she could not do it under anybody's glare. She would not drag herself over desecrated ground, digging and scraping for a meaningful existence. She has too much pride, not enough lenience towards herself, to let anybody witness her *bella figura* so undone.

She even thinks of Mia, despite herself. And him. Ah, him.

She has thought much on fury these last months, the precise nature of the fire inside her. It has consumed plenty, but that which remains surprises her. Her diamond-cut resolve. And a different kind of love.

She walks on, resolutely, her boots squelching in the mud of the lane, and as she rounds the corner, she sees, for the first time, the cottage. This is where they will live, her and her tiny daughter. This will be their home. It's made of grey stone, and has a dark slate roof, but it appears to have been half eaten by the woods that surround it. A good cottage to disappear in. A storybook place, where perhaps one day she'll tell her daughter a tale about a woman who came out of the sea, who thought she was leaving with nothing, who had no idea that she carried the most precious thing of all inside of her; that the fisherman saved two lives that day, not one.

Her baby starts to cry then, and she lifts her out of the pram and cradles her to her chest. Kit. Named for the English-woman who brought her into the world, the midwife who urged Rosa on as she bucked and screamed, and pushed, pushed and pushed. Who said the words, *Miss Costa, you have a daughter* with such matter-of-factness that she had to believe it to be true.

Drizzle has begun to fall, but this is a child who does not mind getting wet. Resilient already, she knows that much. And possessed of her own mind, for just see how she clenches her fists and screws up her mouth and cranes her neck, as if to look about herself and decide if she likes what she sees. This place is a far cry from the London hostel, the crowded, anonymous streets. Rosa sought space for her and her tiny girl, big skies and sweeping quiet. So here they are, way out west, a couple of nobodies in the middle of nowhere. Kit stops grizzling, and stares back at her with her sky-blue eyes. She blinks approval of this place called Deer Leap, this home that will be theirs.

They're his eyes. Not in shape, but in colour. The midwife told her that lots of babies' eyes begin blue, but mostly they change, fade or darken into something else. Despite everything, Rosa finds herself hoping that Kit's will not.

She'll say his name out loud again one day, but only when she knows, beyond all doubt, that it has to be said. This is the promise she has made herself, and along with all the others, she will keep it. For Rosa knows that once she begins to talk of him, even just the two words of his name, her life – whatever kind of a life it is by then – will change in an instant. Maybe, she dares to think, it will be a release, a relief, a kind of peace. Or, perhaps more likely, it will bring inexorable pain. Of only one thing is she certain: life as she knows it will be over. Again.

Acknowledgements

Writing this novel truly was a journey. While all roads (or ferry routes) led to Elba, there was certainly a detour or two along the way, and I've never been more grateful for the enthusiasm and the faith of the people around me. Thank you to Rowan Lawton, my agent, for immense encouragement, guidance, and acumen. Thank you to Leah Woodburn, my editor, for stellar judgement, thoughtfulness, and pin-sharp observation. Thanks also to Millie Seaward, Vicky Palmer, and Amy Perkins at Headline, and to Sherise Hobbs for invaluably bringing the Lovers' Festival to my attention. Thank you to my treasured early readers, Marie Deery, Robin Etherington, and Kate Haines – I'm lucky to have you. Thank you to Annabel Harrison for honest and much appreciated advice on writing about loss. Thank you to Patrick Neate for wise words and inspiring company on a well-timed Arvon week – it was a privilege to be tutoring alongside you this time. Thank you to Danny Hancock for top-notch electrical guidance – any inaccuracies are mine alone. Thank you to Zoe and Gary Colosimo for the use of your splendid name – and for making a mean Negroni (or three). Thank you to my family – the Halls and the Etheringtons – for your relentless cheerleading and boundless support; special thanks to Mum for all the notebooks, and that wonderfully teary phone message upon finishing the first draft. Thank you to my son, Calvin Jack, for leaving me to write in my hut when really you wanted to pull me out to play – you amaze me, little man. Finally, thank you to my husband for giving me the courage to rip it up and start again. For sharing that first sunshine and food-filled trip to Elba back in 2003. For everything, really. *Grazie mille*.